The chance of a lifetime . . .
or just another bad decision?

Delaney Lavender Brooks needs to grow up.
At least, according to her parents. After getting evicted
from her apartment and wrecking her car, Laney is
almost ready to trade in her paintbrushes and
surrender to a more sensible nine-to-five existence.
Almost. Until she's awarded an internship at a prestigious
art gallery in Paris. What else can the free-spirited artist
do but follow her dreams? Even if her latest attempt
at chasing rainbows might cost her a real future . . .

Once in the city of lights, Laney is almost undone by
the glaring truth: maybe she isn't sophisticated or talented
enough to make it as an artist—or an independent woman,
for that matter. And when she's hotly pursued by a
seductive Frenchman, she has to wonder if she's about to be
a fool for love, too. Soon Laney's greatest challenge is
not proving herself to her parents, but having the courage
to live the life—and love—of her dreams . . .

"Leah Marie Brown has a wily way of bringing her stories to
life with sharp dialogue and drop-dead sexy characters."
—Cindy Miles, national bestselling author

"When it comes to crafting clever, intelligent, wonderful
escapist fiction with a heroine every woman wants to know,
Leah Marie Brown is a new voice to watch.
Prepare to fall in love!"
—Renee Ryan, Daphne du Maurier Award–winning author

Books by Leah Marie Brown

THE IT GIRLS SERIES

Faking It

Finding It

Working It

Owning It

Owning It

AN IT GIRLS NOVEL

LEAH MARIE BROWN

LYRICAL SHINE
Kensington Publishing Corp.
www.kensingtonbooks.com

LYRICAL SHINE BOOKS are published by

Kensington Publishing Corp.
119 West 40th Street
New York, NY 10018

All Kensington titles, imprints, and distributed lines are available at special quantity discounts for bulk purchases for sales promotion, premiums, fund-raising, educational, or institutional use. Special book excerpts or customized printings can also be created to fit specific needs. For details, write or phone the office of the Kensington Sales Manager: Kensington Publishing Corp., 119 West 40th Street, New York, NY 10018. Attn. Sales Department. Phone: 1-800-221-2647.

Lyrical Shine and the Lyrical Shine logo are Reg. U.S. Pat. & TM Off.

First Electronic Edition: May 2017

ISBN-13: 978-1-5161-0121-4
ISBN-10: 1-5161-0121-9

First Print Edition: May 2017

ISBN-13: 978-1-5161-0122-1
ISBN-10: 1-5161-0122-7

Printed in the United States of America

*If you hear a voice from within you say, "You cannot paint,"
then by all means paint, and the voice will be silenced.*

—Vincent van Gogh

A musical note from Laney

Have you ever had an emotional moment and heard a song playing in your head? Like, say you have been dating this awesome guy and he brings you a pair of retro Lucite cat's-eye sunglasses he found at a flea market, and you think, "I love him." Suddenly, you hear Cristofer Drew of Never Shout Never singing "I Love You 5" in your head.

Or you have the worst day, like, ever. Crash your car, kill your cat, lose your best friend bad day. You're sitting around dwelling in the negative space and you hear the Beatles singing about how all their troubles seemed so far away, "Yesterday."

Or you're home alone, watching a horror flick and you get this super creepy feeling that someone is standing behind you. Cue Rockwell's "Watching Me."

I hear music in my head all the time, like a soundtrack for my life. I call it: Laney's Life Playlist. I even write the songs down in my journal when I am documenting the important stuff. It's fun to go back and read my journal and play the songs attached to life events. It really puts me back in that headspace. If you want to get in my headspace, listen to the playlist at the start of each chapter.

Prologue

Dear Ms. Brooks,

Thank you for your interest in joining the Colorado Museum of Fine Art team! Although your experience as a volunteer educator of arts with Teach Them to Fish is commendable, I am afraid you lack the qualities necessary for directing major exhibits at a world-class museum. We will, however, keep your résumé on record and get in touch with you about future opportunities that may be a better fit for your skills and experience.

In the meantime, the Museum is always looking for volunteers. Perhaps you might consider contributing your skills to our dynamic volunteer and internship team? I am certain you could help the museum spark creative thinking and expression through transformative experiences with art. If you are interested in a volunteer position, please visit our Online Career Center at www.coloradomuseumoffineart.org to submit an application or call 719-825-2222.

We wish you all the best in your job search and hope we will have the chance to consider you for another role in the future.

Regards,

Eli Prichard, Director, Collections Management
Colorado Museum of Fine Art

NOTICE TO QUIT
(Eviction Notice)

To: Delaney Brooks
Located at: 623b Pearl Street, Boulder, Colorado

You are hereby put on notice that you are delinquent in your rental payments for the premises listed above in the amount of $3,300. This rental debt represents the rent due from August 2, 2016, to November 2, 2016.

Pursuant to Colorado state law, **YOU MUST EITHER PAY YOUR DEBT TOTAL OR VACATE THE PREMISES WITHIN THREE (3) DAYS FROM THE DATE OF THIS NOTICE.** If your total debt is not paid in full by this time—OR—you do not vacate the premises in the prescribed time, you are hereby notified that your landlord will take legal action to recover the debt owed and possession of the premises, including attorney's fees and other costs.

THIS NOTICE IS BEING ISSUED PURSUANT TO COLORADO LAW.

Chapter 1

It's time to relax your mind and ground your spirit. Close your eyes and rest your hands on your knees. Bring your awareness to the touch of your body on your chair. Take a few deep breaths. While you are breathing deeply, relax your shoulders, your arms, your stomach muscles, your leg muscles. Let go of all the tension in your body . . .

The driver in the car behind me beeps his horn. I take a deep breath, open my eyes, glance up at the green light, and put my foot on the gas pedal. My Mini Cooper shoots through the intersection. I am fifteen minutes late for my gig, and my chakras are totally out of whack.

Do you feel that sense of peaceful calmness?

"No," I say, switching lanes.

No? Take another deep breath. Pretend you are looking at a control panel with dials and buttons. The control panel to your life. Reach out and turn the dial that controls your focus on the physical world. Turn it all the way down. Let everything just fade to black until you are left with only the ambient sound of your soul. Listen to your soul.

I pull to a stop at one of Boulder's busiest intersections and close my eyes, determined to let my Positive Vibes! app guide me to a more balanced state of mind. Job application rejections. Eviction notices. Road ragers with horn-heavy hands. I let it all fade to black and tune into the sensei's calm, modulated voice as she tries to lead me to a state of perfect Zen.

Now, imagine you are on top of a mountain. Look up at the sky. Do you see that single, wispy cloud floating above your head? That cloud represents your cares and worries. That cloud is blocking your journey to enlightenment. Take a deep breath and blow that cloud away.

With my eyes still closed, I inhale air through my nose deep into my lungs and release it in one explosive breath. In my mind's eye, I see the cloud skitter across the sky and dissolve into the horizon. My limbs feel warm and heavy. My mind feels clearer. I haven't yet entered satori, the deepest state of meditation, but I am approaching it.

Shift your focus to the ground under your feet. Do you notice how solid the earth feels? If not, push your feet down while imagining . . .

I go with the sensei's words and push my feet against the ground, but instead of feeling solid earth and perfect stillness, I feel my gas pedal and a sickening lurch in my stomach as my Mini Cooper darts forward. Horns beep. Tires screech. I simultaneously open my eyes and slam my foot on the brake, but I am too late. I watch in perfect horror as the hood of my beloved Mini Cooper crumples like a starlight blue-and-white striped accordion. There's a violent popping noise as my airbag bursts out of the steering wheel and slams me back against my seat, knocking the wind out of my lungs.

. . . you should feel a perfect sense of peace and the warmth that comes from the knowledge that everything is right and balanced in your universe.

I hear the sensei speaking, people outside shouting, a car door opening and slamming, but I am still on my theoretical mountain, blowing clouds across the sky with my breath. My thoughts are foggy, my limbs heavy, like when I enter a deep, deep state of meditative relaxation. It takes me a moment to process what has just happened.

Someone knocks on my window. Violent rap-rap-rapping.

I look over and find a middle-aged woman gesturing for me to roll my window down. I comply.

"What is wrong with you?" she screams. "Are you fucking crazy?"

Congratulations! Your chakras are perfectly balanced. You have entered a state of bliss . . .

I open the door and climb out of my wrecked car. A crowd of teenagers and college students have gathered on the nearby sidewalk, snapping pictures and digitally recording my tragedy for future upload to Vine and Instagram. I look at the street signs—Broadway Boulevard and Arapahoe Avenue—and realize I have crashed in front of Boulder High School, just down the street from the University of Colorado, my alma mater.

"You know you had a red light?" the other driver screams. "Right?"

"I'm sorry."

"Sorry? Sorry?" Her voice is shrill, her eyes wide with a manic kind of fright.

I look at her minivan, its side caved in, four chubby, grubby little faces pressed against the rear passenger windows.

"You ran a red light and slammed into the side of my van. Are you a lunatic?"

I shake my head, and a searing pain stabs my neck.

"I get that this is a legit bummer deal, but—"

"Legit. Bummer. Deal," she screams, emphasizing each word with a slightly cray-cray gesticulation. "This is more than a legit bummer deal, you pot-smoking freak . . ."

A police car pulls to a stop beside our wreckage, red and blue lights flashing. A tall, grim-faced cop gets out of the vehicle and approaches us.

"Is everyone okay?" he asks. "Is anyone injured?"

I shake my head again. This time, the searing pain in my neck travels up and over my skull, piercing the backs of my eyeballs. I close my eyes and press a hand to my face.

"Easy," the officer grabs my arm. "I think you should sit down, miss."

I let him lead me to the side of the road and am about to take a seat on the curb when I feel my knees buckle. Everything goes black.

"Youuuu killed Lunariaaaa!"

The sharp cry pierces the thick black veil separating me from consciousness. I try to open my eyes, but the bright mid-winter sunshine feels like a thousand pins pricking my eyeballs.

"Hush," someone hisses.

"But what about Lunaria? Is she d-d-dead?"

I squint, peering at the world through tiny slits. It takes me a minute to make sense of the scene. The cop. The angry soccer mom. The gang of picture-snapping students. The chubby toddler with tear-streaked cheeks and two fingers stuck in her mouth.

I was listening to my Positive Vibes! app. I closed my eyes and then . . . Oh, Snap Crackle Pop! That's right! I was in an accident.

"Who is Lunaria?" the soccer mom snaps.

The toddler pulls her wet fingers from her mouth and points them at me.

Why is that kid calling me Lunaria?

I am about to sit up when a bolt of pain travels up my spinal column, spins a donut in my skull, and races back down my spine.

"Don't sit up," the officer says, pressing his hand against my shoulder. "The ambulance is on the way."

"I'm fine," I mumble. "I don't need an ambulance."

I don't need medical bills.

"Is there a reason you're wearing that getup?"

It is only then I remember what I am wearing a unicorn costume, complete with lavender mane and spiraling silver horn. The unicorn's head is on top of my head and has googly eyes that shake back and forth each time I move.

"I am Lunaria," I whisper, smiling at the little girl. "And we met at . . . Jacob's birthday party?"

The little girl shakes her head, and her curls spring up and down.

"Liam!" she says, sticking her fingers back in her mouth. "We met at Liam's *birfday* party. You sang a song about a *fwog* named *Fweddy*."

The soccer mom grabs her daughter's hand, pulls her close, and stares at me through narrowed eyes, one brow lifted high in accusation. She's looking at me like I am one of those perverts on *To Catch a Predator,* like she's expecting Chris Hansen to stroll up and say, "Excuse me, ma'am, but did you know you were singing songs to minors?"

"I'm Lunaria the Unicorn," I explain to the police officer.

"It's a pleasure to meet you, Lunaria," the officer says, his grim lips twitching at the corners. "Would you happen to have your license and registration?"

His question catches me off guard. I stare blankly at him.

"Or maybe an identification card issued by the Ministry of Mythical Creatures?"

The soccer mom snickers, and the students bust out laughing.

"I'm not a *real* unicorn."

"You're not?" he grins.

"No," I say, sitting up, "I am an entertainer. I perform at children's birthday parties as Lunaria the Unicorn. I sing silly songs, tell stories about life as a unicorn, and paint the children's faces. If it's a big gig, my best friend helps me."

"Your best friend? Ariel the Mermaid?"

I roll my eyes. "Oberon, King of the Fairies."

"I see," the officer says in a somber tone, his expression inscrutable. "And is the unicorn business a lucrative one?"

"It isn't exactly making me rich, but it helps pay the bills."

"So you're saying I shouldn't trade my cuffs for a unicorn horn?"

Ha ha.

"I still think you should take that ride in the ambulance, but in the meantime, if you're feeling well enough, maybe you could show me your license and registration?"

"Of course."

I walk over to my car, broken shards of headlight glass crunching beneath the soles of my sparkly silver Vans, and open the passenger door. The Positive Vibes! app has looped and is playing the "Engage Your Senses" meditation.

Keep breathing deeply, slowly, and calmly. Inhaling serenity and strength. Blowing out negativity and nagging concerns . . .

I wholeheartedly believe in the restorative and regenerative benefits of meditation, but the irony of the situation is simply too great. A bubble of hysterical laughter begins making its way up my throat, and it takes all of my self-control not to burst out with a Camille Claudel cackle. (Camille was this crazy-talented French sculptor and graphic artist who was certifiable. An ex-boyfriend once told me her first breakdown occurred when she was found destroying one of her statues and laughing in a shrill, slightly demented way.)

I reach into my purse, retrieve my iPhone, and silence the sensei. Then I grab my license and registration and head back to the curb. I hand the documents to the police officer and sit back down on the curb. The policeman walks over to his cruiser, opens the door, slides inside, and begins typing on a dashboard-mounted keyboard.

I stare at the oily river streaming out from under my Mini Cooper and pooling on the icy pavement, and my head begins to throb; my stomach roils. The car was a graduation gift from my grandpa.

"You have a lot of dreams, baby," he had said, handing me the keys. *"I hope this little buggy will help you chase them."*

Gramps. My eyes well with tears as I think of the one person in my life who always encourages my dreams. He never judges me, never hits me with, *"Now, Laney, isn't it time you gave up your prepubescent diversions and acted like an adult?"*

What will Gramps say when he finds out I totaled my little buggy?

Tears spill down my cheeks. I have grown accustomed to disappointing my parents. I have even grown accustomed to disappointing myself. But I don't think I could grow accustomed to disappointing Gramps.

The police officer returns.

"I ran your license and am happy to report there are no warrants for Delaney Lavender Brooks or Lunaria Unicorn," he says, squatting down beside me.

He hands back my license and registration.

"Thanks," I sniffle.

"I know things seem bleak, but someday you will look back on this incident and laugh."

"I seriously doubt that."

He reaches into his pocket and pulls out a handkerchief.

"If it makes you feel any better"—he hands me the hankie, and I use it to wipe the snot dripping from my nose—"I am issuing you a traffic citation finding you liable for this accident, but I am not going to charge you with reckless driving, which could have resulted in imprisonment or the revocation of your license."

"Thank you, officer."

The ambulance finally arrives, and a *gorge* paramedic gets out.

"Seriously?"

"Excuse me?" the officer frowns.

I shake my head.

After everything I have been through in the last hour, the universe couldn't have sent me a hairy, slightly mannish female paramedic? It had to send me a six-foot-three, tanned, muscular Henry Cavill lookalike.

Harsh!

The paramedic pierces me with his sexy, blue-eyed gaze but addresses the police officer.

"Did she lose consciousness?"

"Yes."

"How long?"

"Less than two minutes."

Solo squats down in front of me and shines a flashlight in my right eye.

"Hello, beautiful," he says, shifting the beam to my other eye. "My name is Dylan. I am an EMT, and I am going to take a look at you. What's your name?"

My mind goes blank. My tongue freezes to the roof of my mouth. All I can do is stare at the dimple on his chin.

"Do you know your name?"

"Lunaria . . ." I look away, my cheeks flushing with heat. "I mean, Laney. Delaney Brooks. My friends call me Laney."

"Okay, Laney," he says, motioning for his partner. "Do you remember if you hit your head during the crash?"

I shake my head.

"You don't remember?"

"I don't think I banged my head."

"Do you feel dizzy?"

"A little."

But I am pretty sure my equilibrium would return if you would stop staring into my eyes with that baby-making gaze.

"Nauseous?"

I nod my head.

The other paramedic arrives, pushing a gurney.

"Possible C-spine injury," Dylan says to his partner. "Let's board and collar her."

While Dylan peppers me with questions about my symptoms,

medical history, and allergies, his partner tries to put a plastic brace around my neck.

"It won't fit," he says. "We need to get her costume off."

"I am fine, really," I cry, pushing the collar away. "I don't need to be boarded and collared."

My panic is legit. I would rather die of a massive brain hemorrhage than let Solo see what I am wearing beneath my costume: a pair of skimpy boy shorts and my Normal Is Boring tank, sans bra. (Have you ever worn a unicorn costume? Ten minutes of singing and dancing and you are covered in sweat.)

"Laney," he says, putting his broad, tanned hand on my arm. "Everything is going to be okay. I promise. There's a chance you obtained an injury to your spine during the accident. We need to put this collar around your neck to keep you from further injuring yourself. If we don't, I could be in big trouble. You don't want me to lose my job, do you?"

I look at the grayish flecks in his dark blue eyes, perfectly framed by thick, black eyelashes, and shake my head.

Before I even know what is happening, Dylan reaches around and unzips my costume. Cold air nips at my exposed skin. I don't need to look down to know my nipples are as hard as headlights. Dylan pretends not to notice my erect nips as he wraps the arms of my costume around my waist. His partner velcros the brace around my neck and they help me onto the gurney. I hug the unicorn head, now resting on my stomach, as they load me onto the ambulance.

Dylan climbs in after me and is about to close the ambulance doors when the police officer appears. He is holding my Betsey Johnson kitschy panda-head purse. He hands it to me.

"Thank you," I mumble. "This ridiculous scene would not have been complete without you handing me my furry panda purse."

When did my life turn into a slapstick comedy? I feel as if I am starring in a Three Stooges movie. Except I am in this farce alone, and so far, nobody is laughing.

Chapter 2

Ninety minutes later, I am dressed in a hospital gown and lying on a gurney in a curtained ER alcove, my unicorn costume draped over me like a strange security blanket, when my parents arrive.

If you are playing a scene in your head wherein my mother rushes to my bedside, throws her arms around my neck, and wails, *"Thank God you are alive, my darling daughter,"* now would be a good time to push pause.

My parents aren't those kinds of parents. They aren't mushy-gushy affectionate. They aren't hovering helicopter parents, ready to swoop in and rescue their only child from impending disaster. They aren't lovey-dovey Lifetime movie parents baking endless trays of cookies and dispensing wisdom with a hug. They're more like Sheldon and Amy from *The Big Bang Theory,* emotionally reserved, driven by logic, and blunt to the point of being tactless.

There is no conversational give and take with us. They talk (and talk) and I listen. My parents are prone to long-winded, one-sided conversations. They're professors at the University of Colorado, so I suppose the lecturing thing is normal for them. Often, when they're in the middle of one of their monologues, I imagine them standing behind a lectern in a classroom filled with expressionless automatons. I have to resist the temptation to make robotic movements with my arms while saying, *"Does not compute. Does not compute."*

My father stands beside my bed, his hands clasped behind his back. My mother stands beside him.

"We came as soon as we got your message," he says, his voice flat. "You said you were in an accident. Were you driving?"

"Yes."

"Were you at fault?"

"Yes."

"Was the other driver injured?"

"No."

"Good."

"Is your car drivable?"

"No." The tears that filled my eyes the second my parents stepped through the curtains into my ER space spill down my cheeks. "It's totaled."

My father reaches out and pats my shoulder two times. It's the awkward, cold response one might expect from a pointy-eared Vulcan. I am waiting for him to furrow his brow, tilt his head, and say, *"I find your constant display of emotions illogical and highly irritating."*

Please don't get me wrong. I love my parents. They're intelligent, worldly, sophisticated, hardworking, ambitious, and generous. They have instilled in me a hunger for knowledge and a burning desire to broaden my horizons beyond the narrow borders of Boulder, Colorado. *But sometimes I just wish . . .*

"Have you been paying your auto insurance premiums?" Mom asks.

. . . they would give me the cookie and the hug. I could really go for a snickerdoodle and a good squeeze.

I close my eyes, exhale, and flop back against the hard gurney.

"Oh, Laney," my mom cries, "please, please tell me you didn't let your policy lapse?"

"I've been paying my insurance premiums, Mom."

She doesn't say "Thank God" because she is an agnostic, but I can almost hear it in her sigh. *"Thank God my unmotivated, unintelligent, unfocused daughter remembered to pay her insurance premium and didn't spend it on ukulele strings, spiritual growth crystals, sunglasses, or records of obscure French artists."*

Can I help it if I dream about living in an Edith Piaf song? Who wouldn't want to escape this technologically frantic, social media driven, uninspired, impersonal society to live in a place where roses bloom and angels sing from above? I would sacrifice my entire collection of vintage jewelry and sunglasses to live in Edith's world, where everyday words magically turn into love songs. To be measured by the uniqueness of my soul, not my ability to fit in with the Fakebook crowd, that's my idea of heaven.

Hot, fat tears squeeze between my closed eyelids and slide over my temples, soaking my hairline, pooling in my ears. My father shifts his weight from one foot to the other (my eyes are still closed, but I hear his Italian leather loafers squeak) and clears his throat.

"Laney, dear," my mother says, perching herself on the edge of the gurney and resting her hand on my arm. "Obviously, it is terribly disappointing to learn you crashed the car your grandfather generously gifted you, but with steady employment with a legitimate company, it will be possible to extricate yourself from this unfortunate situation."

In Chinese philosophy, *yin* and *yang* are words that describe how opposite or contrary forces are actually interconnected and thus working together. Light and dark. Fire and water. The yin of my personality is sweet, agreeable, eager to please, always seeking peace. Right now, the lesser yang is staging a coup—the infinitesimally small part of me that can be contrary, rebellious, churlish, and childish (though usually only to my parents). My yin is trying to keep my yang from speaking, but . . .

"So, I guess now would be a bad time to tell you that I'm being evicted?" I sit up and fix my mom with a falsely bright smile. "I had planned on living in my Mini Cooper until I could sort things out, but now it looks like I am going to be one of the many indigents lining up outside Bridge House for a mug of watery vegetable soup."

My mother pulls her hand away and stands up. She steps between the curtains and continues walking, her high heels making angry tap-tap-tapping noises against the glossy linoleum floor. Her silence cuts me deeper than any hissy fit she might have thrown.

My father stares at the slit in the curtain, as if mentally willing my mother's return. Several seconds pass, marked by the loud click-click of the second hand of the clock on the wall behind my gurney, before my father clears his throat.

"Well," he says, looking from the curtains to the clock to his loafers—looking anywhere but at me. "I assume your declaration that you planned on living in your car was expressed merely for dramatic purposes, with the intent of rankling your mother." He finally pierces me with his unnerving, professor-like gaze. "Would that be correct, Delaney Lavender?"

"Yes," I mumble, dropping my chin to my chest.

He sighs and shakes his head. "Intentionally needling or upsetting someone who loves you and wishes only the best for you is simply . . ."

"Illogical?"

"Well, yes."

"Pops," I smile, fresh tears blurring my vision, "my entire life is illogical."

Two days later, the universe gives me another opportunity to prove to my parents just how illogical my very existence is.

Chapter 3

Laney's Life Playlist
"My Own Worst Enemy" by Lit
"Don't Cry, Baby" by Madeleine Peyroux

Whiplash is, like, a *wicked* pain in the neck. My sore muscles, tingling fingers, and headaches have made it difficult for me to focus on finding a new car, apartment, job, *life*. The ER doctor gave me a prescription for painkillers, but I prefer a more holistic approach to pain management.

OK, for reals? I have always been a little afraid of narcotics. I knew a girl in high school who overdosed at a pharm party—it's like a BYOB party, only people bring prescription pills instead of booze. The pilfered OxyContin, Adderall, Xanax, Percocet, Wellbutrin—whatever could be pinched from their parents' medicine cabinets—were thrown into a big bowl; then everyone grabbed handfuls and popped them like they were Skittles. Only they weren't Skittles. Audra Lang didn't just taste the rainbow; she swallowed a toxic mix of benzodiazepines and opiates.

Pill-popping junkies, like the two who broke into Fanny's hotel room and stole her overpriced designer luggage, freak me the hell out (Fanny and I became super-tight when we were volunteering in Sitka, Alaska. She's super copacetic!).

I have been gutting through the pain—while wearing a neck brace that makes me look like Joan Cusack when she played Geek Girl #1 in *Sixteen Candles*. I'm not being harsh to Joan: she's *actually* listed in the credits as Geek Girl #1.

Finally, early this morning, I popped a painkiller, chasing it with a shot of Sunny D. I know Sunny D is like the hazardous waste of fruity beverage drinks, jam-packed full of high-fructose corn syrup and ADHD-causing dyes, but the tangerine-orange-lime-grapefruit taste is old-school. It reminds me of rainy days at Sunflower Preschool, sitting cross-legged on my carpet square, munching on Graham Crackers, while Miss Beasley (*totally* her real name) read aloud from *The Rainbow Fish*.

Don't judge. I'm unemployed and shackin' with my parents. I *need* comfort.

My temples are throb-throb-throbbing, and my neck feels like I pulled a serious Heisman. It's been a few hours since my first painkiller and it doesn't seem to be doing a thing for the pain, so I pop another pill in my mouth and chase it down with the last of my Sunny D before padding into my bathroom to take a long, hot bath. I sprinkle some Epsom salts in the tub and add a few caps of my fave organic Moroccan Salvia bath gel. It fills the tub with fat, juicy bubblegum-scented bubbles. It's my adult shout-out to Mister Bubble!

Before slipping into the tub, I open iTunes and queue up my alpha waves playlist. Music with alpha waves has been proven to promote deep mental and physical relaxation, increase creativity, and improve the immune system. I am hoping the waves and the pills will work their magic and chase the pain away.

I step into the tub slowly, gingerly easing my body under the hot water. When I am up to my chin in bubbles, I close my eyes and try not to reflect on the last year of my life. Since returning from my volunteer stint with Teach Them to Fish in Sitka, I have been stagnating big-time. My love life. My career. My art. My life has become a stinky, mosquito-infested swamp.

It's outré. It's not like I came home from my year in Alaska, flopped on the couch, and watched *Big Bang Theory* reruns or crap reality TV. I have really been trying to circulate the waters. I hooked up with my old band, and we have been playing gigs from Fort Collins to Flagler. I have applied for at least a dozen non-suit jobs.

I have finished three canvases, all of which are hanging in a gallery here in Boulder.

Lately, I have been inspired by the pop art movement and the way the artists of that epoch mocked society's obsession with commercialism, while flipping the bird at the established art world. I think I captured that irreverence with my ironic *Begging for Biscuits,* an homage to Edward Hopper's *Nighthawks,* featuring smartly dressed Denverites lined up outside the Denver Biscuit Company truck, waiting to shell out their copious cash for an infamous mile-high biscuit sandwich, while indigent men and women crawl on their knees to catch a crumb.

I even went on two blind dates. Nothing epic. Just no love connection. I am looking, but I still haven't found a smoking-hot lumbersexual to keep me warm on the cold Boulder nights. Truthfully, I don't even think I want a brawny, bearded lumbersexual. The pumped pecs and worn flannel shirts are sexy, but I really want a sapiosexual, a Scoville-scale hot man who values intellect over cup size. Don't get me wrong. I'm not interested in a Sheldon. I don't want an egghead sitting across the table from me each morning, but I would like someone who digs intellectual over physical pursuits, gets my art, and challenges me to think outside my quirky box.

Fanny snagged herself a Scoville-hot guy. Calder MacFarlane is cultured and rugged, a hybrid of a sapiosexual and an ammosexual. He's a search and rescue helicopter pilot with HM Coastguard who appreciates fine whisky and collects black-and-white photos. The perfect mix of brawn and brains.

Fanny's best friend, Vivia, snagged herself a brawny brain, too. Her husband, Jean-Luc, is a French aristocrat and literature professor at the University of Montpellier. He's also a competitive cyclist. Tall, dark, and hella hot.

I love Fanny and Calder.

I love Vivia and Jean-Luc, too.

I lift my arm out of the water. My skin looks like a California grape, wrinkled and puckered.

I love California, and I love grapes.

The warm bath and alpha waves must be working because I am feeling no pain. In fact, I feel warm, content, and . . . well, full of love. I pull the plug to drain the tub and step out onto my thick chenille bathmat. Chenille feels so nice on bare tootsies, doesn't it?

I dry off, slip into my onesie jammies with the bunny ears and cottony tail, and put my hair in braids, wrapping them around the top of my head Heidi-style.

I haven't eaten much since the crash—too stressed about everything—and now I realize I am caveman hungry. My stomach is making angry burbling sounds. All I can think about is my mom's veggie white lasagna and a glass of Chardonnay. *Gaudí* in Heaven! I *loooove* my mom's white lasagna. Spinach, eggplant, carrots, garlic, onions, and broccoli layered between sheets of homemade whole-grain pasta and smothered in provolone, mozzarella, Asiago, and Parmesan.

A primeval growl rumbles around in my tummy. If I don't eat something soon, I might start gnawing on Dalí's leg. Dalí is our schnauzer. He has these wild, bug eyes and a black mustache that make him look like a canine version of Salvador Dalí. He's the best dog ever.

I am halfway down the stairs, Dalí hot on my heels, when I hear clinking glasses and low murmuring. It's eleven-thirty on a Wednesday. My parents should be at work.

They must have left the television on.

I hop off the last step, which makes Dalí yap excitedly. He hops off the last step, too. Told you he was the best dog ever. Together, we hop like bunnies into the living room.

I stop hopping when I realize the murmuring isn't coming from the flat screen. The living room is wall-to-wall eggheads, academics and professors from the university.

Professor Snape takes one look at me in my bunny onesie and spills his drink on his lap. His name isn't really Snape. It's Snapp. Edward T. Snapp the third. But he has black hair and an even darker aura, so I call him Snape.

"I am terribly sorry, Elisabet," Snape intones.

Snape looks so forlorn.

I feel sorry for him, so I fling my arms around him and say, "There's no use crying over spilled merlot."

He stays stiff as a board, his arms at his sides, his back as ramrod straight as Harry Potter's broom, so I squeeze him a little tighter.

Snape pulls away, and I can see that his aura has shifted from black to gray.

Aw! He's sad!

Using the sleeve of my onesie, I dab at the violent purple stain on the front of his shirt while singing the refrain of "Don't Cry, Baby." I am singing it in a smoky, throaty way reminiscent of Madeleine Peyroux's jazzy rendition, rather than Etta James's upbeat, bluesy version. Etta could wail, but this situation calls for a restrained, mournful ballad, don't you think?

"Delaney!" my mother says, stepping between me and Snape. "What is the matter with you? Go to the kitchen and get a washcloth."

"That really isn't necessary," Dr. Ingegerd, chair of the university's Women and Gender Studies Department, interjects in her gravelly voice. "Professor Snapp is as capable of getting a washcloth as Delaney, unless you believe the kitchen is only a woman's domain?"

"I love you, Dr. Ingegerd." I say, throwing my arms around the tall Swedish professor. "You get me, don't you? I mean, you really *get* my struggle."

My mother grabs my arm and pulls me toward the stairs. I blow kisses to the other professors just so they don't feel emotionally shortchanged and follow my mother up the stairs. She leads me into my room and closes the door behind us.

"What is the matter with you, Laney?"

My mom's voice sounds angry, but the frown lines and furrowed brow tell me she is worried.

"I love you, Mom," I say, putting my arms around her and pulling her close. "To the farthest galaxy and back again. Like way, way beyond what the Hubble Telescope can see."

She hugs me tight, then pulls out of my embrace to stare into my eyes. She tilts her head and narrows her gaze.

"You seem to love everyone today . . . even Professor Snapp."

"Poor Professor Snape!" I walk over to my bed and fall straight back with my arms out, like I am doing the Nestea Plunge. "He projects this frigid, intimidating air, but I think it's just his way of keeping others at arm's distance. I'll bet he is afraid of rejection."

"Hmm," Mom says, coming over to sit on the edge of my bed. "That's rather perceptive."

"I am a super perceptive bunny," I say, twitching my nose.

"Delaney Brooks, have you been smoking the ganja?"

"Weed." I giggle. "Nobody calls it ganja anymore, Mom. Well, maybe *some* people still call it ganja."

I start giggling and can't stop. Soon I am rolling around on my bed, holding my tummy, and gasping for breath.

Mom gets up and walks out of my room, closing the door with a deceptively silent click, and just like that, I don't feel like giggling anymore.

Chapter 4

Laney's Life Playlist
"Stressed Out" by Twenty One Pilots
"Starfish and Coffee" by Prince
"Swallow My Pride" by The Ramones

It's seven forty-five in the morning, and I am facedown on my bed, legs and arms hanging off the sides, like some sad little starfish clinging to the beach. Dalí is crashed out beside me, head on my pillow, whiskers trembling with each snuffled exhalation. The scent of maple syrup, fresh brewed coffee, and frying Tofurky bacon snakes up the stairs and through the crack beneath my door, and tickles my nose like a hiss. I am Donner Party hungry, ready to gnaw on Dalí's furry gray paw, but too ashamed by my behavior yesterday to make the journey from my room to the promised land of pancakes.

I've done many things to embarrass my parents—failing second grade, majoring in art and music appreciation, protesting the censorship of street artists by roller-skating through campus wearing only body paint and a piece of duct tape across my mouth, dressing like a unicorn—but snuggling up to Professor Snape while wearing a fuzzy bunny onesie has got to be at the top of the list. I feel like crying just remembering my mom's shocked expression and the feel of Snape's cold, waxen, strangely scentless cheek beneath my lips.

I hear someone coming up the stairs and the shrill creek of the floorboard outside my bedroom door, so I grab a pillow and put it over my head. Maybe I can score a reprieve from the parental verbal guillotine dangling over my neck by feigning sleep.

"Laney," my father says, opening the door, "please come downstairs. We would like to have a word with you."

I let my starfish limbs dangle off the sides of my bed, while opening my mouth a little and making a soft gurgling noise in the back of my throat. It's an Oscar-worthy performance. Don't laugh. If Anne Hathaway could win a statuette for playing a corpse in *Les Misérables,* I'll bet I can convince my skeptical father than I am living in the Land of Nod.

"Laney?"

I am not ready to abandon my quest for the Oscar gold. I smack my lips together and turn my head so the pillow tumbles to the floor, shifting positions just enough to make my parental audience believe my slumber has been ever so gently disturbed, but not broken. *Cue mournful music, strangled gasps, and death rattle. Fantine is about to take her last breath. Soon, she will clutch the statuette in her bony hand and thank all the little people who made her performance possible.*

"You're not fooling me, Laney," my father says, his deep voice rumbling around my room like a pre-Oscar winner announcement drumroll. Dalí hops up and starts licking my face. "You're not fooling the dog, either."

Adieu, Monsieur Oscar. C'est la vie. Who wants to spend a night in Spanx and Harry Winston jewels, schmoozing with Ryan Seacrest and Giuliana Rancic anyway? Anne can keep her Academy Award.

I sit up, yawn, and pretend to wipe sleep from my eyes.

" '*Good morning, said Bilbo, and he meant it,*' " I say, smiling sheepishly at my father.

When I was six, my dad read me J. R. R. Tolkien's *The Hobbit.* Since then, we've made it our morning ritual to recite a scene wherein Bilbo greets Gandalf with a sincere "Good Morning." Pops should respond with the next lines in the book. But he doesn't.

He simply stares at me, his cardigan-clad arms crossed over his chest, his lips turned down, worry lines etched across his forehead.

"I am sorry, Pops," I say, climbing wearily out of bed, shuffling over to him, and giving him a hug. "Please forgive me."

Dad wraps his arms around me, and I rest my head on his shoulder. Dad hugs are the best; they're as warm and comforting as cashmere jammies and smell like nutmeg, leather, and smoky wood.

They can almost make you forget that you are dwelling in the negative space; that you're a single, unemployed, homeless, unicorn with a Depression-era bank account and a devo Mini Cooper.

Almost.

"Mom's making her carrot whole-wheat pancakes," he says, breaking our hug. Dad can only do feely situations in short bursts. "Why don't you run a comb through your hair and join us in the kitchen? We would like to discuss a few things with you."

He leaves before I can respond. Dalí bounds after him.

Traitor in a fur suit.

I pad over to the bathroom, look in the mirror, and groan. My hair looks cray-cray, a dark brown hair hive that's probably become home to a few honeybees. (Pops raises bees, is a proud member of the Xerxes Society for Invertebrate Conservation, and is passionate about protecting the pollinators, so it's a very real possibility that my do has become a condo for flying creatures.)

I shift my gaze from my hair hive to the unbelievable unibrow spanning the length of my forehead. In my poverty and depression, I have seriously shirked my brow-maintenance responsibilities.

I grab my brush and attempt to yank it through my snarled hair.

I strip out of my bunny onesie and hop in the shower. Five minutes and half a bottle of Elava Botanik Papaya Conditioner later (it leaves my hair as silky as a Pantene model's hair *and* is safe for the environment), I am ready for pancakes and the parental verbal guillotine. One must not have split ends when meeting the executioner.

I step into my clean cat onesie and zip it up, before hurrying down the stairs, my damp, environmentally friendly hair still wrapped in a towel. My parents are already sitting at the kitchen table, gazing somberly over steaming cups of coffee. The look my mom gives me when I walk into the kitchen in my cat onesie lets me know I am in one maple-syrup-sticky situation with her. I decide a preemptive apology is the only way to extricate myself.

"Mom," I say, sliding onto the chair across from her, "I know my behavior yesterday was *uggo*. Like, way uglier than those planks who think global warming is just a noisy political battle and not a life-threatening reality."

Mom believed in climate change before Leonardo DiCaprio frolicked with orangutans in an Indonesian ecosystem and John Kerry gave toothy, dire interviews about global warming to *Rolling Stone* reporters. I share her belief, but I would be lying if I said I didn't throw out the climate change analogy to help get me out of this hot-maple-syrup situation.

"Planks?" she frowns.

"Flat, wooden, and lacking depth."

Laney-speak, as she calls it, usually makes my mom chuckle, but today she doesn't even smile. Not a lip twitch or a grin. So I drop the pandering analogies and get real.

"I know you have worked hard to build a respectable reputation in academia." Even though I am feeling what I am saying, deeply, my voice quavers and lacks the conviction I need her to hear. "I know I am not the sort of daughter a distinguished, brilliant professor wants to claim as her own. I am an embarrassment, with my ADD, my dreaminess, my ridiculously dramatic wardrobe. I know that."

I can't look at her. I am too ashamed. I look down at my hands and pretend to pick dried paint from my fingernails. Several painful breaths later, I finish what I need to say, what I need her to hear.

"I am sorry, Mom, for everything I have ever done to humiliate you, but especially for yesterday, for humiliating you in front of people you admire."

A heart-twisting, breath-stealing silence stretches between us, each painful second punctuated by the loud tick-tick-tick of the wall clock. When I finally look up, into my mom's eyes, I see they're filled with glassy tears, not flinty anger. She just stares at me, her hands wrapped around her coffee cup. I want her to say something . . . *anything*.

My dad clears his throat. He is the next to speak, not mom.

"What happened yesterday, Laney?"

I consider telling them that I've been nurturing a secret crush on Professor Snape for years now, that I jones for his broody personality and natty tweed coat collection, because the truth is humiliating.

"Laney?"

I look from Mom's teary eyes to my dad's raised brows and realize I am just going to have to own it. "I'm sorry, Pops. The painkillers made me loopier than Toucan Sam."

My dad stares at me.

"Toucan Sam," I say, grabbing a pancake, tearing it in half, and popping it into my mouth. "The cartoon bird on the Froot Loops commercials?"

"I know who Toucan Sam is, Delaney Lavender Brooks."

Uh-oh. This is bad, like epic bad. Pops has only used my full name maybe a dozen times in twenty-five years. Some kids hate their middle names. Not me. Lavender is hippy-dippy cool. My mom picked it because she says I was conceived while her and Pops were staying at a lavender farm in the south of France and because my eyes are kinda bluish-purple. I would love to stay on a lavender farm, wake every morning with the powdery floral scent . . .

"Laney?" Dad raises his hand and snaps his fingers to get my attention. "Away chasing unicorns again?"

I grin. "Guilty as Gollum."

Pops closes his eyes and shakes his head slowly. This is the second time I have referenced Tolkien this morning, and all I am getting is . . . crickets. Tough audience. It doesn't look like I am going to be able to soft-shoe or joke my way out of this one.

"I am sorry for embarrassing you, Mom," I say, but Mom won't meet my gaze. "I will apologize to Professor Snape and Dr. Ingergerd today."

Pops opens his eyes wide, his mouth opens and closes like the butterfly carp in our koi pond. Open. Closed. Open.

"I don't think your mother cares about Professor Snape . . . err, Snapp," he says, reaching out to cover my mom's hand with his own. "I think she is concerned about *you*. In the last few days, you have been evicted from your apartment, crashed your car, and gotten high on painkillers."

"I wasn't high—"

Pops frowns, and I have a sudden flashback of Professor Snape's pained grimace when I asked him if he wanted to give my bunny tail a little squeeze. "Okay, so the pills might have made me just the tiniest bit loopy. I am talking smaller than an atom, like a pentaquirk or a—"

"Quark."

"Excuse me?"

"It's pentaquark, Laney"

"Sorry." I drop the other half of the pancake onto my plate and push it away, resting my elbow on the table and my chin on my elbow. "You're the physics professor. I'm just the unemployed, dyslexic disappointment destined to become a pill-popping jerry hanging around the res at Valmont."

My mom winces, and I regret my reference to the most drug-infested area in all of Boulder. It's where college kids go to score pills so they can pull all-nighters, addicts get whacked out on heroin, and some sad soul drowned after he smoked meth and tried to walk across the reservoir like Jesus at the Sea of Galilee.

"In light of your recent behavior, do you think making jokes about drug use is appropriate?"

"No," I say, tears filling my eyes. "Probably not."

"Is there something you want to tell us?" He reaches across the table and tilts my chin so I am forced to look into his yes. "Anything at all?"

"I'm not a drug addict, if that's what you're asking!"

"So you weren't high when you crashed your car?"

"*What?*" I leap out of my chair, pace the length of the kitchen a few times, and then sit back down. "You're serious, aren't you?"

My parents clasp hands and stare at me.

"Wow! You are serious."

"Totes," my mom whispers.

"So, what? This is, like, an intervention?"

"I don't know," Pops whispers. "Is it?"

"No!" I shake my head so hard my towel comes undone and falls onto my lap. "No, no, no! I have never done drugs, not heroin or meth or cocaine. Apart from the painkillers I took yesterday when my head felt like it was going to explode off of my neck, the only pills I have ever 'popped' were antibiotics that time I had bronchitis and . . ."

"And?" Mom prompts.

"Birth control."

Pops clears his throat. He looks even more uncomfortable than he did when we were talking about me being an addict. He stares into his coffee mug. Mom stares into her coffee mug.

I can't *even* right now.

For weeks, my life has been circling the rim of the toilet bowl. This morning, it finally splashed down into the commode. I am back-floating in shit. That's what it feels like, anyway, to have my parents ask if I am an addict. Mega craptastic. And what's worse? I don't blame them for wondering if the cause of my spectacularly unsuccessful life is chemical dependency.

"Look," I say, my voice quavering. "I get it. I know how this all looks. I am a twenty-five-year-old who wears mismatched socks and an old-fashioned Minnie Mouse watch. I earn my bread money by dressing like a mythical creature and singing ridiculous songs to toddlers. I don't have a retirement account, renter's insurance, or a plunger."

Pops frowns.

"Adults have toilet plungers!" I cry. "They don't use a fireplace bellows or a vegetable scrubber to unclog their toilets, because they're responsible enough to remember to buy a plunger."

I use the sleeve of my onesie to wipe the tears from my cheeks.

"There's a simple solution to your plunger problem, Lane," my practical Pops says. "Just make a note to buy a toilet plunger the next time you go to the grocery store."

"I did!" I sniffle. "But I got distracted in the candy aisle. Half an hour later, I've got a cart full of chocolate. I felt guilty about the candy, so I went to the produce aisle for fresh veggies. And when I was there, I saw the cutest vegetable scrub brush shaped like a walrus. Before I knew it, I was back home eating Brookside Clusters and scrubbing potatoes."

Pops's lips twitch.

"It's not funny!"

"No," he says, shaking his head. "It's not."

"Laney."

Mom has been so quiet it takes me a few seconds to realize she has spoken.

"We know you're a free spirit and that you identify with the bohemian lifestyle, but it's time you grew up."

Hello? Have you even been listening?

"I don't know how."

"Well." She raises her mug to her lips and takes a sip. Dramatic pause for effect. "You could start by adding age-appropriate garments to your wardrobe."

I look at her sell-out suit—the Ann Taylor slacks, prim sweater set, and leather loafers—and a new wave of tears floods my eyes.

Welcome to Squaresville! You'll be issued a strand of pearls and requisite little black dress. Please leave all originality at the door. Individuality is highly discouraged.

My resistance to conservative clothes goes back to second-grade picture day. I wanted to wear a pair of pants with bright yellow pom-poms hanging along the hem and a T-shirt embroidered with an upside-down daisy and the word *Oopsadaisy,* but Mom insisted I wear a pinafore dress and Mary Janes. It's not about nonconformity for rebellion's sake. I have always believed that your wardrobe is a reflection of your soul. My soul is colorful, quirky, and happy. I wish Mom accepted that.

"I don't like that suggestion." I reach over my shoulder and pull the hood of my cat onesie over my head, low enough to conceal my teary eyes. "What else ya got?"

"You could stop spending so much time on prepubescent diversions."

Ouch. It appears I've just been sniped by a card-carrying pacifist in leather loafers. I would like to say I never saw it coming, but this isn't the first time Mom has hit me with the "prepubescent diversions" speech.

"Like my music, you mean?"

"Yes."

"Music isn't a diversion for me, Mom. It's a serious, lifelong passion."

She sighs and uses two fingers to rub circles over her temples. "Strumming a ukulele and singing silly songs to toddlers doesn't pay the bills, Laney."

"Obviously!"

"And then there's your art. You spend a small fortune in paints and canvases even though you have only sold a dozen paintings. It is time you stopped entertaining these delusions of being a world-famous artist who makes enough money to survive. If you were talented enough to make it as an artist, you wouldn't be dressing up in ridiculous costumes and singing ridiculous songs to earn gas money."

Her first shot winged me, but this one is a kill shot. My heart aches worse than when Tommy Brubaker dumped me the day before the prom.

"If I get accepted to the Cadré, I will be working and living in one of the most prestigious galleries in the world."

"If. If. You hang a lot on that little word." She clears her throat. "*If* you were offered an internship at the gallery, how would you pay for your ticket to France? Your food? We will not fund another trip. Besides, painting is a hobby, not a career."

I feel defeated, and I haven't even been accepted to the Cadré program. Each year, the Cadré Gallery chooses half a dozen artists from around the world to live and work in their awesome space. The cadets, as they are called, must work in the gallery and produce a piece of art for display and sale. It's, like, the alpha and omega of all art internships.

I peek around my hoodie and lock gazes with my mom. I am hoping she will see the pain in my eyes and drop the sniper rifle.

"We just want to see you gainfully employed and capable of supporting yourself."

"You're not the only one." I try to keep my tone on the right side of respectful, maybe just a notch or two away from belligerent. "Do you think I like living here? Do you think I like sleeping in my childhood room, surrounded by reminders of my gross inadequacy? Little Laney Brooks, the special child of the brilliant Doctor Elisabet Brooks."

"That's not fair! I've never made you feel like a 'special' kid"— she looks to my father for support, but he merely shrugs—"at least not in the way you mean it."

I am mentally making the okay sign with my fingers and mouthing, "Okay, sure."

"You know how some parents draw little lines on the door frame to mark their children's growth?"

My mom frowns. "Yes?"

"Well, the lines on our door frame represent all of the ways I haven't measured up. All of the ways I have disappointed you both. They might be invisible marks, but believe me, I see them. I know they are there."

You know that moment after you've launched a verbal nuclear missile, when you wish you could turn back time and stop yourself from pushing the button? That satisfying, sickening moment when you realize the fallout will be great. That's this moment. Right now.

The clock tick-tick-ticks ten, twenty, thirty seconds. Loud ticks that punctuate the post-nuclear silence. I consider apologizing, but the small, defiant voice inside me says, "Why? Why apologize for the way you really feel?" Truth be told, I have felt like a bona fide, documented failure in my parents' eyes for years.

"The thing is," Pops says, leaning back in his chair so he can see beneath my hoodie, "your mother and I don't think you are a failure. In fact, we think you are a smart, talented young lady who has failed to live up to your potential. We accept part of the blame."

Wait, what? I push the hoodie back.

"You do?"

Pops nods. "We have provided you with a comfortable, cozy nest. We paid for your college, helped you fund your volunteer year in Alaska, gave you money to get an apartment, and now we have let you move back home."

"And I appreciate all of it. I really do."

"I know you do, sweetie," Pops says, smiling sadly. "But I think you have become accustomed to the nest."

My stomach drops to my fuzzy-covered feet.

"What are you saying?"

"I am saying," he pauses, and my mom squeezes his hand, her silent show of solidarity "that it's time you learned how to fly on your own—completely."

What does that even mean?

"What that means"—Pops reaches across the table with his other hand and grabs my hand—"is that you have three months to find a job, a real job with benefits and insurance, and a new place to live."

"You're throwing me out?"

"We like to think of it as encouraging you to soar."

Chapter 5

Laney's Life Playlist
"Let It Be" by The Beatles
"Unwritten" by Natasha Bedingfield
"You Can Get It If You Really Want" by Jimmy Cliff

To: Laney Brooks
From: Stéphanie Moreau
Subj: RE: Karma Hates Me

Karma is a hair-flipping, designer-bag-carrying, football-player-dating Mean Girl. She waits until you're walking through the cafeteria with a stack of books and a tray with rubbery chicken nuggets and then she trips you. She can act all innocent, but we know she is a spiteful bitch. The good news? You aren't the first person she's bullied. She will get tired of you and move on.

In the meantime, get out of that onesie. You can't conquer the world dressed in a polyester cat suit. Well, you could, but you would look classier wearing an Armani suit and Louboutin's pink crystal python pumps (coveting).

N'abandonne pas, ma puce. I might not be as good at reading auras as you, but I am sensing yours is greenish. Didn't you tell me green signified growth and change? I think the Cadré Gallery will choose you to be one of their cadets. Think about it! In a few months, you will be living and studying art in Paris! (I would never end two sentences in a row with exclamation points, but Vivia is reading over my shoulder, and she told me to add them because they are "energetic and uplifting.")

I'm not going to lie. The downer convo with my parents has left me bummed. Crawl back into bed, hug Hoppy (my fave stuffed animal from when I was a kid), and pull the covers over my head bummed. Ugly cry bummed. Both of which I did after eating a cold pancake and helping Mom with the dishes. That's where I am now, under the covers, clutching Hoppy.

I stick my hand out from under the covers, feel around for my nightstand, grab my iPhone, and read Fanny's e-mail again, pausing when I get to the part about never giving up.

N'abandonne pas.

That's easy for her to say. Karma is her BFF now. After leaving Alaska, Fanny went to Scotland to track down the man she loved. Now they're engaged, and Fanny has a successful boutique in the Highlands. She also has a ginormous trust fund.

I sound jelly, don't I? I'm not jealous of Calder, her hot lumber-sexual fiancé, or her Trump-sized trust fund. Okay, it would be nice to have a hot boyfriend, but money has never fueled my mojo. If I am jealous of anything Fanny has, it's her focus. She has more focus than the Hubble Telescope. She knew what she wanted, and she made it happen.

I know what I want but can't seem to make it happen. I am focus challenged. I am perpetually distracted. Did you ever see the movie *Up?* I am like Kevin, the dog, who would be focused on his ball and then suddenly . . . *squirrel!*

My life is filled with squirrels. I can't seem to keep my eye on the ball long enough to get it because . . . *squirrel.*

"Dude!"

One minute I am in the fetal position under my blankets thinking about squirrels, and the next I am bouncing three feet in the air as my best friend jumps on my bed like a trampoline.

"Get up! Get up!"

He jumps a few more times before vaulting himself off my bed. When I finally stop bouncing, I kick the covers off, sit up, and look at Theo. He's leaning casually against my dresser, his dark brown hair flopping over his eyes, a grin stretching from ear to ear.

"You're such a freak."

"Guilty"—he reaches over his shoulder and grabs a green paper sack off my dresser—"but I come bearing gifts."

He walks over to my bed carrying the paper bag as if it were an offering to a queen, his head bowed, hands flat.

"You brought me FroYo?"

"Blackberry with chocolate shavings."

My eyes fill with tears. Theo Wilde has been my best friend since kindergarten. He's the yin to my yang. We both love music, art, vintage things, '80s movies, and living life outside the coloring book lines. The only thing we disagree on is whether *Game of Thrones,* the television show, is as good as *A Song of Ice and Fire,* the book series it's based upon. Theo loves the show (probably because of the gratuitous sex), while I prefer the books. I don't like the show because it totally lost the plot in the fifth season, but watching it with Theo has become our Sunday night thing.

"Thanks," I say, taking the bag and putting it on my nightstand. "But I'm too bummed to eat."

"Bullshite," he says, snatching the bag. "You're never too bummed to eat FroYo."

He pulls the carton out of the bag, removes the lid, and hands it to me, along with a spoon.

"Eat." He flops on my bed on his back, grabs Hoppy, and tosses him in the air like a football. "You need sustenance. You're starting to look like Cersei Lannister when she walked from Great Sept of Baelor to the Red Keep."

I snort. Cersei Lannister is a character in *A Song of Ice and Fire.* On the show, she was forced to atone for her sins by walking naked through the streets as hecklers hurled food and insults at her. It was gratuitously sexual and sickening to watch. Theo thought it was gnarly.

"I feel as if I have walked in Cersei's footsteps."

"It can't be that bad." He catches Hoppy by a floppy ear and tosses him in the air again. "Admittedly, crashing your car and getting tossed from your pad aren't the makings of a stellar week, but your 'rents are being cool and letting you stay with them."

I snort again. Between bites of FroYo, I tell Theo about the conversation with my parents.

"Duuuude." He stops tossing Hoppy and rolls on his side so he can look at me. "She didn't really tell you to give up painting, did she?"

I nod my head because I can't talk. There's a huge lump in my throat, and it isn't one of those phlegmy lumps you get after eating FroYo.

"Shame. Shame," he says, mimicking the hecklers in the *Game of Thrones* scene. "Shame. Shame."

"*Right?*"

"I'm sorry, Lane."

He smiles softly, one of his puppy-dog-eyes and dimpled-cheeks smiles that makes most girls melt like a handful of Hershey kisses left in a gym shorts pocket (been there, done that. Third grade. It earned me the nickname Dookie Brooks). The smolder doesn't work on me though, because, well, Theo is like a brother.

"Thanks."

"She's wrong, you know?"

I blink back the tears. "She is?"

"More wrong than Donald Trump. More wrong than complaining about the sex scenes on *Game of Thrones*. Like, *totes* wrong."

I laugh.

"I've never heard you say *totes* before."

"You see what I do for you?"

"You're the best."

"I am." He rolls off my bed and leaps to his feet. "You know what else I did for you?"

I grab my glasses off my nightstand and put them on.

"What?"

He walks over to the dresser, lifts a stack of envelopes and a withered house plant in a hand-painted pot and brings them to me, tossing the envelopes in a stack on the bed and depositing the plant on my nightstand.

"I went to your apartment, moved your boxes into the 'rents' garage, and grabbed your mail before your shady landlord sold everything at the flea market." He flops on the bed again, grabs the FroYo container from my hand, and spoons a frozen lump of black-berries and chocolate into his mouth. "And I rescued Fern."

I look at the withered house plant in the pot Theo helped me paint and smile. Fern, with her brittle leaves and droopy stalk, is a metaphor for my dried-up, sad life.

"I wish all it took was a little fertilizer and some water to revive my withered life."

"Your life isn't that tragic."

"Isn't it?" I scoff. "I have three months to find a well-paying, steady, non-suit job that won't zap my brain from boredom or require me to dance naked on tables."

"Hey, there's nothing wrong with nudity."

"Whatev."

"You could always move to Burlington, Vermont, with me."

"Wait. What?" I shake my head back and forth like a cartoon character. "Why are you moving to Vermont?"

"Remember that old dude I told you I met at the Recycled Arts Festival in Portland? The one who gave me his business card and told me to call him if I wanted to take Wilde Rides to the next level?"

Wilde Rides is the name of Theo's company. He makes bikes from recycled materials.

"The one wearing the Doors T-shirt and Birkenstocks?"

Theo nods his head, and his floppy mop top hangs in front of his eyes. Theo is the lead singer in our band. Whenever we play a gig, women literally throw themselves at him. It's because he has a crazy soulful voice and this whole Ashton Kutcher thing going. He's tall, model-handsome, but with a laid-back, I'm just here to chill 'tude. His hair matches his 'tude.

"I called him a few weeks ago."

"What? Why didn't you tell me?"

He shrugs. "Didn't think it would amount to anything."

Theo's bikes are original pieces of art and totally old-school.

"Well? What did he say?"

"It turns out he was one of the original investors in Ben and Jerry's."

"I. Can't. *Even*." I push my glasses back up on my nose. "Ben and Jerry's has been around since, like, the Jurassic period. He must be a stegosaurus."

"A stegosaurus with loads of cash."

"And you're sure he's not sus?"

"Naw," Theo shakes his head again "nothing shady going on. He's the legit deal."

"What did he say?"

"He wants to invest in Wilde Rides. He's giving me the capital to start manufacturing on a crazy-huge scale in exchange for a twenty-five percent stake in the company."

"That's Van Gogh insane!"

"Fall in love with your cousin and cut off your ear crazy."

We laugh.

But I am conflicted. Theo is a savage artisan with mad skills, and I am happy he is a nanosecond away from realizing his dream, but I'm also a little frightened that if he goes off to Vermont and becomes a focused, successful bike mogul, he won't have time for me. No more midnight FroYo runs. No more bingeing on John Huston movies. No more arguing about whether the writers of *Game of Thrones* have compromised the storyline in order to present an alternate, and more salacious, view of gender, power, and sexuality.

"Laney-Bo-Baney?" He nudges me with his knee. "Stop dwelling in the negative space."

"I'm not."

Yes, I am.

"Yes, you are."

Theo can't read auras. If he could, he would know that the dark, dense colors I am emanating indicate serious self-pity and depression. He can read me, though.

"Are you afraid I will forget you after I become a billionaire? That I'll be too busy posing between Oprah and the queen on the cover of *Forbes?*"

I blink away the tears and shake my head.

He rolls off my bed, grabs my ukulele from its stand, and strums the strings while singing about wanting to be a billionaire "so fucking bad" Bruno Mars–style. When he's finished, he tosses my ukulele on the bed and imitates Travie McCoy's in-yer-face swagger.

I grabby Hoppy and toss him at Theo, and we both laugh.

He sits back down on my bed, and I hug my knees to my chest.

"But why Vermont?"

Theo shrugs. "Something about placement for strategic distribution and access to raw materials."

Theo might act dumb, but there's a super-sharp brain behind that pretty face. I have no doubt he's already memorized every word of the contract binding him to the ice cream dinosaur.

"So you're leaving Boulder?"

I really want to say, "You're leaving me."

"Yes.

"When?"

"The end of the month."

"The end of the month? But that's only two weeks!"

"It's going to take me a week to drive the Bananarama from Boulder to Burlington."

Theo has this old banana-yellow Toyota Land Cruiser he's been driving since high school. It breaks down a lot, but it has tons of space in the back for our band equipment or his bikes.

"What will you do with all of your bikes and tools?"

"I'm renting a U-Haul."

"Wow! This is really happening." I grab the sleeve of his hoodie and pull him into a hug. "I am so happy for you. Wilde Rides is gonna be huge."

He hugs me back, hard. I am going to be lost without Theo, but I'm really glad the stegosaurus saw that he is a savage bike builder and a beautiful soul. Theo deserves a shot at Ben & Jerry's greatness.

We stop hugging. Theo picks up a stack of my mail, reads the return address on an envelope, and tosses it onto the floor.

"So," he says, tossing another envelope onto the floor, "are you going to move to Burlington and help me chase my dream or go to Paris and chase your own?"

"Paris?"

"Paris." He flicks his wrist and another envelope whizzes to the floor. "France."

"I know where Paris is, Theo. Why would I go there?"

"You could go to that snooty gallery and be one of those corporals."

"Cadré. It's an art gallery internship, not a military promotion."

"So, why not go to Paree?" His French accent is really bad. "Eet ees what you want, ees eet not? To be dzee struggling arteest and live in one of dzose"—he snaps his fingers—"how you say, leetle room in dzee attic?"

"Garret."

"Voilà!" He has tossed all but one of the envelopes onto the floor. He holds the last envelope behind his back and grins. "Dzees ees what you want, to leeve in a garret room and be dzee arteest intern at dzee Gallery Cadré?"

"Yes."

"Zhen why not go to Paree?"

"Une idée extrordinaire, Theo," I say, crossing my arms and collapsing against my headboard. "Except they don't want me."

"Yes, they do."

"No, they don't."

"Oh, yes they do."

"How do you know?"

"Eet ees seemple, ma chérie," he says, pulling the envelope from behind his back. "You got a letter from zhee Gallery Cadré."

"What? When?"

"Today."

I take a deep breath and imagine myself inhaling all of the positive thoughts floating around in the collective thought-o-sphere. I hold my breath until my lungs ache and then blow out all of my doubts and negativity in a big, explosive exhalation.

"You open it."

"Are you sure?"

I nod my head.

"Okay, here goes."

He sticks his finger under the flap and begins tearing the envelope.

What if it's another rejection letter like the one the Colorado Museum of Fine Art sent me? What if they say I lack the qualities necessary for being an intern at the most prestigious gallery in the world?

"Wait!"

He stops ripping. I take another cleansing breath.

"Go ahead."

He finishes opening the envelope and removes a thick packet of papers. He hands the papers to me. I close my eyes, say a little prayer to my higher power, open my eyes, and start reading.

Dear Mademoiselle Brooks,

 Over four thousand artists from around the world applied to the Cadré Gallery's Artistes en Résidence Programme d'Excellence this year—the highest number since Jacques-Louis Galliard de Cadré conceived of the bold and altruistic idea to create a program to foster young artists.

"What does it say?"

I look over the stack of papers at Theo.

"They received a record number of applicants to the program this year."

"And?"

"And that probably means I am going to be spending the next year painting murals, hocking my canvases at the flea market, and singing songs to toddlers."

"Oh, ye of little faith," he says, snatching the papers from my hand. "I think it means you are going to be one out of the thousands to join zhee program."

He starts at the beginning and reads out loud. My stomach is in knots.

"As you know, only six applicants are chosen to join our Artistes en Résidence Program. It is with great pleasure that I inform you that Le Conseil de Sélection reviewed your portfolio and application and has voted to admit you to the Spring 2017 Artistes en Résidence Program."

Theo stops reading and looks at me with wide, holy-shit eyes. I snatch the papers from his hands and scan the lines until I come to the part he just read.

"Holy shiatsu balls!" I say, jumping up on my bed and hopping up and down like a giddy six-year-old. "I am going to Paris!"

Theo laughs.

I stop jumping as a pain shoots through my head. The pain travels from my head to my heart as I realize I don't have enough money left in my bank account to buy a luggage tag, let alone an airline ticket from Denver to Paris.

I stop jumping and sink to my knees on the mattress.

"What's going through that crazy brain of yours, Lane? Why'd you put the kibosh on your victory jumping?"

"I can't go to Paris."

"Why not?

"Unless the Bananarama is seaworthy, I have no way to get there." I exhale, and my lips smack together to make a violent raspberry sound. "I am flat busted. Like, outta scratch and without credit."

"I have some extra nuts hidden away I could give you."

"Thanks, but I need to dig up my own acorns. It's time I made it on my own."

Theo grabs the stack of papers I dropped on the bed and reads the rest of the letter. "It says here you don't need to be in Paris for another three months. I have faith in you, squirrel; you'll dig up the acorns by then."

"I don't know how."

"Dude!" Theo punches the air as if he'd just won the Superbowl. "What if you, like, make a CD of the songs you sing to the little dudes?"

"I don't have money to pay for studio time."

"*Duuude,* you're seriously harshing my FroYo mellow." He puts the lid on the empty container and tosses it into my trash can. "Okay, so what if I have a convo with Jared and ask him to donate the studio time and a few CDs?"

Jared is Theo's OBFF (Other Best Friend For, like, Ever), and he owns a multimedia company that produces videos, photography, and audio recordings for nonprofit organizations and businesses committed to "authenticity."

"Even if Jared donates the studio time, how will a few CDs make me enough money to spend six months in France?"

"Hello. Hello." He knocks on my forehead with his closed fist. "Think, McFly. We take the CDs to stores that cater to little dudes and ask the managers to play them when the stores are open. Customers and their little dudes will totally want to be able to listen to the songs when they're not in the store, so they'll ask the managers to hook them up. The managers will tell them *Luna Sings to Little Dudes* is available for download on iTunes."

"Doesn't iTunes charge a fee to list music?"

"Nah, man. They just take thirty percent of sales."

A bubble of hope rises from the murky, despondent depths of my heart. "Do you think I could make enough money from downloads to buy a ticket to Paris?"

"Doubtful."

The bubble pops.

"What's the point then?"

"The point, McFly, is that if you just use your melon, you will probably think of other ways to get to your future."

Chapter 6

Laney's Life Playlist
"Take Off Your Sunglasses" by Ezra Furman and the Harpoons
"Don't Stop Believin'" by Journey
"The Climb" by Miley Cyrus

Close your eyes.

Take several deep breaths.

With each breath, wipe your mind clean, like an eraser on a chalk board, until your mind is a blank space, ready to take in new thoughts.

Are you ready?

Good.

Now, imagine you are magnet attracting all that is good in the world. You attract love through the boundless application of love. You attract beauty and goodness by presenting your most beautiful self to the world. You attract positive growth through positivity and action.

Like a magnet, you can also repel. Negative, self-depreciating, and self-defeating thoughts repel love, beauty, acceptance, achievement.

What does your heart most desire?

Do you see it in your mind?

Good. Now, imagine yourself pulling it to you like a magnet pulls iron. If you can believe, you can achieve. Believe you are a magnet, attracting everything you hope to achieve.

Namaste.

After listening to Theo's Marty McFly pep talk and the Positive

Vibes! app's meditation on achieving, I am feeling motivated. My life might be floating in the crapper, but it's just one flush away from a whole new scene. I am not going to keep floating in the stench of my indecision and failures. I am going places.

The next morning, while I'm eating leftover pancakes with Nutella, I decide to take a page from Fanny's super-organized book and make a list of everything I need to do to be a more mature adult and to make my Paris dream a reality.

Laney's Magnet List:

1. Fill out insurance paperwork for accident.
2. Send card to angry soccer mom, apologizing for crashing into her minivan.
3. Call Jared about making *Luna Sings* CD.
4. Sell all canvases.
5. Call Get Good Press and agree to paint their mural.
6. Sell records to High Fidelity.
7. Go through closet. Pare down wardrobe. Take my reluctant orphans to secondhand stores (sell clothes, jewelry, and *gulp* Lucite sunglasses collection).
8. Apologize to Dad (and Mom) for stressing them out.
9. Buy plunger.

By mid-afternoon, I have filled out the insurance paperwork for the accident and painted a watercolor card for Angry Soccer Mom, aka Bettina Reade of 12622 Lake Shore Drive, Longmont, Colorado.

I have also sold most of my record collection, several boxes of clothes, and all but five pairs of my vintage Lucite sunglasses. Selling my records and sunglasses felt like performing seppuku, the ritualistic act of committing suicide by cutting open the abdomen with a short sword. I read somewhere that samurais committed seppuku to release their spirit to the afterlife. I hope giving up some of my most precious possessions will release my spirit into Paris. The alternative—a long, miserable life spent in Boulder without being able to groove to the Mamas and the Papas' *If You Can Believe Your Eyes and Ears,* while wearing my '60s Jackie O–inspired marbleized pearl and black mod specs—is worse than hell. Seriously? The B-side of that album, with "SomebodyGroovy" and "The 'In' Crowd," is the end.

Now I am wearing my ab fave pair of Lucite glasses, '50s golden-brown femme fatale frames that make me look like Barbara Stanwyck, the shady lady in *Double Indemnity,* and maneuvering the Banarama into a parking space on Spruce Street. The owners of two of Boulder's best-known galleries, Artful Soul and Munch & Lunch, have agreed to take all of my finished canvases. Although galleries usually pay sixty percent and keep forty percent, I have agreed to a fifty-fifty split because I need the cash fast.

Named in honor the Norwegian painter Edvard Munch, Munch & Lunch is a gallery cum sandwich shop that draws Pissers— pseudo-intellectuals with serious scratch. Since Munch's paintings are famous for their psychological themes, the sandwiches at Munch & Lunch are named after psychological disorders. My favorite is the Bipolar, a turkey and hot pepper jelly sandwich served with spicy sweet potato fries. Way better than the Schizophrenic, tuna salad and peanut butter.

I finish pulling into the parking space, feed a fistful of coins into the meter, and drop the first load of canvases off at Artful Soul. I drop the rest of my canvases off at Munch & Lunch, grab a Bipolar to go, and am on the freeway headed to Denver to meet Jared at his studio when my phone rings.

I fish my phone out of my purse. I hit the speakerphone button and set the phone in the cup holder.

"Spread the joy."

"That's an unusual greeting," Fanny says, laughing.

"I like to make my expectations clear."

"Well, I am pretty sure I am going to meet your joyful expectations."

I laugh. "You always meet my expectations, Fanny-Bo-Banny. What's up?"

"I got your e-mail about being accepted to the Cadré and wanted to call to congratulate you."

"Thanks."

"What can I do to help you?"

"Just send me good vibes."

"Always," she says, laughing again. "But I was thinking of more tangible help, like a place to live. I spoke to my father, and he said he would be happy to let you stay in my old room. Our place isn't that far from the gallery."

"Thanks, but the program requires us to live at the gallery."

"Bon," she says in her no-nonsense Fanny tone. "What about a plane ticket?"

"I'm working on it."

"I'll buy your ticket."

"Thanks, but if I go to Paris, I really want to get there under my own steam."

"If? *If* is a weak, passive word. It denotes doubt." Fanny's accent is thickest when she is emotional or impassioned. Right now, it is as thick as my brows. "And doubt is a bug that must be crushed beneath your heel. Crush it, Laney."

I imagine a ladybug fluttering its wings in a vain attempt to escape the heel of my fur-trimmed granny boots, and my stomach lurches.

"Crush it!" Fanny orders. "Crush the fat, ugly cockroach before it crawls into your basket and ruins your picnic. Do it!"

"Okay! I'm doing it! I am crushing the cockroach."

"Bon!" she laughs.

Fanny's innate strength can be intoxicating. Just a few minutes talking with her and I feel drunk with the possibilities looming on my horizon. Maybe my doubts will return tomorrow, like a bad hangover, but today I feel empowered, strong, focused.

"Merci, Fanny."

"De rien."

We chat until I pull into the parking garage near Jared's studio. Fanny tells me about some of the handcrafted items she's selling in her boutique, life in her small Highland town, and her plans for her wedding. Before we hang up, she makes me pinkie-promise that I will tell her if I don't raise enough scratch to buy my ticket to Paris.

"Karma might be a mean girl, but she was super nice when she introduced us," I say, sniffling. "I don't know what I did to deserve a friend like you."

"I could say the same thing, ma chérie."

* * *

"That's great, Laney," Jared says, his voice low and reassuring in my headphones. "I think we got it."

It's after midnight. We've been recording songs for over nine hours. Theo showed up a few hours ago with salads and soup from Uber Eats, a vegetarian place not too far from the studio. He rode his bike from Boulder to Denver. Thirty-two miles. Ninety minutes of intense cycling cardio is nothing for Theo, but it means everything to me.

He grins at me through the window and gives me two thumbs-up. I must have done something right for karma to give me such a to-die best friend. Forget Beyoncé and Jay Z, Jennifer Lawrence and Amy Schumer, Craft Beer and Food Truck Tacos. Theo Wilde and Laney Brooks are the OTP of the decade. We are the one true pairing . . . in the completely nonromantic way.

I take off my headphones and leave the booth. Jared and Theo meet me in the hallway.

"We've got six good tracks," Jared says. "That should be enough to upload to iTunes."

"It sounded good, then?"

"Dude, you were slaying it," Theo says.

"Thanks."

We walk back into the studio. Theo and Jared help me pack up my instruments. I had brought my ukulele, guitar, tambourine, and harmonicas.

"I thought of another way you could make some scratch to fund your PBG," Jared says, grabbing my tambourine and giving it a little shake. "Like, serious ka-ching."

"PBG?"

"Paris Bohemian Goals."

I suddenly see myself living like Manet, minus the affluent parents. Working in my cold garret room from sunrise to sunset to capture snapshots on canvas of bohemian and bourgeois Parisian life. Surviving on cheap red wine and baguettes. Exchanging radical ideas on art in smoke-filled cafés. I can't help but smile.

"Hit me. What's your idea?"

"Start a YouTube channel."

I exhale, blowing my bangs off my forehead, and roll my eyes. "There must be, like, a billion singers on YouTube, with, like, a trillion uploads of covers."

"That's because there's, like, a billion dollars to be made on YouTube if you have a popular channel," he says, rolling his eyes and mimicking my *pff whatever* tone.

Jared means well, and I am being a total Rooney (the creepy principal in *Ferris Bueller's Day Off*. Hail Hughes!). A tyrant in Lucite cat's-eyes. A month ago, I would have been excited about the idea of starting a YouTube channel. It would have been all fairies and pixie dust and big dreams. Life has knocked the pixie dust right out of me.

"I appreciate the idea," I say, smiling. "Do you really think I could be the next Madilyn Bailey or Kurt Hugo Schneider?"

"Doubtful," Theo says, pulling his beanie out of his pocket and putting it on his head. I stick my tongue out at him. "Not before you have to leave for Paris. Just keepin' it real."

"I don't think your channel should just be about songs," Jared says.

"You don't?" I turn my attention from Theo to his friend. "Why not?"

"You aren't a one-dimensional person, Laney. You're, like, multi-dimensional. Your channel should be a platform for you to share your many dimensions."

"I'm intrigued."

"What if you used the channel to document the next year of your life? The broad stroke would be your journey from Boulder to Paris, but the finer strokes would be your journey through life."

"Who would want to watch videos about my life?"

"A lot of people. There are loads of twenty-somethings in the world trying to figure out what colors are supposed to be on their canvases. I'll bet they would identify with your struggle. Think about it"—he holds up his fingers like he is framing a shot—"a down-on-her-luck young artist embarks on a journey of self-empowerment and spiritual enlightenment by going to the City of Lights. You could call it *Illuminated* or *Blank Canvas*."

"Pixie dust."

"What?"

"Pixie dust," Theo interjects. "That means she is feeling your idea."

Jared looks at me. "Are you?"

"Totes."

Chapter 7

Laney's Life Playlist
"My Best Friend" by Weezer
"Bitter Sweet Symphony" by The Verve
"Miles Apart" by Yellowcard

"Well, I'm off like Monica Bellucci's bikini top," Theo says, flashing a toothy grin in a perfect imitation of Duckie, our favorite character from our favorite John Hughes movie, *Pretty in Pink*.

My heart hurts. Maybe not as much as Duckie's heart hurt when Andy blew him off for Squaresville Blane, but it *really* hurts. We are standing in my parents' driveway, beside the Bananarama, just like we did when I went off to Alaska for my volunteer year. But somehow this good-bye feels different. Heavier.

I wrap my arms around him in a final hug.

"We will always be best friends, Theo."

I say it for me more than him.

"Duuude, you're harshing my farewell mellow," he laughs, hugging me back. "You know this isn't a forever good-bye?"

We break the hug and stand across from each other.

"I know we will see each other again, but it feels like it did when I moved out of my parents' house. I knew I would see them for Sunday dinners and holidays, but I also knew there would be this barely perceptible shift from intimate to just close." I shrug my shoulders and smile wistfully. "I'm just going to miss sharing all of the minutia of our lives. That's all."

"What if I promise to keep sharing the minutia?"

"Will you?"

"I promise," he says, placing his hand over his heart. "I, Theodore S. Wilde, promise to call Delaney Lavender Brooks every time the Bananarama craps out, FroYo releases a new flavor, or I watch an '80s flick."

I do one of those sad laugh-sniffle noises.

"Before I go"—he opens the driver's side door and lifts a blue bag off the seat—"I got you something."

He hands me the bag. I don't need to open it. I know what is inside.

"You bought me the Jullian Plein Air Easel?"

"You said all of the artists in Paris use that easel."

"Yes, but—"

"But what?" He climbs into the Bananarama and slams the door. "You're an artist, and you're going to Paris, aren't you?"

I nod my head, and tears slip down my cheeks.

"Okay, now you're really harshing my farewell mellow." He turns the key and the Bananarama rumbles to life. "Duuude, stop crying. Tears are for pussies."

He grins and puts the Bananarama into reverse.

What-the-what? I can't believe the last thing my best friend said to me before driving off to chase his dream of being a bike mogul was not to be a pussy.

I am still standing in the driveway, staring down the street at the Bananarama's fading taillights, when my iPhone vibrates in my pocket. I take it out and stare at the screen.

Text from Theo Wilde:
Look inside the bag.

I carry the heavy blue bag into the house and up the stairs to my room. Unzipping the bag, I find an envelope with my name written on it in Theo's practically illegible script.

Inside the envelope I find a gift card to Sennelier, the oldest and most venerated art store in Paris. A generous gift card that would allow me to buy most of the supplies I would need for my year at the Cadré.

I am about to text Theo to tell him I couldn't possibly accept such a generous gift when I see a folded piece of paper sticking out of the envelope.

Laney Dude,

  I know you think I am being way too generous with this gift card, but it's not really a gift. I'm your Stegosaurus Dude. I am investing in your ice cream. Pay me back when you get Ben & Jerry's big. I know you will rock the Paris art scene.

                    Theo

Chapter 8

Laney's Life Playlist
"Be What You Wanna Be" by Darin Zanyar
"She's Leaving Home" by The Beatles
"Big City Dreams" by Never Shout Never

I am flying to Paris tomorrow morning. Icelandair flight 670, departing at 5:00 with a layover in Reykjavik, and I haven't told my parents I am leaving. I don't think my eggshell resolve could take another of my mom's assaults. Hearing her dismiss my art as a hobby and prepubescent diversion was pretty shattering.

If I were a superhero, my superpower would be avoidance. Able to dodge awkward or difficult conversations in a single bound.

It might not sound like much of a superpower, but it's literally saved my life. Imagine, if you will, a dark alternate universe wherein I confessed my intention to use what little money I have scraped together to fly to Paris to be an unpaid intern in an art gallery. KRASH. BLAM. Holy torpedo! Mom would have brought out her heavy arsenal, the prepubescent diversions speech, and I would have folded like Superman's cape.

Call it rebellion. Call it desperation. Call it determination. Call it whatever you want, but ever since I found out I was accepted to the Artistes en Résidence Program, I have been mega-motivated and focused. I have been fabricating my own pixie dust, and I haven't wanted anyone to blow it away.

In *Peter Pan,* Tinkerbell sprinkles the golden, sparkly dust on Wendy, Michael, and John Darling so they can fly around Neverland.

That's all pixie dust is: something that makes you believe you can fly, that you can chase your dreams.

Mom means well. She doesn't mean to be a pixie dust blower. She's of a world that believes pixie dust is the stuff of childish fantasies. I'm of a world that believes pixie dust exists as long as you believe it exists. It's more than a state of mind; it's a way of life. People who live the pixie dust life dream and encourage others to follow their dreams.

In a few minutes, I am going to have to tell my parents I intend to follow my dreams.

"Hey, Mom," I say, walking into the kitchen and taking a deep whiff. "The pork roast smells to die. Anything I can do to help?"

"Would you set the table, please?"

"Abs."

She looks at me with one brow raised.

"I mean, absolutely."

I take the plates out of the cupboard and the silverware out of the drawer beside the dishwasher, and arrange them on the table. I take the pitcher of iced tea out of the fridge and pour us each a glass. Then I sit at the table and wait for the moment I have been dreading for seven weeks and three days. The moment I say, *"Um, Mom, Pops, thanks for the serious parental talk about getting a paying job, one with bennies and advancement opportunities, but I've decided to disregard it and move to Paris instead, where I am going to work for free and live with five other bohemians in an attic room."*

Mom carries the roast to the table. The scent of sage, apples, and roasted potatoes circles around us like a warm, cozy blanket, and for a second, I wonder if leaving home is a good idea. I wonder if I am making decisions that will keep me from creating my own happy little domestic scenes. Is Mom right? Are my prepubescent pursuits leading me toward a lonely and unstable future of frozen dinners purchased with welfare checks?

It's not too late. I could refund my ticket and use the money to buy a sensible pants suit. I could apply to be a substitute music teacher or an art therapist at a home for at-risk youth.

I could . . .

. . . dance to the beat of my own heart. The beat that has been so loud it has drowned out all other sounds. The beat that has brought me to this very moment, this moment of truth. Will I continue to dance to my own tune, or will I fall in step with everyone else, ignore the music in my soul that compels me to skip while everyone else is marching?

Pops is on his second serving of roasted potatoes and carrots when I tell them I have decided to keep on skipping. I know the news will come as a shock to them, but it shouldn't. I have never been a goose stepper. When my classmates were drinking the conformity Kool-Aid, I was sipping Sunny D and spinning circles in the playground.

"I was accepted to the Cadré Artistes en Résidence Program."

I fork some pork into my mouth and wait for Mom to demand I stop skipping and start marching.

"You were?" Mom asks, brows raised.

It's one of those shocked, I-can't-believe-it questions. She draws the "were" out for several insulting beats as if she needs extra time to absorb a scenario in which I actually succeed at something.

"Of course you were!" Pops smiles. "You're a talented artist, Lane."

"You think so?"

"I know so."

This is absolute amazeballs! The conversation I have been dreading for seven weeks and three days, the one where my parents douse my pixie dust with a bucket of cold, wet reality, is *so* not happening. Pops isn't saying my art sucks canal water.

"So, you're okay with me going then?"

He clears his throat and looks at my mother. If he were a cartoon character, this is when he would sputter, his cheeks would turn fire-engine red, and he would obsessively adjust his collar.

My mom rests her fork on her plate. She lifts the napkin from her lap and folds it three times to form a neat rectangle. When she finally speaks, her voice is low and carefully modulated, like she's speaking to a dim-witted child.

"Don't be ridiculous," she says, placing her napkin on her plate. "You don't have the financial means to fly to Paris, let alone live there for six months."

"I can make it work."

She inhales. "How, Laney? How will you make it work? Will you sing a happy song that summons your woodland creature friends, who will bring you forest berries and a basket full of cash?"

"Wow." I lean back in my chair and exhale. "That's totes harsh."

"Life can be harsh, especially if you spend most of it chasing dreams. We aren't living in a happily-ever-after Disney cartoon."

I open my mouth to respond, but all I can do is stare at this alien creature who supposedly hatched me. I look at her. Really look at her. The down-turned lips. The frown lines. The blouse buttoned to the chin.

"How did it happen, Mom?"

"How did what happen?"

"How did you lose your pixie dust?"

She rolls her eyes.

"How did you forget that you can fly?" My voice wavers. "Wasn't there a time when you had a dream?"

"I am not a dreamer, Laney."

Tears flood my eyes.

"Yes, you are," Pops says, reaching for my mom's hand and squeezing it. "You had a lot of dreams when you were Laney's age. We used to spend hours at The Sink, drinking that Golden Ale they had on tap and sharing our dreams."

Wait! *What?* The Sink is a restaurant and bar in Boulder that's been around for, like, ninety years. It's a quirky dive, known for making amazing burgers and attracting famous customers, like Madeleine Albright and Anthony Bourdain. Now, if that's not the quirkiest pairing in the world, I don't know what is.

"You used to go to The Sink?"

I stare at my mother, blinking back the tears. I can't imagine my mom and pops chillin' at The Sink. And they drank Golden Ale on tap? Pops has no idea how much his revelation is giving me life.

Pops nods his head. "That was our place. I even wrote our names on the ceiling near the air vent. Elisabet and Grant, in purple Sharpie."

Theo and I wrote our names on a wall. Everyone writes their names on the walls of The Sink. Everyone, but Professors Elisabet and Grant Brooks? I can't *even* right now.

Mom looks at Pops. Her gaze softens. Her frown lines disappear. The corners of her mouth turn up in a half-smile for just a nano-second.

"That was a long time ago, when we had the luxury to do silly things." Mom looks back at me, frown lines firmly in place. "You're twenty-five, Laney. You've done a lot of silly things, but you don't have the luxury to do many more."

"Being an artiste in résidence at one of the world's most prestigious galleries isn't a silly thing, Mom."

Tears fill my eyes again. As corny, rom-com-worth as it sounds, I want her to love me . . . *just as I am*. I have always wanted her to love me, quirks, lack of focus, habitually late habit, and all.

"You don't have the money for a ticket to Paris."

"Yes, I do."

"You do?" Mom frowns. "A ticket to Paris must be over a thousand dollars. Where did you get that kind of money?"

"Eight hundred and sixty-nine dollars and fifty-two cents," I say, wiping a stray tear with the back of my hand. "And I paid for it with money I earned."

"Earned?" Pops leans forward, resting his elbows on the table. "You didn't tell us you got a job."

"I didn't get a job. I took a gig painting a mural on the wall of Get Good Press. It's an organic juice bar and news agent in the Pearl Street Mall."

"A mural?" Mom asks.

I nod my head.

"And you made enough money painting a mural to buy a ticket to Paris?"

"I made enough to buy *four* tickets to Paris!"

"Good for you, Lane," Pops smiles. "You see what you can accomplish when you put your mind to it? I am so proud of you. My daughter's artwork is on the wall of a business right here in Boulder, for thousands of people to see."

Pops is sprinkling some serious pixie dust on me. It doesn't matter that my artwork has been hanging on the walls of several galleries here in Boulder for months now. I am sparkling with happiness and ready to fly.

"That's great, honey." And now Mom is sprinkling the dust. "I can't wait to go to Get Good Press and see your mural."

Whee! I am floating, free-falling, flying.

"Thanks, Mom."

"But"—she takes a deep breath and blows my pixie dust clean away—"you will need to paint a lot of murals to earn enough to spend a year in Paris."

"I am going to Paris." I see myself making a superhero landing, knee bent, scowl fierce. "Nobody is going to stop me."

"We aren't going to fund your year in Paris."

"I'm not asking you to fund me."

"How will you pay for food, toiletries, art supplies?"

"Munch and Lunch sold four of my canvases, and Artful Soul sold two more." I can't keep the self-congratulatory note from my tone. "I also liquidated my record and sunglasses collections. Added together with the money I have left from doing the mural, I should be able to live like a starving artist in Paris."

I don't bother telling them that my newly padded bank account contains only enough to allow me to live like a starving artist for four of the six months. The last two months I will just be starving. I don't tell them that I am banking on getting a royalty check from iTunes. And I sure don't tell them that I am banking on them floating me a loan if things get Toulouse-Lautrec bad (I am referencing, of course, the artist's struggles with poverty, not syphilis).

Pops sits back in his chair and lets out a long breath. "We hoped she would show some initiative and motivation, Elisabet. I think she's met our hopes."

Mom looks at Pops with her you-can't-be-serious expression, before staring at me, eyes wide, disbelieving.

"I have accepted that you don't want to be a lawyer or doctor, but starving artist? Really, Delaney? Is that really what you aspire to be?"

I remember my conversation with Fanny last night, and a strange sort of déjà vu washes over me.

"Face it, Laney-Bo-Baney, you won't ever be a lawyer or doctor. You have an artist's soul, so own it. You are meant to bring beauty and light into this world. Own your destiny. That's when the magic will happen."

"I'm owning it."

Mom frowns. "Excuse me?"

"I want to be an artist, Mom."

Fanny's voice whispers in my ear. *"Stop saying want. It's a weak, passive word. Own that shit, Laney."*

"I am an artist, Mom."

Chapter 9

Laney's Life Playlist
"Nerd Lust" by Schäffer the Darklord
"Pumpkin Soup" by Kate Nash

"You are not an artiste. You might desire, long, yearn to be an artiste, but you are not truly an artiste until you 'ave suffered for your passion."

I have been in Paris for exactly three hours and fourteen minutes, and I have managed to eat two *pains au chocolat* and anger one Frenchman. Monsieur Alexandre Galliard de Cadré is the gallery manager. He's tall, lithe, intimidatingly sophisticated, and a stickler for punctuality. He didn't say he was upset over my tardiness, but his aura, which is mostly the blue-black of a powerful intellectual, definitely showed some angry red when I walked into the gallery.

I missed the shuttle the gallery had arranged for the *artistes en résidence* because I was buying the aforementioned croissants. Missing the shuttle meant taking a taxi. Taking a taxi meant getting to the gallery an hour after the other artistes and earning Monsieur Alexandre's disapproving tsk-tsk.

"You will suffer while you are 'ere," Monsieur Alexandre says, lifting his chin and looking down his nose in a very Gallic manner. "We demand it! In return, we will give you unprecedented access to some of zhee world's finest artists, living and dead. Zhis is not a summer camp for spoiled infants. Zhis is where you will metamorphose from a moderately talented caterpillar into a magnificent butterfly."

I glance at the *artiste* to my left, a towering, solidly built blond with slicked-back hair and a square jaw. His face is expressionless, his gaze fixed forward. He's wearing a black turtleneck and black skinny pants, and looks like he should be dancing with Mike Meyers in the old-school *Saturday Night Live* Sprockets skit. *Now we dance.* Just the thought makes me want to laugh out loud, so I bite my lip and return my attention to Monsieur Alexandre.

"Modigliani. Cézanne. Manet. Picasso." Monsieur Alexandre waves his hand, gesturing at the walls around us. His accent is as thick as oil paint. "Many of *the* greats have hung on these walls . . ."

No words. There are no words to describe the emotions swirling around inside of me right now. I'll bet if you were to look at my aura it would resemble a Monet painting. Maybe *San Giorgio Maggiore at Dusk,* with its bold infusion of motivated orange and cheerful yellow.

Why haven't I ever thought of comparing auras to famous paintings? It's kind of a genius idea. From now on, when I read someone's aura, I am going to mentally assign them a painting.

"Zhis gallery has an impressive history. It was established by my three times great grandfather in 1802 and is a labor of love for zhee entire Galliard de Cadré family—"

The door opens, and a tall, handsome man enters the gallery. The stranger nods at Monsieur Alexandre, who returns the nod without interrupting his *histoire de gallery.*

I want to pay attention to what Monsieur Alexandre is saying, but I can't hear him. I can't hear anything but the loud thump-thump-thump of my heart. The stranger smiles at me, and the thumping increases in speed and volume. My chest hurts, and I suddenly realize I have been holding my breath from the moment he walked into the gallery. I exhale, and my fringy bangs lift off my forehead.

The stranger chuckles.

Heat flushes my cheeks and spreads down my body. It reminds me of the time I had a crush on Mr. Thomas, my eleventh-grade art history teacher. How I would flush all over whenever he called on me to answer a question.

Whoa. What is happening here? I am not crushing on a suit-sexual, am I?

I lower my chin and study the stranger from behind the safety of my bangs. He's definitely wearing a suit, and I am definitely feeling that flushy-crushy Mr. Thomas feeling. He wears his expensive suit as casually as if it were a pair of jeans and a ripped sweater. He runs a hand through his longish hair, and it falls to one side. The dark stubble shadowing his chin and upper lip, the floppy hair, the roguish grin contrast with his squared-away suit style.

I try to read his aura, but the colors are moving so fast around him they don't make sense. He's like Van Gogh's *Starry Night,* swirly happy colors with dark spots full of mystery and excitement.

"Now," Monsieur Alexandre says, walking toward the back of the gallery, "please follow me, and I will show you to zhe atelier and your rooms."

I grab my easel and follow the other artistes, rolling my suitcase behind me. The wheels make a thunk-thunk noise as they roll over the parquet floor.

Monsieur Alexandre stops walking and pivots on his heel, staring at me with an aghast expression.

"Mademoiselle Brooks, these floors have been here since Madame de Sévigné was writing letters about life in the court of Louis Quatorze. They are older than your country. Kindly carry your case."

I look down at my plastic suitcase, patterned with bright daisies, and heat flushes my cheeks again. It isn't the flushy-crushy kind of heat, either.

Chapter 10

Laney's Life Playlist
"Why Can't We Be Friends?" by Smash Mouth
"Mean" by Taylor Swift

My psychology professor at the University of Colorado Boulder said there are only sixteen personality types. It's a theory that still blows my mind because it means that seven billion people can be neatly sorted into sixteen well-defined categories. I answered the one hundred and thirteen questions on the quiz and was neatly sorted into the ENFP category. The Inspirer. According to the printout my professor handed me, ENFPs are enthusiastic, idealistic, and creative people who live life according to their inner values. They become excited by new ideas, but quickly become bored with details.

Even though there might be some truth to that description of my personality, I don't believe the entire human population can be sorted into one of sixteen categories. That would be like living in a Mondrian painting.

The minimalist approach to analyzing personalities isn't for me. People aren't Mondrian paintings. They're made up of more than a few colors, and their shapes are always changing. We are complex, colorful, textured, shaded canvases.

When I meet new people, I don't feel a need to quickly sort. I prefer to remain open. Otherwise, it's like getting a present and being told what it is before you open it, isn't it? A total bummer.

I hope Monsieur Alexandre and the other artistes aren't sorting me into any one particular category. I've been sorted before. Hipster. Nerd Girl. Space Cadet. ENFP.

Monsieur Alexandre leads us through the gallery, an elegant space with white walls and glossy wood floors, until we come to a grand staircase with gilded wrought-iron railings. We climb the stairs to the second floor.

"Zhis is our upper gallery, where we display sculptures and paintings by lesser-known, up-and-coming artists. And through here"— he pushes on one of the mirrored panels covering one wall to reveal a hidden door—"is zhe private gallery. Entrance to zhis gallery is by invitation, extended to our most esteemed collectors."

I am digging that Monsieur Alexandre calls his clients collectors. It implies they are cultured connoisseurs instead of crass consumers. Art should be collected, not consumed.

He steps through the secret door and invites us to follow him. Stepping into the private gallery is like stepping back in time, into the opulent salon of an eighteenth-century aristocrat. Fabric-covered walls. Subtle lighting. I can almost hear the tinkle of a harpsicord and see the candlelight reflected off the gilded frames showcasing a rococo masterpiece, like by Fragonard or Boucher.

Monsieur Alexandre leads us through another hidden door, and we find ourselves in a narrow stairwell.

"Zhis is the original stairway used by zhe servants. It is also the way you will come and go. Down zhere"—he gestures down the stairs—"you will find a door leading to our private courtyard and zhe street beyond. We will give you the code to zhe cypher lock. It is also zhe way to our vaults. Naturally, zhe vaults are off limits."

Monsieur Alexandre begins climbing the stairs, and we, like pilgrims eager to behold the Promised Land, shift our heavy suitcases and art kits to scramble after him.

To, like, say I had a spiritual moment when I stepped into the atelier would not be an exaggeration. The dove-gray walls and floor faded to the color of driftwood. The old cabinets that have probably contained artistic treasures since before Michelangelo took his first breath. And the wicked old pyramid-shaped ladder that nearly touches the ceiling—something you would expect to see in Cézanne's studio—is seriously giving me life right now.

Monsieur Alexandre strides over to the far side of the room, opens bifold shutters covering floor-to-ceiling windows, and we are suddenly bathed in glorious, golden light from heaven. I feel a peace that passes all understanding. It's nearly as powerful as when a great gray owl swooped out of nowhere, landed on a fence post nearby, and fixed its yellow gaze on me. Since owls are spirit animals sent to remind us that we must move out of the shadow of our fears to fully step into the light of happiness, and I was trying to decide if I should leave the comfort of my parent's home to volunteer in Sitka, I pretty much consider my encounter with the winged one a defining spiritual moment.

I listen as Monsieur Alexandre explains that welcome packets, including city maps, Metro passes, and an itinerary of our work and lecture schedules, have been left for us in our rooms above the atelier. I listen, but just enough to absorb the most important details, because my mind is already flying over the city, mentally surveying the many sites I want to visit, absorb, re-create with oils, crayons, and watercolors.

I look out the window at the neat grassy park enclosed by tall wrought-iron gates and linden trees—place des Vosges, the oldest planned square in Paris, where Henri II once practiced jousting and indignant noblemen met at dawn to duel with pistols or swords.

If I took a short walk down rue des Francs Bourgeois, I could have another spiritual moment at Museé Carnavalet, staring up at the seventeenth-century, Venetian-inspired ceiling painted by Charles Lebrun. Farther down rue des Francs-Bourgeois is Hôtel Herouet, where Brigitte Bardot lived when a *Life* magazine photog arranged for her to meet Pablo Picasso.

I sound like a crazy art fangirl right now, don't I? Some kids memorize baseball statistics or Guinness world records; I memorized the places where artists lived, worked, partied, and died. Back home, I have spiral notebooks full of notes from a lifetime of gathering obscure art trivia.

Let's put it this way: if the art world held conventions like Comic-Con, I would be the one attending dressed like Mary Cassatt (who died blind and miserable at Château de Beaufresne, just outside Paris).

Someone taps my shoulder, and I nearly jump out of my ballet flats. I don't know how long I have been staring out the window, but it must have been a while because Monsieur Alexandre isn't talking anymore. In fact, he isn't even in the atelier.

"Welcome back," says one of the other artistes, a petite blonde with a fierce pixie cut and thick, fluttery lashes. "You were traveling in another dimension, not only of sight and sound, but of mind."

Wait! Am I hallucinating, or did she just quote the opening lines to *Twilight Zone,* season three?

"A journey to a wondrous land of imagination," I say, smiling. I look at the other artistes, but their confused expressions tell me they're not *Zone* fans. "Sorry. What did I miss?"

"Did you hear the part about the welcome packets?"

I nod, and my glasses slip down my nose.

"What about the part about meeting the Galliard-Cadré family for dinner tonight?"

I shake my head.

"Seven p.m. at Bâtard de Valadon on rue Saint-Paul." She smiles and blinks, her lashes fluttering like butterfly wings against her cheeks. "In the meantime, we are supposed to select our rooms and unpack."

"Thank you."

"You're welcome. I'm Rigby Larson, by the way."

"*Rigby. Rigby. Bo-bigby. Banana-fana, fo-figby. Fee fi, mo-migby. Rigby,*" I sing. "*Rigby, rhymes with Twiggy, and you look like Twiggy. Rigby!*"

Rigby laughs. "What was that?"

"My short-term memory is totally Dory, so I sing a little name-game song to help me remember people's names when I first meet them."

The other artistes stare.

"Have you tried drinking green tea with ginseng and rosemary? It helps with focusing and memory loss. My mom sells a blend at her store. She has an herbal supplements shop in Tacoma. That's where I am from." Rigby speaks so fast her sentences run together to form one super-long sentence. "What's your name?"

"Delaney Lavender Brooks, but my friends call me Laney."

"*Laney. Laney. Bo-baney. Banana-fana, fo-faney. Fee fi, mo-maney.*

Laney!" Rigby grins before finishing her song. "*Laney rhymes with zany, and my favorite people are zany. Laney!*"

Rigby has one of the purest auras I have ever read, so I know she's not teasing me.

"You know the opening to *The Twilight Zone,* didn't need me to explain the Dory reference, and sang the name-game song without missing a beat. You are on your way to becoming my PBFF, Rigby Larson!"

"Paris best friend forever?"

"Yes!"

The other female artiste groans and rubs her temples with the tips of her fingers. She's tall with blue-black hair scraped back into a high ponytail. She is one purge away from emaciated.

"Please, stop talking." She speaks with the nasal accent of a New Yorker and *talking* comes out as *tawking.* "You're killing me."

"Sorry," Rigby says. "Wanna pop a squat and get to know each other a bit before we claim rooms?"

"I don't squat."

The fifth artiste, a slight Italian with eyes the color of melted chocolate and a cheerful aura, frowns.

"Pop squat?" He says. "What is this pop squat?"

I drop my suitcase and sit on the floor cross-legged.

"Ah," the Italian says, dropping his suitcase and sitting across from me. "I like to pop squat."

Rigby and Sprockets join us.

The New Yorker stands her ground, towering above us in her six-inch heels, arms crossed, brow furrowed. Her aura is intense, with a lot of competitive, aggressive, ambitious red. It reminds me of Caravaggio's dark and dramatic *Taking of Christ.* I think she will be the one to infuse our group with a motivating energy.

"Why don't you start," Rigby says, smiling up at the New Yorker. "What's your name? Where are you from? What medium do you prefer?"

"Julia. Manhattan. Clay." She spins on her heel and heads for the door. "I'm going to get a cup of coffee."

"Wait!" Rigby cries. "Don't you want to know about us?"

"I know your names. If I wanna know anything else, I'll google you."

Rigby waits until the echo of Julia's footsteps in the stairwell fade away. She is smiling brightly, but I know from having read her aura that she is taking Julia's behavior personally. Rigby has an abstract tan aura. Abstract tans are friendly, cheerful, and sensitive. They are the people-pleasers, the peacemakers.

"I'll bet Julia is a Strider," I say, referencing one of my favorite Lord of the Rings characters. "Menacing at first—"

"—but friendly upon further acquaintance?" Rigby says, finishing my thought.

"She is a Saruman," Sprockets declares. "Self-serving and an enemy to the Fellowship."

I laugh. Rigby laughs. The cheerful Italian laughs. Sprockets does not laugh, but I think I see the corners of his lips twitch.

"I am Giorgio," the Italian says, gesturing to himself. "I am from Bedizzano, Italy. My family, she owns a marble quarry. My father wishes for me to work in the quarry, but I wish to work with the marble. I am a scultore."

"A sculptor?" Rigby says. "That's awesome."

"Grazzi." Giorgio grins. "What about you, Rigby?"

"I am a watercolor painter and glassblower."

"You do the watercolor and the glassblowing?" Giorgio claps his hands. "Bravisma, bella! Bravisma!"

Rigby blushes. My love-dar might be off, but I am picking up strong signals that tell me Giorgio and Rigby are going to make an international love connection before this year is over.

Sprockets is the next to speak.

"My name is Gunthar, and I am from Aachen, Germany," he says, in flawless English. "I am a street artist and painter. I prefer oils."

"Your family?" Giorgio asks. "Do they approve of your painting?"

"I don't have a family." Gunthar's expression remains as unreadable as a physics textbook. "I am alone."

"That's so sad," Rigby says. "You don't have anyone? Not even a distant aunt or uncle?"

"I was left in front of a hospital in Aachen when I was an infant."

"Technically, Frodo Baggins was an orphan because his parents died in a boating accident"—I pat Gunthar's back—"but he didn't let that stop him from embarking on a marvelous journey and joining a remarkably loyal fellowship. We'll be your fellowship, Gunthar,"

"Yes, we will," Rigby says.

Giorgio nods his head.

Gunthar lifts his lips in the briefest, most self-conscious smile I have seen, like, ever. I don't need to read his aura to know that he is a reserved man, as uncomfortable showing his emotions as I am hiding mine.

"I am a painter," I say, steering the conversation back to neutral ground. "My parents are professors. My mom teaches philosophy and reasoning, and Pops teaches physics. I am definitely the octagon in their square world. Being accepted to the Artistes en Résidence Program is, like, the end. I might as well make my funeral playlist because I seriously can't imagine my life getting any better than it is right now, right here."

"I feel you," Rigby says. "When they write my obit, it will say, 'Rigby Larson was a girl scout, museum guide, Loot Crate subscriber, and artiste en résidence. That is all.'"

We are all laughing—all except Gunthar, who has only managed to emit a grunt and a chuckle—and sharing our hopes for the next year when Julia, her long, slender fingers wrapped around a paper Starbucks cup, strides back into the atelier.

"Can we go to our rooms yet, or did you want us to make daisy chains and say what kind of tree we think we are?"

"Great idea, Julia!" Rigby says. "What kind of tree would you be?"

Julia rolls her eyes.

"A tree." Giorgio laughs. "I love it! I would be a lemon tree, because she is a happy tree."

"I would be an umbrella tree because it defies logic," I say. "What about you, Gunthar? What kind of tree would you be?"

Gunthar shrugs.

"You don't talk much, do you?" Julia says.

"Words are highly overused and overrated. I prefer the beauty of silence." Gunthar lifts his bag. "But I like to curse."

"So you don't speak, but you like to fuck," Julia says, assessing

Gunthar over the rim of her coffee cup. "You sound like all of my exes."

Julia doesn't wait for a reaction. She grabs her suitcase and heads up the stairs. We leave our art kits where they are, grab our bags, and follow her. Gunthar, following close behind Julia, bangs his head on a low-lying beam at the top of the stairs.

"Scheisse!" He rubs his forehead with his free hand and curses again. "Scheisse."

The attic is divided into six rooms—a common area, bathroom, and four bedrooms. The two larger bedrooms are designed to house two people, with double beds and wardrobes. The smaller rooms each contain a twin bed and are situated below the eaves, with steep, sloped ceilings and porthole-sized windows.

"I am claiming my territory," Julia says, walking to one of the larger bedrooms and tossing her suitcase on one of the beds. "No offense, but I am not here to make braid buddies. I won't be sitting around in my jammies and eating s'mores. I am here to improve my art."

People-pleaser Rigby is about to follow her into the room when Julia pushes the door shut with her foot. A second later, the sound of the lock clicking into place echoes in the attic. It's like a big exclamation mark at the end of her bold statement.

Rigby looks at us through wide eyes.

"Is it me, or is she just the rudest person ever?"

"She's definitely raining on our Paris parade." I instantly feel guilty for voicing such an ungenerous thought. The soothing sensei on my Positive Vibes! app would recommend I balance the negative with a positive. "But I bet she will hop on the float just as soon as she gets some rest."

"She is, how you say, arrogante," Giorgio says.

"She's confident."

Turning the negative into a positive.

"What's wrong with s'mores?" Rigby asks.

"Like, not a thing," I smile. "I dig s'mores."

"Me too!" Rigby returns the smile, but there's still a shadow of pain in her expressive eyes.

"I'll be your braid buddy, Rigby."

"You will?"

I push my glasses up my nose and nod.

"We take the small rooms"—Giorgio carries his suitcase into a room with a single bed—"so you can be braid buddies, no?"

"No," I say, rolling my daisy case into the room. "The ceilings are way too low for you guys. Gunthar will bruise his spätzle every time he gets out of bed."

"My spätzle?" Gunthar asks from the doorway.

"Your noodle."

He frowns, so I make a fist and knock on my head.

"Ah, mein kohlkopf!"

"You take the big room, no?" Giorgio asks.

"Are you kidding?" I flop on the bed and stare out the round window just over the iron headrail. "A garret room with a view of the Parisian skyline is my happy place."

"She is very small," Giorgio says, holding up his fingers as if measuring an inch.

"She is cozy."

"And there's less space to clean," Rigby says, carrying her suitcase into the room beside mine.

"Danke," Gunthar says.

"No worries."

Giorgio carries his suitcase out of the room, and I close the door. I pull my iPhone out of my purse and send a text to Mom and Pops, letting them know I am safe and sound in Paris. Then I snap a picture of the view outside my window and send it to Fanny on the free texting app I downloaded before leaving Colorado. Thankfully, the gallery offers free Wi-Fi (pronounced *we-fee* in France) because Mom turned off my account when I told her I was leaving on a jet plane to Paris. I prepaid for one month of the cheapest international plan so I could make emergency calls.

Fanny's response hits my phone in seconds.

TEXT FROM STÉPHANIE MOREAU:
Didn't I tell you life would look better after you stepped out of your onesie?

Chapter 11

> TEXT FROM THEO WILDE:
> Have you done it yet?

> TEXT TO THEO WILDE:
> Done what?

> TEXT FROM THEO WILDE:
> Rocked the Paris art scene.

> TEXT TO THEO WILDE:
> I just got here.

> TEXT FROM THEO WILDE:
> Right. So I'll give you another day.

I unpack my clothes, kick off my flats, and am chilling on my bed, listening to a guided meditation on realizing your dreams when someone softly knocks on my door.

"Come in."

The door opens, and Rigby sticks her head in.

"I thought I heard you moving around," she says, coming into my room and gently closing the door. "I can't sleep. Wanna blow this Popsicle stand and take a walk?"

"Shyeah!"

I jump up, slip my feet into my flats, and grab a sweater from the dresser, a vintage store find made of cashmere and embroidered with ladybugs. I think the ladybugs add a whimsical touch to my outfit—a polka-dot Peter Pan collar dress with black tights.

We hurry down the stairs and out the door into the courtyard. The late-afternoon sun is flirting with the clouds, slipping coyly behind one and then another, and a chilly spring breeze is flirting with the delicate petals of a potted hydrangea atop a bistro table in the center of the courtyard. Purplish-blue petals float on the breeze before swirling to the ground.

We walk across the courtyard and exit a set of heavy, blue-painted doors into the street.

"Was there somewhere you wanted to go?" I ask, slipping my arms into my sweater and buttoning it up to my collar. "Or do you just want to wander and see what serendipity has planned for us?"

"Let's wander."

We walk by *boulangeries,* the scent of buttery bread hanging seductively in the air, like perfume spritzed before the arrival of a lover, and *fleuristes,* their buckets of flowers artfully arranged beneath green canopies.

We come to a brown storefront with a wrought-iron sign: a cherub holding an ice cream cone and the words *Amarino, Artisenal Gelato.*

We look at each other and grin.

"Bienvenue Amarino!"

A pretty girl in an apron greets us.

I order two scoops of *amarena et chocolat*—cherry and chocolate. Rigby orders two scoops of *amarena et fiordilatte*—cherry and Italian vanilla. The girl behind the counter scoops the gelato with a little paddle, molding it on the cone until it resembles a flower in bloom.

I think of the FroYo Theo and I would get back in Boulder, artlessly dispensed from large humming machines, like Play-Doh squeezed out of a plastic Play-Doh extruder, and decide I prefer my frozen dairy desserts served with panache.

We take our cones and continue exploring the Marais.

"So how did you get the name Rigby?" I say, licking my cone. "I've only ever heard it in the Beatles song *Eleanor Rigby.*"

"That's my name."

"Rigby?"

"Eleanor."

"Wait." I stop walking and grab her arm. "Your name is Eleanor Rigby?"

She nods. "Eleanor Rigby Larson."

"Serious?"

"As Whistler's mother."

We keep walking.

"Your mom must have been crazy about The Beatles."

"Moved to the compound, drank the Kool-Aid crazy." Rigby keeps walking. "She holds candlelight vigils at the park near her store every year on the anniversary of John Lennon's death."

"Way to represent, Moms!"

"You think?"

"Totes." I pluck a fat cherry out of my cone and pop it into my mouth. "It sounds like your mom is a free spirit."

"The freest." She holds her cone out to offer me a bite, but I shake my head. "What about you? How did you get the name Lavender? Are your parents hippy-dippies, too?"

I snort. "I wish. They conceived me while they were visiting a lavender farm in the south of France—their idea of a wild time before joining the rank and file of academia."

"Your parents sound pretty amazing."

"My parents are pretty amazing, but . . ."

"But?"

I hear my mom's voice in my head, saying, *"Now, Laney, isn't it time you gave up your prepubescent diversions and acted like an adult?"*

"They're academics, especially my mom. She just doesn't have an artist's soul, you know?" Rigby nods her head, so I continue sharing my tale of woe. "She doesn't get me. Sometimes I think I see a tiny flicker of light in her eyes, a glimmer that tells me there is a bohemian just trying to break out of those conservative clothes, but . . . *nope*. I think my mom came out of the womb clutching her twelve-year plan. What about your mom?"

"My mom is cool," Rigby says. "She supports my art and is proud of me for making it into the Artistes en Résidence Program, but she doesn't support my . . . lifestyle."

"Oh, I get it. There are a lot of parents who don't accept the LGBT plus community. I think that will change as . . ."

"What?" Rigby laughs. "I am not part of the LGBT community."

"Then what's the deal? Do you read wicked-trashy erotic fiction, get blitzed on the weekends, and shoplift Nutella?"

Rigby laughs again. "Why would anyone shoplift Nutella?"

"Oh, it's a problem."

"You're serious?"

"Totes." I shiver, but it's not from the gelato or the cool spring breeze. I am randomly remembering Monsieur Tall, Dark, and Hot's flirty gaze, and it's doing things to me. "I heard on NPR that, like, there is a shortage of hazelnuts. People all over the world have been stealing jars of Nutella."

"Shut up!"

I put my hand over my heart and raise three fingers in the air in the Girl Scout pledge of honor. "Some Nutella nuts lifted eleven thousand pounds from a parked cargo truck last year. Swear it."

Rigby shakes her head. "Well, I can promise you I don't jack jars of Nutella in my spare time."

"I didn't think you looked like the sort."

"I'm more of a Goober girl."

"Ohmygod!" I grab her arm. "I love Goober!"

"Me too."

"Whoever thought to put peanut butter and jelly in the same jar—"

"Genius."

"Right? Goober on white bread with the crusts cut off and a bottle of Sunny D." I close my eyes and moan. "Old-school fat fest. It would be faster to inject fifty ccs of sugar directly into your veins, but—"

"—but then you wouldn't have the fun of sticking your knife into the swirls of peanut butter and strawberry jelly."

"Exactly!"

We are laughing as we link arms and hurry across the busy rue de

Rivoli. We keep walking until we come to a tree-lined road leading to the river.

"So, if you aren't a Nutella nabber, what's the deal with your mom?"

"She doesn't like Matthias."

"Who is Matthias?"

"My boyfriend. We met in college but never dated. We ran into each other eighteen months ago, and he asked me out on a date. We went to lunch and spent the next eight hours talking." She sighs one of those dreamy, I'm-in-love-love-love sighs. "We've been inseparable ever since."

"So why is she harshing your Matthias mellow?"

Rigby laughs. "Harshing my Matthias mellow. That's a good one. I am going to use it the next time I talk to her."

"You're welcome." I grin. "So, she doesn't like Matthias. What's wrong with him? Does he sniff glue? Wear your panties? Drive an SUV? Vote republican? Hate The Beatles?"

"He's a man."

"Okay?"

"That's it. He's a man, and she doesn't like men."

"She must have liked them at one time, because you're here. That, or she made a deal with the fey ones to bring her a pixie child. You look like a little pixie with that haircut. It's adorbs, by the way."

She touches her head. "Really? Thanks. I just got it cut."

Rigby explains that her mom doesn't hate men, not exactly. She simply doesn't believe a woman should alter her life in *any* way for a man.

"She's a card-carrying, bra-burning feminist who believes women should pay their own way, hold their own doors, and keep their own names after marriage." Rigby takes a deep breath and exhales. "Actually, she doesn't even believe in marriage. She thinks it's an archaic, chauvinistic tradition meant to subjugate women. She says women cheapen their worth when they exchange their autonomy and power for a ring."

"Are you engaged?"

"No," Rigby says, handing me her gelato so she can button her sweater. "But she says I've changed since I started dating Matthias."

"Don't we change a little every time we let a new person into our lives?" I think about how I became aware of my lack of focus after I met super-focused Fanny. "Friends should broaden our horizons and challenge us to be better than we already are, especially *boy*friends."

"I agree."

She takes her gelato back and tells me how Matthias scored a suit job with Starbucks Corporation right out of college. She says he worked in Seattle until three months ago, when the company transferred him to Paris.

"He's part of a team tasked with running a multimillion-dollar campaign to make Starbucks more appealing to the café culture." She smiles, and her eyes sparkle with pride. "Apparently Europeans think Starbucks' employees are impersonal and the coffee is mediocre. Matthias is studying the variations in coffee consumerism in Europe and coming up with brilliant ideas to make the stores more appealing to the French. It's serious anthropological marketing."

"It sounds like it."

I don't tell Rigby that I am pretty anti-Starbucks. I think it is a bottom-line-oriented, soul-sucking corporation that propagates conformity. Also, after Starbucks bought Teavana, they started sourcing the tea from cheaper, less healthy sources. They totally messed with the Samurai Maté blend, my fave. The spicy peppercorns were gone, and the lead value was way, way up.

"I can't drink their coffee because it makes my stomach ache, but last spring my mom bought me a Cherry Blossom Green Tea Matcha Frappuccino. I died." If I wasn't anti-Starbucks, I would have become a Cherry Blossom addict. No lie. "So, this internship will let you see the OOYA more."

"Ooyah?"

"Object of your affection."

"Totally," Rigby says. "I am swinging on stars."

The existence of Matthias the Marketer tells me my love-dar is way off. I was picking up life forms on planet Giorgio, but it must have been a blip because Rigby is way gone for Matthias, like crazy out there gone.

We are walking down a narrow road not lined with cafés and bistros. Rigby grabs my arm and squeezes it.

"Ohmygod. There he is."

"Who?" I look around. "Your boyfriend?"

"No, *your* boyfriend."

I snort and take a bite out of my cone, getting some chocolate gelato on my nose. "I don't have a boyfriend. If someone kept track of my love life in a checkbook, I would be in the red. Like way, way in the red."

"I think someone wants to make a deposit."

I follow her gaze, and my cheeks flush with heat. Flushy-crushy heat.

Monsieur Tall, Dark, and Hot, the suitsexual from the gallery, is sitting at an outdoor café, watching me devour my cone. He smiles, the slow, confident smile of one proficient in the art of seduction. A smile that says, *"I am in no hurry. I will savor this moment as I am savoring my wine and you are savoring your gelato."*

My stomach drops to my flats, and I look around to see if he is smiling at someone else, maybe his French supermodel girlfriend just returning from a lingerie shoot. It's a reaction worthy of a John Hughes heroine. Remember that scene in *Pretty in Pink* when Andie is in the library working on a computer and she receives a message from Blain, the OOHA (object of her affections)? Remember how her eyes widened and she gasped? How she looked around the library to make sure she wasn't the target of a cruel high school prank? Right now, Andie is my Hughes spirit heroine.

Monsieur Tall, Dark, and Hot's cell phone is sitting on the table. It rings, but he doesn't immediately reach for it. He continues to stare and smile.

"I think he wants to talk to you," Rigby says. "You should go over there."

I look at Rigby. "Are you crazy?"

"Maybe paint myself blue and walk around with a loaf of bread strapped to my head Salvadore Dalí crazy, but not slice off my ear Vincent van Gogh crazy."

Rigby grins and waggles her eyebrows, and I can't help but laugh. She's definitely going to be my PBFF.

When I look back at Monsieur Tall, Dark, and Hot, he has his cell phone pressed to his ear and is jotting furiously in a notebook.

I clutch Rigby's arm and pull her down a narrow, cobblestone street, away from Monsieur Makes-Me-Flushy-Crushy hot.

We make another turn and find ourselves in the shadow of the spires of the Cathédrale Notre Dame. We both stop walking and stand in the shadows, staring up at the headless statues of the twenty-eight kings of Judah.

"Did you know the heads of the twenty-eight kings of Judah were chopped off during the French Revolution?" Rigby asks.

"Yes," I say, continuing to walk toward the southernmost point of the Île de la Cité, the island in the middle of the Seine. "Did you know the heads were found in 1977 and are on display in the Musée de Cluny?"

"Shyeah."

We continue walking until we arrive at the end of the Île de la Cité. I point to a green park behind the cathedral.

"Do you know what used to stand on that spot?"

"The Morgue," Rigby says. "Art students from the nearby Académie would sneak in at night to study and sketch the corpses."

"Eugène Delacroix is rumored to have purchased corpses so he could use them as models while he was painting *Liberty Leading the People*"—I ball up my napkin and toss it in a nearby garbage can— "which was put on display at—"

"—Luxembourg Palace, just a little to the south of here."

"I can't *even* right now!" I look at her through wide, worshipful eyes. "You are seriously giving me life."

"You're giving *me* life."

We lean against the stone wall that stands between the cathedral and the river and stare into the breeze-rippled waters of the Seine. A *batobus* filled with picture-snapping tourists glides by, the cathedral and clouds above reflected in its glass-topped roof. We keep watching even as the sun sinks low behind the mansard roofs and streaks the bruised sky with angry orange welts.

The cathedral bells begin ringing. *Dong-dong-dong* . . . Six haunting dongs that echo in the dark night.

"We better get going if we want to make it to the restaurant in time to meet the Galliard-Cadré family," I say, taking a last look at the river. "Monsieur Alexandre might have me sent to the guillotine if I am late again."

We have made it back to the Marais and are only a few blocks from the restaurant when I decide to share a warm fuzzy with Rigby.

"I am so glad you're here, Rigby. I think we are going to be super-tight friends."

"Me too."

"I don't have many girlfriends."

"Get out."

"I'm serious. I have a Theo."

"Oo, who is Theo? Your boyfriend?"

"Eww!" I shudder. "That is disgusting. Theo is my BFF."

"So you have a BFF, but not a BF?"

"Nope."

"What about the suit guy?"

I play dumb. "What suit guy?"

"Don't even." Rigby hits my forearm. "I saw the way he looked at you, like a starving man looking at a jar of Goober."

"I'm not sure how I should take being compared to a jar of Goober." I laugh. "Destiny has brought me to Paris to study art."

"Maybe destiny has brought you to Paris for more than one reason. Art and love."

"I will be happy with art and friendship."

"You don't strike me as a lonely person."

"I am too happy to be lonely, but sometimes I wish I had a girl-friend who gets me the way Fanny gets Vivia."

"Fanny?"

I tell Rigby about all about Fanny, about how we met in Alaska, how she introduced me to her outrageously funny best friend, Vivia, and about how I envy their super-tight friendship because I have never had that with another woman.

"People don't get me."

"I get you," Rigby says, linking her arm through mine. "At least, I think I do."

"I think you do too."

Chapter 12

"Bienvenue dans Bâtard de Valadon, mesdames."

A large man with slicked-back black hair and an aura indicating cheerfulness and mischief greets us as soon as we step into the foyer of the elegant restaurant. Rigby tells him we are with the Galliard-Cadré group.

"Ah, but you are early."

I look at my Minnie Mouse watch. 6:22.

"Je suis desolée, monsieur. Nous reviendrons."

"Nonsense," he says, dismissing my offer to return at the appointed hour with a flick of his wrist. "If you would like, you are quite welcome to sit in the winter garden. Perhaps you would like a glass of wine?"

We follow him down a long, dark-paneled hallway, passing a curio cabinet filled with strange objects, to an enclosed courtyard topped with an art deco glass dome.

"Voilà! Le jardin d'hiver."

The winter garden is an intimate space with gray-painted walls, clear Lucite tables, and dramatic black-and-white photographs of flowers in bloom.

"What a beautiful room."

"Merci." He holds his hand out, inviting us to be seated at one of the tables. "My name is Robert, and it would be my pleasure to bring you a glass of wine. Which would you prefer, red or white?"

"Merci beaucoup, Monsieur Robert." I take a seat on one of the Lucite chairs and repeat our host's name in my head several times to commit it to memory. "I am a starving artist. L'eau de la vie is not in my budget."

"Une situation tragique." He clucks his tongue and shakes his head. "Please, allow me to bring you a complimentary glass of wine."

"Thank you, but—"

"Mademoiselle." Robert presses his hand to his heart. "I am a Parisian, born and raised. It pains me to think of you spending your first night in my city without at least one glass of l'eau de la vie. S'il vous plâit?"

"That would be lovely," Rigby says. "Merci."

"Red or white?" He holds up his hand. "Non, leave it to me."

Robert returns carrying two glasses and a bottle of wine on a silver tray. He places the glasses on the table, pulls the cork out of the bottle, and pours us each a glass of white wine. We thank him.

"Bâtard de Valadon," I say, taking a sip of my wine. "Valadon's Bastard. That's an interesting name for a restaurant."

"Oui."

I am waiting for Robert to elaborate, but he merely crosses his arms and rests them on his rotund belly, smiling at me with a twinkle in his eye. I haven't decided which painting represents Robert's aura, but it is definitely one with a lot of yellow. Maybe Van Gogh's *Wheat Field with Reaper and Sun.*

"You know this name, Valadon?" he asks.

I nod my head. "Suzanne Valadon was a painter and popular artist's model in the late nineteenth century. She sat for many famous artists, including Renoir."

"In fact, she is the woman dancing in his painting *Dance at Bougival*," Rigby says.

"Brava!" Robert uncrosses his arms and claps his hands together. "Now I shall tell you the story of how this restaurant came to be called Bâtard de Valadon."

Robert drags another chair over to our table. He takes his time situating himself. He leans leaning back in the chair and sticks his legs out, crossing them at the ankles. He forms a steeple with his fingers and takes a deep breath. Robert is definitely a showman, a natural-born storyteller who knows how to build suspense.

"You are correct, mademoiselles. Suzanne Valadon was a popular artist's model. In the days of Renoir and Degas, it was common for models to pose nude. It is only natural a man should feel a stirring of desire if he spends hour after hour staring at a naked woman." Robert pauses, his stomach rising and falling several times before he resumes his tale. "Artists, they often practiced more than just painting, eh? They practiced the art of séduction."

I look at Rigby and know what she is thinking. Robert's story is basic. Every art history student knows artists often seduced their models. Rose Beuret spent fifty years as Auguste Rodin's muse and lover before he finally put a ring on it (she died two weeks later).

"You are thinking, but Monsieur Robert, this is common knowledge, eh?" He chuckles. "Nine months after modeling for Renoir and Degas, Suzanne Valadon gave birth to a bâtard. She took the infant to Renoir, and do you know what he said?"

I know the answer, but I shake my head.

"Renoir lifted the blanket, looked at the squalling infant, and said, 'He can't be mine, the color is terrible!'" He clucks his tongue and shakes his head. "Then she went to see Degas. He lifted the blanket, looked at the squalling infant, and said, 'He can't be mine, the form is terrible!'"

Robert pauses again, giving us time to sip our wine.

"Poor, miserable Suzanne, cast off by Renoir, discarded by Degas, went to a café to drown her sorrows in wine, but while she was there, she saw another artist, Miguel Utrillo. She told him her unfortunate story, and Utrillo said, 'Call the baby Utrillo. I would be glad to put my name to the work of either Renoir or Degas!'"

Robert crosses his arms and stares at us expectantly, his eyes twinkling.

"Wait," I say. "Is this the café where Valadon told Utrillo her sad story? Here?"

Robert shrugs his shoulders. "It is believed by some. Nobody knows for certain, but it makes for a very good story, no?"

He looks down the hallway.

"Ah, I see Monsieur Cadré has arrived."

* * *

Monsieur Alexandre arrived along with his intimidating family, two well-known Parisian artists, the Ministre de la Culture, the curator of the Musée d'Art Moderne de la Ville de Paris, and a journalist for one of France's most popular art magazines. Gunthar, Giorgio, and Julia followed close behind.

Bâtard de Valadon's dining room is beyond elegant—way, way beyond—with wood floors stained black, plush velvet upholstered chairs, and art deco chandeliers. I am seated between an elderly woman wearing a Pucci scarf tied artfully around her orange hair and the journalist.

Would it be negative if I said I wished I were back in the jardin d'hiver enjoying Robert's infectious bonhomie, or back in Boulder at Munch & Lunch noshing on a Bipolar sandwich? Yes, yes, it would. I take a deep breath and remind myself that every minute brings a new opportunity, and every new opportunity brings a chance to connect in a meaningful, spiritual way. Breathe in positivity, breathe out negativity.

Monsieur Alexandre is seated at the head of the table. He stands and clears his throat.

"I would like to thank zhe Ministre de la Culture for taking time out of her busy schedule to join us tonight." Monsieur Alexandre nods at the minister, a petite, dark-haired woman with Michelangelo-worthy bone structure, and she nods back. "Two hundred and fourteen years ago, Jean-Baptiste Galliard began collecting superlative works of art by young masters in what would become zhe Galliard-Cadré Gallery. Sixty years ago, my grandfather, zhe distinguished gentleman seated at zhe far end of zhe table, conceived of an idea to foster young artists by giving them an opportunity to live in a working gallery. Zhe Galliard-Cadré family is proud to act as patrons to a new group of talented young artists. It is our pleasure, our passion, our destiny to nurture your talent, and so, we welcome you, our artistes en résidence."

Monsieur Alexandre introduces each person seated at the table. Jacques-Louis Galliard de Cadré, the patriarch of the family, nods his head but does not smile. He is everything I imagine the head of an art dynasty to be—reserved, watchful, dignified, discerning. He is tall, like Monsieur Alexandre, but with silver streaks through his dark hair. His wife, seated beside him, is equally dignified. Madame

Galliard de Cadré is an accomplished watercolorist, and her artwork has hung in Europe's most prestigious galleries.

Monsieur Alexandre's parents stare at each of us as if assessing our value. Madame Galliard catches me staring and regally nods her head.

Monsieur Alexandre introduces his sister next. Impeccably dressed in a black pencil skirt, a sheer black silk blouse, and high heels that lace up her ankles, Celine Galliard de Cadré is the embodiment of every woman's fear when they imagine themselves visiting a Parisian boutique. Her dark hair has been cut in a sharply angled bob that frames her beautiful face. Celine has made a name for herself by organizing pop-up exhibitions of edgy contemporary artists. Her art raves are held in abandoned buildings and draw heiresses with money to burn and bad-boy princes. The young elite attending her events sip expensive champagne, listen to technopop spun by millionaire DJs, and spend small fortunes on paintings by artists they hope will be the next big thing.

Finally, there is Aunt Fantine, the Pucci-wearing elderly woman seated beside me. Fantine Galliard, known simply as Fantine, has been an eccentric figure on the art scene for over fifty years. She partied with the Rebel Painters, the post–World War II artists who challenged the aesthetic establishment with their radical abstract expressionism and shifted the world's focus from Paris to New York. She's rumored to have been Adolph Gottlieb's muse and Jackson Pollock's mistress. Until her retirement a few years ago, she was the most coveted guest speaker at museums and art schools on the subject of abstract art.

"My brother had other obligations and could not join us, but you will meet him at some point," Monsieur Alexandre says, finishing his introductions. "Now let us dine and get to know each other better."

I divide my time between Aunt Fantine, who turns out to be as colorful as an Andy Warhol painting, and the journalist, Henri, who asks me about my art and seems genuinely interested when I tell him about my exhibit at Munch & Lunch.

"Munch and Lunch is like McD, only with art on the walls?"

"McDonalds?" I laugh. "No, Munch and Lunch is not a fast-food restaurant. The chef is classically trained and serves farm-to-table, organically grown food. He makes a turkey sandwich called the Bipolar that literally gives me life."

I look down at the lamb chop with balsamic vinegar and creamy carrots on my plate and feel a pang of homesickness.

"You don't like zhe lamb chop?" Henri asks. "You would rather have Big Mac?"

"I am morally opposed to the eating of baby animals." I take a bite of the carrots and swallow. "The carrots are delicious, though."

"But you aren't morally opposed to eating turkey?"

"No, why?"

"You must know turkeys raised on farms for gastronomy are hatched in incubators. Zhey do not see zheir mothers." Henri clucks his tongue and shakes his head. "Zheir beaks are cut off and zhey are forced to eat only antibiotic-laced cornmeal. Most of zhem die young, starving zhemselves from zhe stress of zheir environment."

"Is that true?"

"Oui."

"That's depressing."

Henri shrugs, as if to say, "Eh, what can you do?" He turns his attention to Julia, who is seated on his other side.

I look down at the pinkish lamb chop on my plate. Truthfully, I don't know why I boycott lamb and not pork, beef, or chicken. Did I imagine poultry farmers to be more humane than sheep farmers? I guess I never really thought about it. The anti-lamb bandwagon was big in Boulder, so I jumped on. Truthfully, I don't know how I feel about eating lamb. It's just another thing I am trying to figure out. In college, it's easy to follow the crowd onto the bandwagon. Maybe it's time I figured out if I want to keep riding or get off.

I glance down the table at Monsieur Alexandre and notice he has been watching my exchange with Henri. This spread probably cost the gallery several hundred euros. I don't want Monsieur Alexandre to think I am an ungrateful, uncouth American, so I cut my lamb into small pieces and pretend to fork some into my mouth. When he looks away, I hide the meat under my greens.

Aunt Fantine elbows me and crooks her finger. I lean closer.

"I do not like lamb, either," she whispers in French. "What they do to those poor animals is barbaric. I preordered a steak. Would you like some?"

I told you Aunt Fantine was a cool old bird. In another life, we were probably best friends.

"I am all good, but thank you."

"De rien." Aunt Fantine lifts her wineglass and tosses back the contents. "My nephew doesn't eat lamb."

"Monsieur Alexandre?"

"Non, his brother, my other nephew." Aunt Fantine nods at a waiter. He hurries over and refills her empty glass. "He is a nonconformist, like me."

I look at Monsieur and Madame Galliard de Cadré, the very picture of decorum, and find it hard to believe that one of their children is a rebel. Aunt Fantine tilts her head and squints, peering deep into my eyes, as if reading my soul.

"You are a nonconformist, aren't you?" She doesn't wait for me to answer. "Bon! The world needs more people who aren't afraid to march to the tune of their own drum."

"Sometimes it would be a lot easier if I marched to everyone else's beat."

Before I realize it, I am metaphorically stretched out on a couch, unloading my life story on Aunt Fantine Freud. I tell her about my life back in Boulder. I tell her how difficult it was for me to be the disorganized, dyslexic, attention-challenged child of two highly organized and focused college professors. I tell her about my gigs as Lunaria the Unicorn and singing with my band at nameless dives around Denver. I even tell her about crashing my car, getting evicted, and having to move back home with my mom and dad.

"My parents would like me to be more like them, conservative, responsible, mature, professionally ambitious, but I am not trying to be different. I am just being . . . me."

Aunt Fantine pats my arm. "The biggest challenge in life is to be yourself in a world that is trying to make you like everyone else."

"Wow. You get my struggle."

"Ralph Waldo Emerson gets your struggle, ma cherie. That was his quote, not mine." She tenderly squeezes my arm before letting it go. "I will tell you what I used to tell my nephew: You are not alone in this world. You are part of a minority of souls who are truly unique. The Divine One used more crayons when he sketched you. Do not be ashamed of your different colors."

Chapter 13

I am thinking about Aunt Fantine's words the next morning as I set up my easel in the gardens of the Tuileries. I have found a quiet spot in the shadow of the Musée de l'Orangerie, the museum that is home to eight of Monet's *Water Lilies* murals, and I am watching the early-morning sunlight spill from the sky like liquid gold.

I woke up before the fairies had sprinkled the morning dew, my body clock all jacked up from jet lag, and decided to get a jump on the day. I am not scheduled to work in the gallery until after lunch, which means I have several hours free to paint, people watch, and absorb the atmosphere.

I lean back in one of the many green lawn chairs scattered around the park and lift my face to the sky. It's too early to get a suntan, but the warmth feels good on my cold cheeks. I am waiting for my muse to suddenly materialize like a gossamer specter, to float on the breeze and whisper in my ear a language that is all our own, a language of whimsical ideas and unspoken poetry. But it is the ghost of Aunt Fantine that whispers in my ear.

"You are part of a minority of souls who are truly unique. The Divine One used more crayons when he sketched you. Do not be ashamed of your different colors."

I see the garden in my mind's eye. I see people—featureless silhouettes, really—standing around the fountain, their faces turned to the sky as if in supplication. Then, suddenly, the silhouettes explode like fireworks. Bright, beautiful colors that re-form into the shapes of angels rising to the heavens.

I grab a charcoal pencil and begin sketching the scene on my canvas. I often use a charcoal pencil to sketch out a scene; then I use acrylics, and then oils. Vermeer used a similar technique when he created *Woman Holding a Balance.*

Soon the outline of the scene I had imagined in my head covers the canvas, and I am feeling that familiar excitement that comes with the genesis of each new work. Anticipation and hope mingle. I squirt some paint on my palette and begin to make my artistic hope a reality.

Theo says painting is my form of Transcendental Meditation, that my mind literally leaves my body to travel to a nonphysical realm of creativity and insight. I definitely get in a zone. I am in the zone now, focused on the colors and shapes that will bring my vision to life. The gardens and tourists fade away, and I am one with the paints. I work until my stomach growls loud enough for the sound to reach the nonphysical realm. I haven't eaten anything since dinner last night, and I am starving.

I rest my brush on the tray attached to the easel and lean back to assess my work. It's pretty spec. Or it will be spectacular once I finish it.

I bought a ham and cheese crêpe and a lemon San Pellegrino from a street vendor on my way to the gardens this morning. I pull the crêpe out of my backpack and devour it. I had finished my San Pellegrino and returned to my work when someone taps me on the shoulder.

It's like being woken from a dream. That wistful feeling you have when are lying in bed, trying to snatch the wispy string of your dream before it floats away, like a balloon on the breeze, but realize it is too late. It is out of your grasp, floating, floating, floating away.

I look over my shoulder and discover a middle-aged tourist in bright white sneakers, a fanny pack strapped around her waist.

"Excuse me," she says, smiling. "Do you know what time it is?"

I look at my watch and see that Minnie's little hand is pointed to one and her big hand is pointed to five. It can't possibly be 1:25. No way. I have thirty-five minutes to pack my easel and run almost four miles back to the gallery. It took me an hour to walk here this morning, before the streets were crowded with tourists.

"It's one twenty-five," I say, tossing my supplies inside my kit, closing my easel, and throwing my backpack over my shoulder.

The tourist thanks me and hurries off.

Nearby, there is a girl selling ice cream from a stand. I run over and ask her for directions to the closest Metro station.

She points across the park. "The Concorde station. Walk straight down this path until you come to the rue de Rivoli."

"Merci, mademoiselle."

I run through the park, clutching my easel and wet canvas, taking the Metro station stairs two at a time. I look at the map hanging on the wall, dissected by dozens of colorful lines, and see that I need to take the yellow line, Metro line one, in the direction of Château de Vincennes. I feed coins into the automated machine until it spits out a ticket. I snatch the ticket, stick it in the turnstile, and run down through the station, my steps echoing in the tiled tunnel. The train squeals to a stop just as I arrive.

The doors slide open. A steady stream of passengers flows by me. Finally, I wade through the mass onto the train and collapse into one of the empty seats, my easel banging painfully against my shins.

Thank Gaudí! I don't even want to imagine what Monsieur Alexandre would have done if I had arrived late for my first shift at the gallery. Isn't the guillotine still used as the preferred method of capital punishment in France? I'm not sure, but I think it is. And I think insulting a gallery owner's sensibilities is pretty much a capital offense in Paris. I am willing to suffer for zhe art, but decapitation is taking it way, way too far.

The train rumbles along, stopping at the Palais Royale, Louvre, Châtelet, Hôtel de Ville, and finally Saint-Paul, the stop closest to the gallery.

I grab my belongings and race through the station, out into the bright afternoon sunshine, pausing only to slide on my femme fatale sunglasses.

I run down the rue de Rivoli until it turns into the rue Saint-Antoine, hang a left at the Hôtel Sully, and keep running until I reach place des Vosges. My side aches, and I am breathing so hard the lenses of my glasses are fogged over. I stop to catch my breath and check Minnie. Eight minutes and twenty-seven seconds left before I am officially late, and all I have to do is cut through the park.

Phew! I set my easel on the ground and wipe the perspiration from my forehead. You wouldn't believe how sweaty you get when you're racing to beat the blade.

I grab my easel in one hand and my painting in the other and hurry through the wrought-iron gates, down the gravel path toward the statue of Louis XIII on horseback. I am congratulating myself for conceiving of a completely brilliant new canvas and navigating the Metro like a boss when I collide with someone, the impact causing me to drop my easel and slam my canvas into them.

"Je suis desolée . . ."

I snatch my foggy glasses off my face and look at the stranger. Heat scorches my cheeks like a late-summer sun on asphalt, blistering and unexpected. Flusy-crushy heat.

I didn't just collide with someone. I collided with . . .

"Monsieur Tall, Dark, and Hot," I whisper.

Up close, Monsieur Tall, Dark, and Hot is even hotter than he was standing across the gallery from me, with slate-blue eyes, smooth, tanned skin, and a chiseled, stubble-covered jaw. He notices me staring at him, and his full lips curve in a smile.

"Pardon?"

Do I own it or lie? Do I tell him I named him Monsieur Tall, Dark, and Hot because he is as beautiful as Michelangelo's *David,* or do I act like Fanny, cool and indifferent to the charms of *l'homme beau*?

He bends over and retrieves my easel. When he stands back up, I notice paint from my canvas is smeared across the front of his otherwise pristine white shirt.

"Oh my god!" I try to rub the paint from the front of his shirt, but a new wave of heat washes over my cheeks when my hand moves over his sharply defined pec. "I have ruined your shirt."

He smiles again, and sparks of light ignite in his eyes, like when you strike two pieces of flint together. He looks down at the blue, purple, and black blotches of paint on his shirt. I stop rubbing and pull my hand away.

"On the contrary," he says in flawless English. "You have improved my shirt, dramatically."

The flushy-crushy cheek heat blazes down my body like a crackling bolt of electricity.

David doesn't understand English. He doesn't speak. He sure doesn't flirt. He just stands on his pedestal looking sexy and unattainable.

"Merci," I whisper, unable to look away from his hypnotic gaze. "But I promise I will pay to have it cleaned."

He waves his hand dismissively. "Where are you off to in such a hurry?"

"The gallery. I am an intern. Today is my first shift, and I am going to be late. Monsieur Alexander already thinks I am a slacker because I was late the day I arrived."

"You are a painter." He wipes a small blob of purple paint from his shirt. "An oil painter, it would seem. May I see the canvas?"

I nod and hand him the canvas. Some of the paint is smeared, but the charcoal outline is still visible.

"C'est bon."

"You think?"

He stares at the canvas for several more seconds and then looks at me, his lips curving softly, his eyes sparkling. "Oui. You are very talented."

His gaze is too intense. I have to look away. I pretend to study my feet, and this is when I realize he is not wearing a suit, but worn dark jeans and a leather jacket that fits him like a glove. When my cheeks cool and my pulse slows to a normal beat, I look back up.

"What will you call it?"

I stare blankly, because I saw his lips move, heard the sounds coming out of his mouth, but I am too fixated on the lock of black hair that has fallen across his forehead and cheek. I want to run my fingers through it and smooth it back off his beautiful face. He doesn't look like a suitsexual today, with his floppy hair, seductive gaze, and battered leather coat. He looks as dangerous as the devil.

"What will you call your painting, mademoiselle?"

I shove my glasses back on my face. "I am calling it *Minority of Souls*."

His eyes narrow. "That is an unusual title."

"I was inspired."

"I think you were," he says, looking back at the canvas. "Forgive me, I haven't introduced myself. I am Gabriel."

"Bonjour, Gabriel." Just saying his name causes my heart to skip a beat. "I am Delaney Lavender Brooks."

"Lavender, like the flower?"

I nod my head. "My friends call me Laney, though."

"It is a pleasure to meet you," Gabriel smiles, exposing straight, white teeth, and a dimple only on his left cheek. "Are you working in the gallery tomorrow, ma fleur?"

I don't know anything about Gabriel or if I will ever see him again, but hearing him call me *his flower* makes me feel like I have come out of the rain and slipped on a warm fuzzy robe. *You feel that way because you belong with him. Maybe Rigby was right when she said Destiny brought me to France for more than one reason. What? This is coconuts. Like off the tree and rolling toward crazy land. He's gorgeous and I'm . . .*

Gabriel frowns. "Ma fleur?"

"I am sorry." I shake my head to clear my thoughts. "I was chasing unicorns."

"Uni-corns?"

I try to think of the French word for unicorn, but my mind is too loud to focus. "You know, a horse with a horn on its head?"

"Ah, licorne?"

"Oui," I say, smiling. "Je poursuivais licornes."

Gabriel laughs, a warm, throaty laugh that fills the space between us. He is one of those full-body laughers. His eyes light up. He throws back his head and presses his hand to his chest, over his heart. It's unguarded and organic, and it makes me happy.

"You are funny."

I scrunch my nose. "I don't know about that."

"Trust me," he says, smiling. "You are funny. I need more funny in my life."

"People in France aren't funny? Come on!" I say, punching his arm. "What about Nicolas Sarkozy? Remember when he teased Angela Merkel, the German stateswoman, for eating two helpings of cheese after declaring she was on a diet? Now that is funny stuff."

Gabriel laughs. "Sarko is unintentionally, oftentimes embarrass-ingly, funny."

"Okay, what about Fabrice Luchini?"

"The actor?"

I nod.

"I love his movies."

"Me too!" We grin at each other. "Have you seen *Bicycling with Molière*?"

Gabriel shakes his head.

"What about his latest? The one where he plays an inspector."

"Non," Gabriel smiles sheepishly and looks down at his feet. "I have to travel for my work. I am afraid it doesn't leave me a lot of time for movies or . . ."

"Or?"

He looks up, focusing his intense gaze on my face.

"Relationships."

"Oh."

Oh. Oh. I get it.

"Most women don't like dating a man who is gone half the year. They become bored and lonely. Paris is filled with men who will ease a woman's boredom and loneliness."

"It sounds like you haven't met the right women." I want to stay here, in this moment, in the shade of the linden tree, with this strangely familiar and thrilling Frenchman, but I can't be late to the gallery.

"I am sorry, but I really have to go."

"Mais bien sûr."

He smiles and bows his head, like a leading man in a classic Hollywood flick. If this were a movie, our meeting in place des Vosges would be called a meet-cute. We would fondly recall our serendipitous collision for years to come.

But my life isn't a Hollywood flick.

He hands me my canvas and steps aside.

"Au revoir, Gabriel."

I smile and brush past him.

"Ma fleur?"

I turn around to look at him. "Oui?"

"Would you like to run into each other again, say tomorrow around one o'clock?"

I can't *even*. Did Monsieur Tall, Dark, and Hot just ask me out on a date, or am I still back in the gardens, lost in a transcendental meditation? I look into his eyes, and my heart practically explodes in my chest.

I nod. "I will see you tomorrow at one o'clock, and I promise I will not assault you with my canvas."

"That is no fun."

He winks and walks away. I watch him for a few more seconds, trying to memorize his slow, confident gait, the broad expanse of his shoulders, the sunlight shining on his black hair.

Even if I live to be an ancient dinosaur, with dentures and blue hair, I won't forget the day David descended from his pedestal and called me his flower.

Chapter 14

"I told you destiny brought you to Paris for art and love, didn't I?" Rigby tears off a piece of her croissant and dips it into her *chocolat chaud*. "Oh my god! What if you end up marrying Monsieur Tall, Dark, and Hot? Wouldn't that be, like, the craziest thing ever?"

"We aren't getting married!"

"But you could."

I shrug and strum the strings of my ukelele. I am trying to keep it ultra-chill, or at least project an ultra-chill vibe, because inside I am a gawky, geeky mess, twisted up in knots and writing silly love songs in my brain.

They say I am quirky and free,
Because I fell in love with a statue,
In a park under a linden tree.

Rigby had bounded into my room this morning before the sun stretched and spread its first rays. "Let's break our fast," she said. So, here we are, sitting in an outdoor café around the corner from the gallery. The boutiques, galleries, and wine bars that line the narrow streets of this quaint *quartier* are still closed, their windows black against Dawn's first yawn. It's the perfect time to quietly strum a ukulele and let inspiration stir your resting spirit.

"You said your mom hassles you about being late, right?" She dips another piece of croissant into her chocolate and offers it to me. "But if you hadn't been late twice, you wouldn't have met Gabriel, aka Monsieur Destiny."

I stop strumming long enough to take the chocolate-drenched croissant and pop it into my mouth.

"We haven't been on a date, and you've already got us married and mortgaged."

"Oh, I am shipping you." She grins. "I am shipping you *so* hard! Harder than Samwise and Frodo—and I shipped Samdo hard."

I stop strumming and look at my new friend through the fringe of my bangs. "You did not make a smoosh name for two of my favorite LOTR characters."

"Oh, yes I did," she laughs. "And I am gonna make a smoosh name for you and Gabriel."

"That's okay."

"It's happening! Gabaney? Delriel?" She tilts her head and focuses me with an intent gaze. "Those aren't working for me. What's his last name?"

I shrug. "Dunno."

"Gabrooks?"

I groan.

"I might have to hold off on the smooshing until you get his last name."

"Yeah," I laugh. "That might be a good idea, because Delriel is epically bad."

"Play me a song."

I strum an upbeat tune, reminiscent of Cristofer Drew before he bought a one-way ticket to the negative space and extinguished his cigarette on a reporter's head. I was, like, totally in love with Cristofer and Never Shout Never. It's so tragic when someone does something to make you fall off the infatuation cloud, isn't it?

I close my eyes and keep strumming. I hear lyrics in my head that haven't been written, so I just start riffing.

Oh, let's run away to the south of France,
Where the music of love makes us want to dance.
We'll eat olives by the light of a silver moon,

And sing silly songs and kiss 'til we swoon.
Oh, let's run away to the south of France.

When I finish playing and open my eyes, Rigby is grinning like the Cat in the Hat after he wrecked Sally and Conrad's house, and a small group of passersby have assembled around our table.

I have played my music dressed as a mythical creature. I have played to a crowd of totally wasted frat boys. I have played some pretty embarrassing gigs and sung some pretty ridiculous songs, but I've never once felt the embarrassment I am feeling right now, sitting in a café in the heart of Paris, exposing my most private dreams.

Rigby claps.

The waiter claps.

A passerby tosses a handful of Euros into my ukulele case.

"Laneriel is happening," Rigby says. "It is so happening!"

Chapter 15

Laney's Life Playlist
"You and I" by Ingrid Michaelson
"La Vie en Rose" by Daniela Andrade (cover)

TEXT FROM VIVIA PERPETUA DE CAUMONT:
Thomas Merton said, "Art enables us to find ourselves and lose ourselves at the same time." I hope you find yourself and lose yourself in Paris. Bon chance, Laney!

I am retro Friday Night Dream Date Barbie. I have scooped my hair up in a high, glossy ponytail. I am wearing my fave pleated black-and-white striped A-line skirt and a short-sleeved top with a Peter Pan collar. I just need Ken to swing by in his plastic convertible.

I am trying to decide between wine-colored ankle-strap pumps or my black flats. The pumps say, in a sultry voice, *"Have we met? I am a goddess."* They're very Rita Hayworth. The flats say, in a sweet voice, *"Hands off. I am an innocent."* They're Olivia Newton-John singing "Hopelessly Devoted to You" in *Grease*.

The question is, do I want Gabriel to see me as Mame or Sandy? *Neither. You want him to see you as Laney. Just plain old Laney.*

I sit on the floor, cross my legs, rest my elbows on my knees, close my eyes, and take several deep, cleansing breaths. I replay the Good Vibes positive affirmations meditation in my head.

Your worth is not measured by your appearance. You are

worthwhile as a person, just the way you are. If you accept yourself, others will accept you just as you are.

I take two more deep breaths and open my eyes. My chakras are feeling more balanced already. I am relaxed and confident.

I let my hair down, wipe the lipstick from my lips, and slide my feet into my flats. At the last minute, I reach into my purse and pull out my necklace. It's a silver chain with an oval pendant engraved with the words, "Faith, trust, and pixie dust" and a small glass vial filled with pink and silver glittery fairy dust.

Gabriel is sitting on a bench in the shade of a linden tree. He is wearing worn jeans and a slouchy roll-neck sweater. His black hair is hidden beneath a beanie, and he has a scarf tied around his neck. He looks the way I imagine Modigliani would look if he were living in modern-day Paris, cool and a little dangerous.

I suddenly feel like a loser for having no chill and worrying about my shoes. Gabriel has tons of chill. Gone is his conservative suit and crisp white shirt.

He glances my way, and my breath catches in my throat, my cheeks flame with heat. He makes me feel like a gawky teen, and I kinda dig it.

"Bonjour, ma fleur," he says, standing.

He greets me the way Parisians greet each other: by pressing his cheek close to mine and kissing the air near my ear. His stubbly cheek grazes mine, and my heart flips over in my chest. I catch a whiff of his spicy cologne and imagine a moonless night in an exotic land, sultry breezes tinged with the scent of nutmeg, swaying palm trees, shadows that promise intrigue. His cologne matches his aura, dark, thrilling, mysterious, and romantic, with a hint of danger.

He wraps his long, tanned fingers around my hand and leads me back to the bench. We sit facing each other, close enough for me to notice his long, thick eyelashes and the flecks of silver shimmering in his blue eyes.

"How was your first day at the gallery?"

"It was good, except . . ."

"Except?"

I shrug. "I made it to the gallery with a minute to spare, but

Monsieur Alexandre was still pissed. He's a stickler about tardiness. and punctuality just isn't in my bag."

He chuckles low in his throat. "Are you always so candid?"

"Guilty."

"So you were late?"

I hold up my hand and make a pinching gesture to indicate just a little.

"That reminds me," he says, reaching into the pocket of his leather jacket, which he has tossed over the back of the bench. "I brought you a gift."

"Get out!" My cheeks are hot enough to boil coffee. "I should have brought you a gift or at least a new shirt. I am sorry about that."

"It was nothing," he says, handing me a box wrapped in colorful paper. "Now, open your gift, s'il vous plait."

I take the box and look at the shiny paper covering it. "Did you wrap this in comic book pages?"

"Guilty."

I can't *even* right now. A handsome Frenchman who reads comics and is into me? It seems obvious. Fate has stopped being a Mean Girl. She likes me again. She *really* likes me.

I carefully remove the comic page from the box and smooth it out on my lap. There's half of a superhero in red and gold and a lot of French words in small comic script.

"Who is this? Iron Man?"

"Non," he shakes his head. "It is Exodus, also known as Bennet du Paris. Do you know his origin story?"

I shake my head.

"He was born in the twelfth century and always felt as if he had a deep hidden power. When he grew up, he became a crusader and discovered his mutant abilities. He was stripped of his powers and sealed in a crypt in the Swiss Alps. Years later, Magneto frees him. Exodus became one of Charles Xavier's most powerful mutants." He stops talking and gives me this charming, slightly self-conscious smile that literally makes my heart ache with its sweetness. "Anyway, I do not read the comics anymore. I had a pile of them I was going to give to my cousin and thought they would make good wrapping paper."

He ripped up one of his favorite comics to wrap a gift. A gift for me.

"I love vintage comics," I say, folding the wrapping paper into a neat square and slipping it into my purse. "Some of the artwork is next level, like Brian Bolland's iconic Joker image. So Warhol-inspired."

He stares at me so intensely I think I might melt away, like chocolate in a fondue pot. My sensei would call it a look into the soul, an intermingling of spirits. I hope he likes what he sees because I would like our spirits to intermingle some more.

I break eye contact, shifting my focus to the box in my hands. I lift the lid and find a pink Swatch watch with a band that looks like those stretchable candy bracelets I used to wear when I was a kid.

"I love it!" I take it out of the box and slip it onto my wrist. "It's the coolest gift anyone has ever given me."

"You really like it?"

"I love it." I can't help myself. I throw my arms around him and give him a big squeeze. "Thank you, Gabriel."

I pull away quickly, before it gets awkward. The hug was organic and so me. I just went with what I felt. I doubt the sophisticated, cool French girls I see strolling around the Marais give spontaneous hugs, but then, I doubt they've ever been given a candy bracelet watch.

"Now, you don't need to worry about pissing off the Stickler."

I don't bother telling him that my trusty Minnie Mouse watch has been strapped to my wrist for several years now, and it's never kept me from being late. I am perpetually time challenged.

"Thank you, Gabriel."

I remember I don't even know his last name. In fact, I don't know anything about him. My cheeks flush with heat, only this time it's caused by shame, not embarrassment.

"What is it, ma fleur?" He reaches out and brushes a hair from my cheek. "The eyes are the windows to the soul, and your windows just darkened with shadows."

"I'm ashamed."

"Ashamed? What do you have to be ashamed about?"

"I ruin your shirt and then accept a gift from you before I know anything about you."

"What do you want to know?" He holds out his hands. "I am an open book for you to read."

"Well, why don't we start with your name?"

He takes a deep breath and exhales slowly. Now it is my turn to watch the windows of *his* soul darken with shadows. Why doesn't he want to tell me his name? What could he possibly have to hide?

Chapter 16

Laney's Life Playlist
"Anything Could Happen" by Ellie Goulding
"First Date" by Blink-182

"I don't want there to be dishonesty between us, ever," he says, reaching for my hand and wrapping his warm fingers around mine. "My name is Gabriel Galliard."

My palms begin to sweat.

"Gabriel Galliard? As in Gallery Galliard de Cadré?"

He nods his head, and I pull my hand away.

Fate is back to being a wicked mean girl. I should have known our newly fostered friendship was as sketchy as a Da Vinci drawing.

"My family owns the gallery. The Stickler is my brother."

"Are you kidding me?" I stand up. "We can't do this."

"Do what, exactly?" He grabs my hand again and pulls me back onto the bench. "Meet in the park? Sit on a bench? Get to know each other? What can't we do, Laney?"

It's the first time he has used my name, and it sends a shiver of pleasure over my skin. I want him to hold my hand and say my name until the leaves fall off the linden trees and snow swirls around the statue.

"You're Monsieur Alexandre's brother? What are the odds? That's, like, epic, epic bad luck. He already hates me."

He rubs his thumb over my knuckles. "Who could possibly hate you, ma fleur?"

"Stop calling me your flower."

"Why?"

"It's unethical."

He laughs. "How is it unethical?"

"I am an intern in your family's gallery."

"Exactement!" He lets go of my hand and sits back, crossing his legs at the ankles. "You're an intern in an art gallery, not a recruit for some top-secret military organization."

"Still, don't you think we should get Monsieur Alexandre's permission first?"

Gabriel throws back his head and chuckles.

"I am not in the habit of seeking my brother's approval before conducting a love affair."

"Love affair?" My heart is thudding against my ribs so hard I am sure he can hear the thump-thump. "Is that what this is, a love affair?"

"It might be. We will have to wait and see, won't we?" He winks and my cheeks flush with heat. "Now, shall we get something to eat?"

"Eat?"

"Oui." He stands, grabs his leather coat, and holds out his hand, pulling me to my feet. "I promised you lunch, did I not? I know a place that makes superb pita sandwiches."

"I crave pitas sandwiches. They're, like, the alpha and the omega of sandwiches."

He laughs.

"Bon." He holds my hand, and we walk toward the wrought-iron gate leading out of the park. "It is not too far."

We leave the park and walk side by side on the narrow sidewalk, passing an old-fashioned *tabac* shop with jars of pungent tobacco, a luxury *perfumerie* called Diptyque, and a hat shop selling outrageous fascinators.

Gabriel sees me looking in the window and stops walking. "Do you like des chapeaux?"

"Do I? Did Degas like little dancers? I love hats!"

"Would you like to try one on?"

Is he kidding? Of course I would like to try on a quirky, artistic hat, but it probably costs more than my Mini Cooper.

I shake my head.

"Why not?"

"I am kinda klutzy. I would probably rip the delicate netting or ruffle the feathers." I smile at his reflection in the window. "Besides, where would I wear a fascinator? I don't exactly move in the Ascot circle."

I suddenly remember Gabriel is a Galliard. He probably moves in the Ascot circle.

"You could wear it while you paint," he says, giving my hand a little squeeze. "It could be your signature piece."

"Like Vigée Le Brun and her turban? Picasso and his onesie?"

"Exactement."

I laugh. "Such eccentricities are only allowed after one has become a genius."

"Ah, I was unaware of the rule for eccentrics," he says, smiling. "Nevertheless, if you had to choose a hat to wear as your eccentricity, which of these would you choose?"

I look at the hats. One catches my attention, a small green felt cap with a spray of peacock feathers held in place by a diamond-encrusted hat pin.

"That one," I say, pointing to the peacock cap.

"The one with the feathers?"

I nod my head.

"Why that one?"

"The colors of the feathers remind me of Gustave Klimt's painting *Portrait of Emilie Flöge*." I look at Gabriel and realize his gaze is fixed on my face. My breath catches in my throat. "Have you seen *Emilie Flöge*?"

Gabriel shakes his head.

"Emilie Flöge was a member of the Viennese bohemian society and Gustave Klimt's . . ." I let my words trail off because I don't think I can say the word *lover* while looking into Gabriel's eyes. ". . . lifelong partner. In fact, he spoke her name with his dying breath."

"Romantique."

"Oui."

Gabriel is still holding my hand. He begins making circles on my palm with his thumb—slow, absentminded circles, as if it were the most natural thing in the world to be standing on a street in Paris, holding hands with a strange girl, and talking to her about hats. I wonder if seducing gallery interns is his thing. I hope not. My heart is clutching onto the slender hope that this is one of those rare, serendipitous encounters, the kind that seems fated by the stars and can't be explained, just felt.

"Tell me more," he says, his voice low. "I like to hear you speak."

I swallow hard. Most people tell me to be quiet, chill, take it down a few notches.

"In the portrait, Emilie is wearing a cobalt-blue gown patterned with shapes that look like the eye of the peacock feather. Klimt painted her against a green background." I take a deep breath to calm my erratic pulse. "It's ethereal, yet powerful, truly breathtaking."

"You're breathtaking," he whispers, staring deep into my eyes. "I've never met anyone like you, Delaney Lavender Brooks. You're so . . . so . . ."

"Quirky?" I laugh. "Random?"

"Vivant."

"Alive?"

He nods his head. "You are like the most wonderful painting, full of color and movement, drawing the viewer in with your singular beauty."

Someone stick me with a hat pin because I am trapped in an unbelievable dream, a dream where a thrilling, charming, gorgeous man tells me he likes my quirky personality and thinks I am beautiful. Me. Laney. Beautiful? I've been called cute and adorkable, but never beautiful.

I chuckle. "You say that now because you hardly know me. You haven't seen the ridiculous riot of colors I can be. I am completely bonkers."

What is wrong with me? Why did I just tell him I am crazy? Am I trying to talk him out of liking me? Fanny would never respond to a compliment in such a self-depreciating way. Think Fanny! Think Fanny! What would Fanny say?

Yeah, I got nothing.

Gabriel smiles one of those sad, lips-turned down smiles, and I realize I have ruined the moment. Before I opened my stupid mouth, we were surrounded by a warm, intimate blanket, sheltered in our own little world, oblivious to the people bustling around us.

"I know what it is to have people think you are"—he tilts his head and looks at me through his thick, dark eyelashes—"what was the word you used? Bonkers?"

I nod.

"My family thinks I am bonkers."

"Get out."

"I am serious."

I stare at him, trying to find the chink in his perfectly beautiful armor, a wonky eye, a tic, something.

"Why would they think you are bonkers? You're perfect."

He chuckles, but it is one of those slightly bitter, wounded laughs that hint at a deeper pain. "À chaque troupeau sa brebis galeuse."

There is a black sheep in every flock.

"Come," he says, pulling me along. "Sandwiches, and then I must get back to work."

"You work?"

He chuckles. "Mais bien sûr."

I wonder what kind of job would allow him to hang around the gallery and take long lunches. "Are you an artist?"

"That depends."

"On what?"

"On who you ask." His words come out as a growl. "My family doesn't think I am an artist."

"I feel you. My family doesn't appreciate my art, either. What kind of artist are you? What's your medium?"

"I am a photojournalist."

"Are you kidding me? That's awesome."

He glances over at me, and I can read the skepticism written all over his handsome face, feel the negative shift in his aura. "You really think so?"

"Absolutely!"

"My parents say photojournalism, it is not art."

"Are you kidding me? What about Margaret Bourke-White? Her images are pure art, evocative stories painted with light and shadow." I feel his aura shifting again, the dark, cloudy colors moving away to reveal his natural sunny state. "Have you always wanted to be a photojournalist?"

"Non," he says, his tone less gruff. "I studied law at Katholieke Universiteit Leuven in Belgium. In my junior year, I began working as a stringer for a Belgian newspaper, covering local and national news. After graduation, I was hired by Reuters to cover international stories."

"That sounds exciting."

He shrugs. "It was at first, but taking photographs of soldiers blown apart by IEDs took a lot out of me. Reuters had me stationed in the Middle East."

"What an admirable way to apply your talent."

He slants a look at me. "Admirable?"

I nod my head. "You are the man on the ground, taking the pictures that provoke the conscience and persuade people to take action."

"Merci."

"De rien."

He holds my hand, and we walk together in silence. I feel this strong simpatico with Gabriel. We have a lot more in common than I realized. We are both black sheep, going against the flock. I express my rebellion through my outlandish wardrobe, music, and art. Gabriel appears as cultured and sophisticated as his family, but his leather jacket and long hair suggest he has a definite rakish, rebellious side.

We arrive at L'As du Fallafel, a small green storefront at the start of the pedestrian-only portion of rue des Rosiers, and take our places in the long queue of students and hip, young locals. The scent of grilled meat and exotic spices hangs in the air like a delicious cloud.

Gabriel orders for both of us. A minute later, we are each handed a large sandwich wrapped in paper and a plastic cup of minty lemonade. We walk to a nearby square—really more of a triangle formed by the convergence of three pedestrian streets—and lean against a building covered in the most beautiful seafoam-green tiles.

The sandwich is, like, crazy good. The pita bread is crunchy on the outside and soft on the inside. The meat—tastes like pork (but can't be)—is tender and buttery and slathered in this creamy white sauce.

"Do you like the sandwich?" Gabriel asks.

"Are you kidding me?" I moan and roll my eyes. "This is, like, nine point five on the Richter scale of deliciousness. Maybe even better than Munch and Lunch's Bipolar."

"Munch and Lunch?" Gabriel frowns. "Bipolar?"

"Sorry," I say, opening my eyes and smiling. "Munch and Lunch is this gallery cum diner back in Boulder. They make a turkey and hot pepper jelly sandwich called the Bipolar."

"It is good?"

"Mythically good. Like, conceived by a genius in an otherworldly place of unicorns, fairies, and rainbows. Just wait until I take you there and—"

Heat flushes my cheeks. I am talking as if Gabriel and I have serious history, as if we have a serious future.

He fixes me with his solemn, breath-robbing gaze and smiles with his lips closed, a sly, unnerving smile, the lazy smile of a clever cat who knows he has trapped the mouse.

"And?"

And? And, what, Laney? My heart is thump-thump-thumping so fast, so loud, I can't hear my own thoughts. I have never felt like this around a man. I am all flushy-crushy and cotton candy brained.

"And, do you still work for Reuters?"

Gabriel chuckles low in his throat.

"Non, I work for the European Pressphoto Agency."

"What sorts of stories do you cover?"

"Pfff." He shrugs. "One month, I might be sent to cover the migrant crisis on the French-Italian border and the next month to Cannes to snap pictures of Hollywood stars posing on the red carpet. Revolutions, ecological summits, bike races, workers' strikes, soccer matches. Take your pick."

I shake my head. "That's impressive. I can't believe your family doesn't take your work seriously."

He doesn't look at me. Instead, he balls up his empty sandwich wrapper in his fist and tosses it into a nearby trash bin. He does the same with mine.

I remember the bold indigo streak I saw when I first read Gabriel's aura and realize his independence was born from rejection. I get that. In that respect, we are kindred souls. Gabriel seems like he has mastered the focus thing, though.

"My Aunt Fantine takes it seriously."

"I met your aunt."

"Elle est remarquable, est-elle pas?"

"Oui," I say, smiling. "She is remarkable. I am pretty sure we were best friends in another life."

He laughs. "Do you believe in reincarnation?"

I take a sip of my lemonade to stall for time.

"Truthfully?"

"That's the only way we shall ever be, ma fleur."

"I don't know what I believe. Christianity. Judaism. Hinduism. I believe there must be a higher power who keeps order in the universe through the use of karma, or something like that."

"Good deeds are rewarded and bad deeds met with misfortune?"

I shrug. "My father would say it is a spiritual twist on the principle of cause and effect. He's a physicist, though, and doesn't believe in things that can't be seen or proven. I believe in karma because I have seen it in action in my own life."

Gabriel smiles at me, and I have to fight the urge to reach out and touch the dimple on his stubbly cheek.

"I wonder what good deed I did to bring you into my life?"

He stares at my mouth and leans in close enough for me to catch another whiff of his exotic cologne.

Chapter 17

"So, did he kiss you?"

Rigby was waiting in the courtyard when I returned from my lunch with Gabriel. We are scheduled to have atelier time this afternoon, but we are sitting in the sun-filled courtyard talking about boys.

"He tried, but I made some stupid comment."

"What? What did you say?"

I flush. "I said, 'Is this one of those smooth French guy seductive moves American mothers warn their daughters about?'"

"You did not!"

"I did."

"Oh, Laney! Why?"

"Because he's so hot he breaks the Scoville scale."

"Uh, hello?" Rigby reaches out and knocks on my forehead with her fist. "We want hot guys to kiss us, not uggos."

I am dying of mortification. My eyes fill with tears, and I look away, at some shadowy corner of the courtyard.

"Oh my god!" Rigby cries. "Laney, are you a virgin?"

I nod and a tear slips down my cheek.

"How is that even possible?"

"What do you mean?"

"Look at you, Lane," she says, holding her fingers up as if framing a camera shot. "You're stunning."

"Shut up."

"Stuh-ning."

I look at her and frown.

"I'm serious."

"Thanks," I sniffle.

"How is it possible that nobody has tried to take your V card?"

"Oh, I've had some boyfriends who tried, but . . ."

"But?"

I shrug and sniffle again. "I don't know. It's never felt right."

"Never?"

I shake my head. "I know what I am about to say is going to set the women's movement back, like, a trillion years, but I believe in the Disney Princess stories."

Rigby smiles and sighs.

"Remember Sleeping Beauty?"

She nods. "It's my fave."

"Mine too!" We reach out our hands and touch our wiggling fingertips together. "Twin power."

"Activate," Rigby says.

"I always wanted to be Princess Aurora, because she is so gentle and loving. Plus, she is raised by three fairies!"

"Right?" Rigby pulls her knees up to her chest and wraps her arms around her legs. "She lives in the deep, dark forest surrounded by her woodland creature friends until Prince Phillip, her one true love, rescues her with a kiss."

"Exactly. She was sheltered and protected by the fairies, kept pure until a man worthy of her beauty arrived." My bottom lip trembles. "I've never met a man I thought was worthy of my . . . you know."

"V card?"

I nod.

She laughs. "Oh, Lane. You are the best."

"You don't think I'm a loser?"

"No way! I think you are rare."

"Thanks," I say, swiping the tears off my cheeks.

"I think Gabriel thinks you are rare too," she says. "Do you think Gabriel might be able to fit into Prince Phillip's boots?"

"Maybe, but I've probably ruined everything with my stupid smooth French guy comment."

Rigby jumps up and wraps her arms around me.

"It's all good, Lane."

"It is?"

"Heck yeah." She stops hugging me and sits down again, pulling her chair closer, and lowering her voice to a whisper. "French guys don't like girls who are open books. They want to learn the plot slowly."

"How do you know?"

"Earth to Love-Struck Laney," she says, laughing. "I am dating a French guy. And, I read the book."

"What book?"

"*La Seduction: How the French Play the Game of Life* by Elaine Sciolino."

"You're kidding?"

"I'm not." She plucks a petal from the potted hydrangea and rubs it between her fingers. "It's been super helpful in helping me understand the cultural differences between Matthias and me."

"Really?"

She nods enthusiastically. "It's, like, the American girl's bible for dating a French guy. I left my copy at home, but I'll bet you could pick up one at Shakespeare and Company."

Every artist, whether of the written word or painted scene, knows about Shakespeare and Company, the left-bank bookstore opened by Sylvia Beach and visited by Hemingway, Fitzgerald, and various expat bohemians.

"I'll have to check it out."

Rigby stands and holds out her hand. I give her my hand, and she pulls me to my feet.

"We will both check it out after our atelier session. You need that book, because Gallaney is so happening."

We spend the remainder of the day in the atelier. I work on my *Minority of Souls* painting while Rigby works on a brill watercolor of a Paris street scene in shades of purple. By the time we clean our brushes, the sun has slipped behind the mansard roofs, casting the atelier in woolen shades of darkness.

We grab our sweaters and purses and leave the gallery behind. A vigorous twenty-minutee walk later and we have crossed over the Seine from the Right Bank to the Left Bank.

Shakespeare and Company takes up two green-and-yellow storefronts in an old, Baron Haussmann–era building a stone's throw from the river. The shop is practically in the shadow of Notre Dame. We arrive as a poet begins reading aloud from her book, titled *Dirty Verse*. A crowd has assembled on the sidewalk around her, tourists with iPhones held aloft, a homeless man leading a scruffy terrier by a rope, a few Parisians on their way home from work.

"Pussy," says the poet, in a loud, defiant voice. "Come, come lose yourself in the forest of my femininity, where darkened thatches conceal a feline ready to devour your masculinity . . ."

My cheeks flush with heat.

"I'm going to look for that book," I whisper to Rigby.

"Cool, I'll see you inside in a bit."

I work my way through the titilated crowd and into the dimly lit bookstore. The scent of musty pages greets me. Wooden shelves from floor to ceiling strain under the weight of countless books, some classics, some completely forgotten by everyone save the authors who wrote them.

I climb a red staircase to the second floor. The first room I come to has a small wooden table situated beneath a window overlooking the street. An old Olympus typewriter sits upon the table. I wander through the rooms until I come to a bookcase filled with books about art. I see many familiar titles—*In Montmartre: Picasso, Matisse and the Birth of Modernist Art* by Sue Roe, *Shocking Paris* by Stanley Meisler, *The Judgement of Paris: The Revolutionary Decade That Gave the World Impressionism* by Ross King—and several that make me wish I could bust my meager budget—*The Lady in Gold: The Extraordinary Tale of Gustav Klimt's Masterpiece* by Anne-Marie O'Connor and *Creative Madness: Radical and Totally Mental Artists* by Madeleine Magdelene.

"Can I help you find a book?"

I turn to find a pretty girl with shoulder-length dark-blonde hair, wide blue-gray eyes, and impossibly deep dimples standing beside me holding a small stack of paperbacks. She's wearing a pair of distressed boyfriend jeans and an Oakland Raiders tee.

"Yes, I am looking for the book *La Seduction* by"—I scrunch my nose and snap my fingers—"Ellen . . . Sicilian?"

"Close," she laughs. "Elaine Sciolino."

"Right."

"If you follow me, I will show you where to find it."

I follow her to another room. Without hesitating, she walks to the back wall and pulls a book off the second shelf from the bottom.

"Here ya go," she says, handing it to me.

I look at the price tag and grimace.

"Ouch! Twenty-four euros will totally pummel my budget." I hand it back to her. "I'm going to have to wait until I sell a painting."

"Are you an artist?"

I nod my head. "I'm interning at the Cadré Gallery, in the Marais."

"That's awesome." She takes the book from my hand and slides it back on the shelf. "Internship? So you're a starving artist, then?"

"Totes. My bank account is scary malnourished."

"But you're chasing the dream."

"I am."

"My name's Rachelle, by the way."

"I'm Laney."

"Nice to meet you, Laney."

"Likewise." I smile. "So, how did a Raiders fan end up working in a bookstore in Paris?"

"I'm a tumbleweed."

I frown. "What's a tumbleweed?"

"George Whitman, the man who owned this shop, started allowing aspiring writers to sleep among these shelves way back in the fifties. He called them his tumbleweeds, because they would tumble in, write, and tumble out again." She takes a book from her stack and wedges it onto a crowded shelf. "Since then, thousands of writers have lived and created within these walls, tumbling in and out."

I look around. "Where do you sleep?"

She motions for me to follow her. We walk to a room in the back of the store filled with bookshelves and threadbare sofas.

"Bienvenue à l'Hôtel Tumbleweed!" she says, holding out her arms. "This is the library. It's where a lot of the tumbleweeds crash. I've got an alcove one floor down, though. It has curtains that close and is super cozy. I fall asleep with the scent of old books in my nose and wake to the sound of the bells of Notre Dame ringing in my ears."

"That's amaze!"

"Right?"

I nod. "So you just get to live here for free?"

"We are required to work in the store and write a one-page biography." She takes another book from her pile and slides it on a shelf wedged between a battered leather sofa and a worn velvet sofa. "I work part-time at a souvenir shop across the river just to earn my bread money. So, I dig you when you say you're starving for your art."

"I'm glad you feel my pain."

"Oh, I feel you."

We laugh.

"Where are you from?"

"California. What about you?"

"Colorado."

Rachelle tells me she was born and raised in a small town outside Sacramento, attended UCLA majoring in English, and earned her PhD from Columbia University.

"You're really a doctor?"

She smiles and nods.

"You're so young."

"I'm thirty."

"You're only thirty years old and you have a doctorate in philosophy?"

She nods again.

"I am impressed."

"Thanks."

"You earned it."

"Hey," she says, lowering her voice, "I have an idea. I own a copy of the book you want. Why don't we make a barter?"

"What were you thinking?"

Rachelle shrugs. "Let me tag along with you when you paint. I want to absorb as much of the expat culture as I can for a novel I am thinking of writing."

"Okay, but only if I can call you Dr. Phil."

She laughs. "It's a deal."

I follow her down one floor and over to a curtained alcove, tucked beneath the stairs, like Harry Potter's cubby in the Dursley's house.

"Here you go," she says, handing me a copy of *La Seduction*. "I hope it helps net you a sexy guy."

My cheeks flush.

"She's already netted a sexy guy," Rigby says, joining us. "Monsieur Tall, Dark, and Hot."

"Sweet," Rachelle says. "Bon chance avec Monsieur Tall, Dark, and Hot. Fall in love, have a mad affair, and then tell me all about it so I have authentic material when I write the next great American novel."

"Well," I say, sighing heavily, "I guess I could help you out. I mean, if it's in the name of art . . ."

We all laugh.

"Rigby, this is Dr. Phil," I say, gesturing to my new friend. "She's a brainiac writer from California. She lives and works in the store. Dr. Phil, this is my friend, Rigby. She's a talented glassblower and watercolorist."

"Nice to meet you," Rachelle says.

"Nice to meet you," Rigby responds.

"Hey, Laney," Rachelle says, "I just thought of another book you might want to check out."

She crosses the room, pulls a slender paperback with a white cover from a shelf, and hands it to me. I take the book and stare at the illustration on the front cover. It's a cartoon drawing of a couple embracing beneath the Eiffel Tower.

"*French Women Don't Sleep Alone: Pleasurable Secrets to Finding Love*," I say, reading the title.

"Look, I better get back to work. Stop by the front desk before you leave, and I will give you my contact information."

"Okay." I hold up the book. "Thanks."

Rachelle hurries back down the stairs.

"She seemed cool," Rigby says.

"Totes."

"Are you going to get the book she recommended?"

I shrug.

Rigby takes the book from me, turns it over, and reads the back-cover blurb aloud.

"'Did you know that French women don't date?'" She waggles her eyebrows. "'French women don't worry about the care and feeding of their boyfriend. And they certainly don't travel to Mars to communicate with men. On the contrary, French women's love lives are romantic, sensual, playful, and intense. They conduct their relationships with the same unique sense of originality and artfulness with which they choose their clothes and accessories . . .'"

What am I doing? Who comes to the City of Love and signs up for a crash course on *L'art de la Séduction?* Sadly unprepared virgins, that's who! I wish I were more like Fanny, calm, cool, and completely confident in my ability to catch a man. Her designer boots had barely hit Alaskan ground and she'd already snagged herself a hot lumbersexual.

Or I wish I could be more like Vivia. Fanny's beautiful, audacious best friend lied about her virginity and was dumped by her fiancé when he discovered the truth. She went on the honeymoon anyway and met Jean-Luc, a super sexy bike guide and literature professor. A year later, they were engaged and planning the most romantic wedding in his family's château in the south of France.

"So, what do you think?" Rigby holds the book close to her face and bats her thick, fringy eyelashes. "Are you ready to take 'a guided tour through the corridors of French love'?"

Fanny wouldn't need a book on how to seduce, care for, and feed a man, and Vivia would probably write the book! *But you're not Fanny or Vivia.*

"It sounds like a great book, but I think I'm going to skip that tour and strike out on my own."

"Going solo?"

"That's the way I roll, my friend."

Rigby puts the book on a shelf. "Guided tours are great, but some of the best moments happen when you skip the itinerary and let serendipity take the lead. Besides, you don't need a French woman to tell you how to be with Gabriel. Just be yourself."

"Thanks, Rigby."

On our way out, Rachelle hands me a receipt with her e-mail

address written on the back. She is living old-school—without an iPhone. We make arrangements to meet next week and say good-bye.

We are almost back at the gallery when my iPhone begins vibrating in my pocket.

"Chagall!" I pull my iPhone out of my pocket. "I forgot to turn my phone to airplane mode. I just got a text."

"Maybe it's important."

I look at the screen, and my heart skips a beat, my lips curve skyward.

"It's from the other half of Gallaney, isn't it?"

I nod.

"Well, what's he say?"

I read the text aloud.

TEXT FROM GABRIEL GALLIARD:
Want to let me to practice some of my smooth French man moves on you tomorrow night?

"What do I say? Do I ignore it and keep him waiting? Do I say something flirty?"

"Play it cool, totally cool and casual." Rigby takes my phone and taps out a message. "Send that."

I look at the screen.

TEXT TO GABRIEL GALLIARD:
Sorry. I am busy tomorrow night.

"But I'm not busy."

"It doesn't matter. You can't be too available. You want to make him chase you. It builds the anticipation."

"I don't know," I say, scrunching up my nose. "This seems gamey. I'm not into games."

"Love is a game, mon amie, and the French are the most skilled players on the planet. They are masters at seduction."

I hit SEND and hold my breath. What if he doesn't text back? What if he shrugs his shoulders and moves on to the next girl? A few seconds pass, and my phone vibrates again. I exhale.

TEXT FROM GABRIEL GALLIARD:
I leave on an assignment at the end of the week. I want to see
you before then. How about the day after tomorrow? 7:00 at
La Belle Hortense?

I don't ask for Rigby's advice this time. My fingers frantically tap
the screen.

TEXT TO GABRIEL GALLIARD:
That sounds great. I will try to be on time. ;)

TEXT FROM GABRIEL GALLIARD:
Don't worry. I will always wait for you.

Chapter 18

Laney's Life Playlist
"You've Got Me Wrapped Around Your Little Finger" by Beth Rowley
"Teenage Dream" by Katy Perry

TEXT FROM THEO WILDE:
I am working on something for you. Should be ready soon.
Text me your address.

TEXT FROM VIVIA PERPETUA DE CAUMONT:
Fanny told me you met an über-hot French guy. Freaking
Awesome! She also said you are reading some book to learn
how to act around him. Throw the book away, girlfriend. If
he's asked you out on more than one date, you already know
how to act. Do you, Girl!

The next morning, I am working in the gallery with Julia when
Monsieur Alexandre calls me on the carpet.

"Mademoiselle Brooks," he says, standing to the right of a large
canvas hanging near the front of the gallery. "Parlez-moi de ce
tableau, s'il vous plaît."

A gallery catalog listing all of the pieces of art for sale with
details about the artists was part of our welcome packet. We were
supposed to memorize the entire contents by our second shift, but I
have managed to memorize only half of them. Fortunately, Monsieur
Alexandre chose one of the paintings I studied.

"*La Diversité,* oil on canvas by Jean-Jacques Dupin, is a bold
statement about our need to retain that which makes us truly unique,

while assimilating into a society that desires our conformity." I pause and look at Monsieur Alexandre, but he merely rolls his wrist for me to continue. "Dupin used a palette knife instead of a brush, resulting in complex, textural images with a three-dimensional effect. The layers of paint reflect the light, giving the illusion of great depth. It's, like, totally inspired."

He nods his head and moves to the next painting.

"Mademoiselle Abbott, s'il vous plait."

Julia rattles off the description of the painting as if she were reading from the catalog. Title of the piece. Artist's name. Size of canvas. Medium used. Unlike me, she doesn't go off script.

"Très bien," Monsieur Alexandre says.

Très bien? Are you kidding me? Julia scores a very good for her lackluster recitation, and all I get is a brusque head nod? Monsieur Alexandre hates me.

"I must go down to zhe vault. I will be gone for at least 'alf an 'our," Monsieur Alexandre says. "I am leaving you in charge, Mademoiselle Abbott. If you need anything, please ring me in zhe vault."

He doesn't wait for us to respond, striding across the gallery and disappearing through the back door. I look at Julia. She's leaning forward, her long, talonlike nails pressed against the Louis XV desk that serves as a counter, her lips parted in a half-smile, half-snarl. I'm not trying to go to a dark place, but she reminds me of one of the gargoyles that sits perched upon the pediment of Notre Dame. Any second now, she will spring off her perch, swoop down, and suck the soul from my body like a ring-wraith.

Imagining Julia as a ring-wraith, sucking my soul through her thin, colorless lips, makes me feel super guilty. The sensei I used to meet with for one-on-one spiritual elevating sessions said uncharitable thoughts are like tossing concrete blocks on a rubber raft. We need to remove the blocks with loving, uplifting thoughts. I look at Julia's arched, artfully plucked eyebrows, as dark as raven's wings. They really are quite pretty.

I swallow hard. "Um, I dig your eyebrows, Julia. How do you get them to lift in the middle like that? Do you use a stencil or something, because they are super arched?"

She narrows her eyes, fixing me with an even more frightening gargoyle stare. I am about to tell her that I'm being sincere, that my brows are so thick and fast-growing I need to use an electric trimmer, like the kind old men use to weed-whack their nose hairs, when the phone rings.

I reach for it, but Julia's reach is faster. She snatches the handset off the receiver and grins at me with fiendish delight.

"Galerie Cadré, bonjour."

Julia's perfectly arched brows knit together.

"Un moment, monsieur." She covers the handset with her hand and lowers her voice. "It's for you."

"Me?"

"Yes, you."

She thrusts the phone at me.

"Hello?"

"Bonjour, ma fleur." Gabriel's low, throaty voice hums in my ear. "Don't say anything. I know you are working, but I can't wait until tomorrow night. I have to see you today. I am at the end of the arcade, near Victor Hugo's home. Come to me, please."

"I'm sorry, monsieur, but—"

"It will only take a minute, I promise."

The line goes dead.

I hand the phone back to Julia. She takes it from me and places it on the receiver with exaggerated care.

"So," she says, smiling tightly, "who was that?"

I don't think I mentioned this before, but I am a horrible liar. Lies fall from some people's tongues like rain from the sky. Not me. I dry up. My thoughts. My mouth. Dry as the Sahara.

"Who?"

"Yes. Who?"

"Who who?"

"Who just called you?"

My dentist? My ex-boyfriend? The cab driver that brought me from the airport?

"My uncle."

"Your uncle?"

I nod my head with such eager conviction my glasses slide to the end of my nose.

"Your uncle speaks fluent French?"

I push my glasses up my nose. "Um, yes."

"You call your uncle monsieur?"

I nod again. "My family is super formal. I call my dad monsieur, too."

Julia rolls her eyes. "Whatever."

I pretend to organize the brochures on the desk while trying to think of a believable reason for suddenly needing to leave the gallery.

"Um, Julia," I say, keeping my gaze averted, "I need a smoke break. Do you think I could pop outside for, like, two minutes?"

"*You* smoke?"

I nod.

"Cigarettes?"

I nod again.

"Okay, but don't be gone more than two minutes or I will have to tell Monsieur Alexandre."

"I won't," I say, hurrying around the desk. "I promise."

My hand is on the door, ready to push it open, when Julia stops me cold in my treacherous tracks.

"Laney?"

I turn around. "Yes?"

"Where are your cigarettes?"

And this, mesdames et messieurs, is why I do not lie.

"My cigarettes?" I ask, stalling for time.

"Tobacco rolled inside paper that you light with a match, put to your mouth, and inhale."

"Oh, yeah." I force a laugh. "I am trying to quit smoking, so whenever I have the urge, I take a break and just pretend to smoke a cigarette. Invisible Lights. They're cheaper than real cigarettes and way, way better for your lungs."

Julia scoffs and rolls her eyes. I don't wait for her to fling another pointed question my way. I push the door open and leave the gallery as fast as my Mary Janes will take me.

Gabriel is waiting at the end of the arcade, his shoulder resting against a pillar, one arm behind his back. He's wearing distressed jeans, his leather coat zipped up against the unseasonably cold day, a scarf wrapped around his neck. He sees me coming and smiles.

My cheeks get flushy-crushy hot, and I hear Katy Perry's song

"Teenage Dream" in my head. I wonder if Gabriel will always make me feel like a starry-eyed teen? Will I always feel that roller-coaster, stomach-dropping-to-my-feet sensation when we meet? I hope so.

I stand on my tiptoes and give air kisses to each of his stubbly cheeks. His bangs are finger-combed to one side and hang almost to his chin, giving him a slightly rakish appearance. The silky black hairs tickle my nose. He's wearing the same spicy cologne he wore yesterday. The moonlight and midnight kisses cologne.

"Bonjour, Gabriel. I can only stay for two minutes or Julia is going to stick my neck on the block and call Monsieur Alexandre to release the blade."

He pulls his arm out from behind his back and presents me with a bouquet of daisies wrapped with a wide blue polka-dotted ribbon.

"I love daisies!" I take the bouquet and hold them close to my chest. "How did you know?"

He grins, and I remember he was in the gallery when his brother scolded me for rolling my daisy suitcase over his ancient floors.

"Oh, yeah."

My cheeks flush with new heat.

He leans close, his stubbly cheek grazing mine, his lips brushing against the shell of my ear.

"Thank you for meeting me, ma fleur."

He kisses my earlobe. The heat from my cheeks shoots like lighting down my body, leaving a blazing path down, down, all the way down to my most private part.

I close my eyes and swallow hard. I have held my V card clenched in my fist for twenty-five years, but two days with Gabriel Galliard and I am ready to shred it to pieces and toss them in the air.

I step back, putting distance between me and Monsieur Tall, Dark, and Dangerous to my Chastity.

"I am sorry you came all of this way and I can only stay for two minutes."

"I am not sorry, ma fleur. I would travel a lot farther just to look at you. You're beautiful, candid, smart, and funny. You make my heart smile."

Chapter 19

Laney's Life Playlist
"Somebody That I Used to Know" by Gotye
"Want U Back" by Cher Lloyd

. . . Let's take sixty seconds to relax your body, quiet your mind, and reduce your anxiety. Lean back in your chair, close your eyes, and take several deep breaths, in and out. In . . . and out. In . . . and out. Keep breathing in for three seconds. Hold it for one . . . two. Exhale for one . . . two . . . three . . . four. Good, now imagine there's a large vat of warm honey over your head. Imagine the vat tipping over, spilling on your head, down your shoulders, slowly, slowly down your body until you are covered, from head to toe, in comforting warmth. This warmth is healing, calming, protective . . .

When I was growing up, I would spend the day before the start of a new school year curled up in the fetal position in my bed, hugging Hoppy, and imagining every possible worst-case scenario. I imagined myself reporting to my new homeroom only to discover I had forgotten to put on my clothes. I imagined myself tripping in the hallway in front of Tiffany Parrino, arguably the most popular and spiteful girl in school, or suffering a sudden bout of diarrhea, or vomiting in the cafeteria. A disturbing number of my horrifying imaginings involved the sudden, uncontrolled expulsion of bodily fluids.

I couldn't eat. I couldn't sleep. And there wasn't anything anyone could do—Mom, Pops, Gramps, Theo—to interrupt my painful thoughts.

I have been experiencing a wicked cased of déjà vu all day. The knotted stomach. The overpowering need to hug Hoppy. The obsessive gloom-doom scenario scenes flickering in my head. I barely made it through my shift in the gallery and had to practice anchoring to get through the afternoon's workshop, led by Camille Fabriano, an intuitive painter who lectures at art institutes around the world on breaking inhibitions.

Anchoring is a meditation technique that trains your body to quickly relax through a specific touch, say a touch on your wrist or between your eyes. After following the advice of pediatricians and child therapists, Mom stepped outside her traditional box and sent me to meditation specialist, who taught me anchoring the day before I started middle school.

My date with Gabriel is messing with my chakras. I am totally out of whack. I've run through the 60-Second Meditation for Relaxation, Chakra Healing Meditation, and the Deep Healing and Balancing Meditation. They helped, but every once in a while I find myself imaging worst-case scenario scenes.

What if we are sitting in La Belle Hortense, gazing into each other's eyes, and I vomit, explosively, all over the table and Gabriel? What if I develop a sudden allergy to wine and my face turns as puffy and purple as a grape? What if we are standing beneath a linden tree in place des Vosges and I think Gabriel is leaning in to give me a kiss, but he's not, and I lean forward and kiss his tooth?

It could happen.

It *did* happen.

Not with Gabriel.

It happened with Johnny Josephs, my first boyfriend. It was the summer of freshman year. We were hanging outside a music store on Pearl Street, talking about Justin Timberlake's new CD, *FutureSex/LoveSounds*. Justin was Johnny's "god," and I was arguing that he was kind of an asshat for releasing "Cry Me a River," which everyone knew was a completely unveiled jab at poor Britney Spears. I was leaning with my back against the building. Johnny was also leaning against the building, but he had his shoulder against the brick wall and was facing me. He was staring at my mouth so intensely, I just knew he was about to kiss me. When he leaned closer, I closed my eyes and went for it. It wasn't the leg-lifting, fireworks-exploding kiss I had dreamt it would be because I miscalculated the trajectory and slammed my lip into his front tooth.

Later, I found out he had been staring at my mouth because my lips were lined in green from the handful of lime Skittles I had eaten before meeting him. To this day, I can't hear "SexyBack" without feeling a little sick.

I walk over to the mirror hanging on the wall in my cubby room and stare at myself.

"Think positive thoughts. Say something good to yourself."

I might be a proud, card-carrying virgin, but I've made out with *a lot* of guys since Johnny. Relatively speaking, that is. I know not to consume candies or beverages with a lot of dye in them and not to try to preempt the guy on the first kiss. So, I should be okay if Gabriel makes his move.

"I am okay. Everything will be okay."

I take a deep breath and repeat the mantra in my head. Then I brush a little more mascara on my lashes and dab Burt's Bees Evening Glow lip gloss on my lips.

There is a knock at my door.

"Entrez."

The door creaks open, and Rigby sticks her head in.

"I've brought you the perfume I promised." She pushes the door all of the way open and steps inside, whistling. "You look incredible!"

"Thanks."

"Here you are, mademoiselle."

She pulls her arm out from behind her back and presents the perfume with a flourish, bowing as if she were a lady-in-waiting serving a queen.

My signature scent for daytime is Pink Sugar by Aquolina, because it smells like cotton candy, but Rigby said it was too sweet for a date with a spicy-hot French man.

I take the heavy, rectangular perfume bottle adorned with colorful, hand-painted flowers and read the words printed in fancy black script.

"Balenciaga Rosabotanica." I remove the lid and bring the bottle to my nose, inhaling. "It smells expensive, like hothouse roses growing in a greenhouse owned by a wealthy Italian countess."

Rigby laughs. "It was a gift from Matthias. The scent drives him wild. Hopefully, it will drive Monsieur Tall, Dark, and Hot wild too."

I spray some on my wrists and rub them together.

"Not like that," Rigby says, taking the bottle from me. "You'll bruise the scent. French women spritz their perfume into the air and walk through the scented cloud."

She spritzes the air, and we both walk through the scented cloud, laughing.

Gunthar and Giorgio are on their way out but pause in my doorway. Giorgio looks at me and whistles a catcall.

"Rigby, she tell me about your date," Giorgio says, winking. "You are going out with a French man, no?"

"Yes, I am going out on a date with a French man."

"Why not an Italian?" Giorgio sighs and shakes his head, fixing me with a mournful expression. "The French, they have the reputation for being clever, fashionable, and romantic, but everyone knows they steal from Italians. Napoleon, Corsica, the *Mona Lisa,* Carla Bruni. The mirrors hanging in the Hall of Mirrors at Versailles? All Italian!"

"The heart fancies who it fancies, regardless of nationality."

"True, bella." Giorgio brightens. "If things don't work out with the French man, you will let me sit you up with a nice Italian, yes?"

"Sit me up?"

"I think he means *set* you up," Rigby laughs.

"Si! I set you up."

"Okay."

I don't really want Giorgio to *sit* or *set* me up with another man, but I have found acquiescing to be the fastest way to end a humiliating conversation.

"Ciao, bella."

Gunthar gives an awkward wave and follows Giorgio. A second later, there's a loud, hollow thud, like the sound of a ripe cantaloupe being thumped . . . or Gunthar's head striking a low-lying beam.

"Verdammt," Gunthar curses.

"Don't worry," Rigby whispers. "I told them you were going on a date, but I didn't reveal the identity of Monsieur Tall, Dark, and Hot."

"I'm not worried," I say, smiling. "I know you aren't the type to blab."

"How?"

"How?"

"How do you know I'm not a blabber?"

"I read your aura when we first met."

"You did?"

I nod.

"What did it look like?"

"Loads of loyal blue, sensitive purple, and honest yellow. It was pure."

"Gee, thanks."

Rigby smiles so big, her upper lashes touch her brows and her cheeks look like two shiny apples. It's the kind of smile that makes others feel like they swallowed sunshine. All warm and glowing.

"I have to go. I am meeting Matthias for dinner." She gives me a hug. "Come to my room when you get back and tell me all of the juicy details."

"Okay, but I doubt I will have much juice."

"Yes, you will! You're meeting a French man for drinks and you're dressed like a wide-eyed sex doll. You'll have big, fat, juicy details, my friend," she says, walking out the door. "I am sure of it."

"Wait!" I hurry over to the door. "A wide-eyed sex doll? Is that a good thing or a bad thing?"

Rigby laughs and disappears down the stairs.

I walk back into my room and take a last look in the mirror. I am wearing a black baby doll dress with cap sleeves and my ankle-strap pumps. It's the most va-va-voom outfit in my wardrobe, and I am worried it might have one *va* too many.

My heavy bangs hang to my eyebrows, and my thick lashes emphasize my round blue eyes. My lips look like a wine-colored bow fastened to my pale face. I am a giving off a serious doll vibe. One of those unblinking, slightly creepy porcelain dolls that sat perched on shelves in Victorian nurseries, but not a naughty sex doll. I don't even know what a sex doll looks like. I saw a plastic blow-up doll at a bachelor party once. The bassist for our band booked the gig and didn't tell us what it was until we got there. Awk-ward.

I blink several times, clearing the memory of the bachelor party and the blow-up doll. I really don't want to meet Gabriel with images of sloppy drunk men pretending to hump a sex doll in my head.

Maybe I should change into something less . . .

My iPhone suddenly starts emitting a loud foghorn sound. *Bwah-wah-wah-wah.* I grab my iPhone and slide my finger across the screen, silencing the alarm.

Great! It's seven o'clock, which means I am late, late for my very important date. Hopefully, my baby doll dress and Rigby's big-girl perfume will distract Gabriel from my tardiness.

Gabriel is standing beneath a wide, green-striped awning outside La Belle Hortense when I arrive. He's wearing a suit with a crisp white shirt opened at the throat and a black trench coat. His hair has been combed back in a serious, suitsexual style. He looks devastating in his suit, but I think I dig him more in jeans and with his hair flopping over his forehead.

He steps off the curb and meets me in the middle of the street, casually wrapping his arm around my waist and leading me back to the sidewalk in front of La Belle Hortense. The weight and heat of his arm makes me feel breathless with a nameless anticipation.

When we reach the sidewalk, Gabriel kisses my cheeks.

"I thought you had changed your mind," he whispers, his breath hot against my ear. "I'm glad you didn't."

"Sorry," I say, flushing when he fixes his slate-blue gaze on me. "I'm punctuality challenged."

"You're worth the wait, ma fleur."

He laces his fingers through mine and lifts my hand, kissing the tips of my fingers. He opens the door, and I follow him inside.

I had assumed La Bella Hortense was a bistro or brasserie, but it's a funky wine bar situated inside a bookstore. Shelves line walls filled with artfully arranged books and bottles of wine. Slow, sexy jazz is playing softly in the background. The vibe is totally chill, and the crowd is young, urban, artsy. My kind of people. We take a seat at a small table near the back of the bar. I untie my raincoat, and Gabriel helps me out of it. He folds my coat over the back of his chair and appraises me, his unnerving gaze moving from my face to my toes and back again.

"You make my heart ache with your beauty," he says, pressing his hand to his chest.

The first thing that comes into my mind: *Now, that is just the sort of line a smooth-moving French man would say to a naïve American girl*. Not wanting to spoil the mood, I keep my ungenerous and untrusting thought to myself.

"Merci beaucoup." My cheeks flush with heat. "I like your suit. You look like you were born to wear Armani."

I like your suit? I never thought I, Delaney Lavender Brooks, would tell someone I liked their suit, but I am being one hundred percent genuine, as real as the heavy, expensive Rolex on Gabriel's wrist.

"Merci." He shrugs out of his coat and rolls his shirtsleeves up to his elbows, exposing corded, muscular forearms. "Truthfully? I hate wearing suits, but I had a meeting with my boss."

"About your upcoming assignment?"

"Oui."

"Where are you going?"

"Damascus."

I gasp. "Isn't it dangerous?"

"It's no big deal," he says, dismissively.

I have noticed Gabriel is dismissive about important, emotional issues and wonder if avoidance has become his coping mechanism.

"No big deal?" I search my memory for stories I might have read recently about the city. "Wait a minute! Didn't a radical Islamic group just send suicide bombers to Damascus? Wasn't there a big explosion?"

"There are always suicide bombings in the Middle East. Sadly, it has become a part of daily life in the region."

"That isn't very reassuring. What if you are hurt, or worse, killed?"

"Would you care?"

I grab his hand and squeeze it. "Of course, I would care."

"Bon," he says, rubbing my hand with his thumb. "But you have nothing to worry about, I promise."

"You can't make that promise."

"Ah, but I can, ma fleur. I am good, very good, at what I do. This time next month, we will be right here, toasting my return."

"We will?"

"Bien sûr." He grins. "You will wear this dress again, and I will kiss you and tell you how much I missed you, that the thought of seeing you gave me a new purpose."

My heart melts. Literally melts inside my chest, a warm pool of sentimental mush.

The waitress appears.

"Bonsoir, monsieur et madame. Would you care to order an aperitif or something to eat, perhaps?"

"Would you like a glass of wine?" Gabriel asks.

"Sure."

"Du vin rouge ou blanc?"

I remember Johnny Josephs and the green Skittles debacle and imagine my lips and teeth stained an unsightly bluish-purple with wine.

"Blanc, s'il vous plaît." Even though I took French in high school and college, and was told by Fanny that my accent is impressive, I feel self-conscious speaking it in Paris, especially to order wine. The city is populated with oenophiles, people who were weaned off milk in favor of eau de vie. "Can you recommend a white wine?"

"Bien sûr!" Gabriel says, shrugging his shoulders and holding out his hands, a gesture and phrase that I have learned is the Gallic equivalent of "You must be joking because the answer is an obvious yes."

He orders the wine and two appetizers: pork rillettes, rich, slow-cooked pork served with pickled dried apricots on grilled bread, and a plate of assorted cheeses.

I sit quietly, my hands folded in my lap, listening to Gabriel speak in French, feeling like an imposter, a pretend grown-up in false lashes and strappy pumps. If you had asked me a year ago if I saw myself sitting in a chic bar in Paris, drinking wine with a gorgeous French man, I would have told you that you were out of your melon.

Yet, here I am. In Paris. Drinking wine. With an otherworldly gorgeous French man who has a voice that makes my knees feel as wobbly as green Nickelodeon slime.

The waitress moves to the next table, and Gabriel refocuses his gorgeous gray-eyed gaze on me.

"What do you think of La Belle Hortense?"

"Are you kidding me? Books. Wine. Music. What's not to love?" Gabriel's smoldering gaze is making it impossible for me to vibe off the chill atmosphere. The room feels suddenly warmer, the jazz slower, more seductive. "It reminds me of a place I would go to in Denver, a gallery that serves artisan cocktails."

"What are artisan cocktails?"

"Oh, super unusual cocktails, like rum set afire and tossed between two frozen glasses. A martini made of foamed Earl Grey tea. Or a margarita served with a lime covered in what appears to be caviar, but it's really pearls of tequila that have been frozen to look like caviar. That was Theo's favorite."

"Theo?"

"Theodore Wilde. He's an amazingly talented bike designer, musician, and skier. He's funny and loyal and . . . well, I just love him."

Gabriel's lips press together, and the smolder in his gaze extinguishes, but he doesn't say anything until after the hostess finishes serving our wine.

"Il est votre copain?"

He is your boyfriend?

The laugh that burst from my lips is explosive and loud. Several of the chic, urban set look our way. I press my hand to my mouth because the thought of Netflix and chillin' with Theo makes me want to laugh again—or toss my cookies.

"Theo is my best friend," I say, lowering my voice.

"You are sure?"

I lean forward, resting my forearms on the edge of the table, and look Gabriel in the eye. I am detecting some trust issues with Gabriel.

"I am positive. Theo is not my boyfriend. He was never my boyfriend, like ever. Just the thought makes me want to . . ." I crinkle my nose and pretend to shudder. "*Eww.* It would be like snogging my cousin, Leo, or my Uncle Milt. No. Just, no."

Gabriel chuckles. "Okay, okay. I believe you."

I lift my glass of wine, give it a little swirl like Fanny taught me, inhale the bouquet, and then take a deep drink, the sweet, slightly spicy liquid sliding down my throat and warming my belly.

"What about you?" I wiggle my eyebrows. "Do you have an Amélie hidden away in some quaint corner of Paris?"

"Amélie?"

"Amélie Poulain, the wide-eyed, naïve beauty in the movie *Amélie,* who dreams of love."

Gabriel shakes his head, chuckling. "Non, ma fleur. I do not have an Amélie, Stéphanie, or Alexandrie. There is no one."

I make a raspberry noise and roll my eyes.

"What?"

"I don't know," I say, taking another sip of wine. "It's just . . . you're a total marlin."

He frowns, obviously confused by my Laney-ism.

"A marlin. One of the fish most prized by anglers."

"Are you an angler?"

"No, but you're definitely a catch."

The smile that spreads across his face is as potent as the glass of sweet, spicy wine I've nearly consumed.

"On my honor," he says, pressing his hand to his heart, "I swear there is not an Amélie, Stéphanie, or Alexandrie who lays claim to my heart, but I am hoping there will be a Laney."

I look from him to my empty wineglass and back into his blue-gray eyes. I am mentally doing one of those cartoon head shakes because I think he just said he wants me to be his girlfriend. I must be drunk; the fumes from the wickedly overpriced white wine must have muddled my brain and my hearing. I decide to pretend like I didn't hear what he said.

"Do you like to read?"

Something unrecognizable glimmers in his eyes—humor, irritation, pain? I might not be punctual, organized, or focused, but I have mad skills of perception. I can read people and comprehend their emotions like Pops reads and comprehends Stephen Hawking's *A Brief History of Time.* It's my gift. Or I thought it was my gift. Gabriel is giving me serious Sphinx face, stony and unreadable.

"Oui." He smiles, a Sphinx-like smile. "Do you?"

I nod.

"What are some of your favorite books?"

"I love anything by J.R.R. Tolkien. He's, like, the end. C. S. Lewis. George R. R. Martin. I devour fantasy and science fiction novels. I read Madeleine L'Engle's *A Wrinkle in Time* when I was, like, six, and it completely blew my mind. I secretly believe that government scientists have developed a tesseract and someday we will all be able to travel through time. I also read a lot of books about artists and art history. What about you?"

He rests his forearms on the edge of table and leans forward, close enough for me to smell his cologne, to see the small, crescent-shaped scar just below his hairline.

"I love Tolkien too." His words come out like a seductive whisper, as if he were pledging his fidelity, or declaring his intention to make slow, passionate love to me. "Alexander Dumas is my favorite author, though."

My heart is thud-thud-thudding so violently in my chest I am sure he can hear it, even over the mellow jazz, clinking glasses, and steady buzz of conversation.

"Do you know, I don't think I have ever read an Alexander Dumas novel?"

"Quelle? Il est criminal!"

"Is he that good?"

"Est-il bon? Est-il bon?" Gabriel emits a noise that can only be described as a half-incredulous, half-outraged grunt. "Horatio Georges's books are good. Alexandre Dumas's books are brilliant! Romance, revenge, redemption cleverly woven through plots filled with action and adventure. Incroyable! Brilliant! We must rectify this tragic situation."

I laugh, but Gabriel is quite serious.

"Can you read French?"

I nod.

"Bon." He stands up. "One minute, s'il vous plait."

He walks back to the bar and speaks to the hostess. She leads him away from our corner of the bar, to a shelf in the opposite corner, filled with leather-bound books, and points to the second shelf from the top. The hostess is too short to reach the shelf, but Gabriel is able to retrieve the book with little effort.

Gabriel returns to the table, leather-bound book in hand, and a wide toothy, dimpled grin on his face.

"Voici *Le Comte de Monte-Cristo*," he says, setting the book on the table. "It is, perhaps, my favorite Dumas novel. Would you have a pen in your purse? I would like to inscribe it."

I open my purse, remove my purple roller pen, and hand it to Gabriel. He stares off, his brows knitted together, and then opens the cover and scribbles on the half-title page, the pen making scratching noises against the heavy paper. A few seconds later, he closes the book and hands my pen back to me.

I reach for the book, open the cover, and read the inscription, written in beautiful, loopy French.

Ma fleur,
In this book you will find one of Alexandre Dumas's most famous quotes: "All human wisdom is contained in these two words—wait and hope." I wait and hope for a day when you are as familiar to me as Edmond and Mercedes, the characters in this story.

Yours,
Gabriel Galliard

I don't realize I am holding my breath until my lungs begin to burn and tiny black dots dance around the periphery of my vision. Gabriel's inscription is simply the most romantic thing anyone has ever said to me. It's breathtaking. It's the kind of thing a charming, slightly rakish hero in a rom-com says to the beautiful, slightly naïve heroine.

Am I naïve? Is Gabriel a sincere Mark Darcy or a shameless Daniel Cleaver? Will I write good or bad things about him in my diary?

"Gabriel!"

I look up from the inscription in time to see a tall, willowy woman with sleek black hair and an even sleeker black designer dress kiss Gabriel on both cheeks.

"Giselle?"

Gabriel's tone is flat, but his expression is much, much less Sphinx-like. His cheeks are flushed red, and his aura is swirling with so many colors it looks like a muddled watercolor rainbow. I am having trouble reading him again, but I think he's embarrassed.

Or angry.

Or aroused.

"Delaney Brooks, this is Giselle Sournois DéLoyalle. She is a . . . friend."

"Come now," Giselle says, laughing and pressing her hand against Gabriel's bare, muscular forearm. "We are more than mere friends, are we not?"

Gabriel looks up at Giselle, his gaze as flat and gray as slate, his lips a grim line across his handsome face. He raises a single brow, but doesn't speak. Giselle, I notice, has lost all color in her high, knifelike cheeks.

"It's nice to meet you, Giselle," I say in French, hoping to ease the awkward tension. "Are you here with a date? Would you like to join us?"

Giselle continues to stare into Gabriel's eyes, but her full, pink bottom lip quivers a little. She finally tears her gaze from Gabriel and narrows her smoky, black-rimmed eyes on me. It's a look that takes my breath away. Not the way Gabriel's inscription took my breath away, but in a fierce, furious, I am going to reach into your body and rip your heart out with my pointy fingernails kind of way. I don't need to read Giselle's aura to know she is projecting some serious hate my way.

"Thank you, but I have a prior engagement. I should leave soon if I am to make it," she says, her voice soft and sibilant like a snake. She looks back at Gabriel, dismissing me with a flick of her gaze. "Au revoir, mon cher."

She turns on her slender heel, snatches a silver, fur-trimmed coat from the back of a bar stool, tosses it over her shoulders, and walks out of the bar.

"Awk-ward," I say, emphasizing both syllables.

"Oui."

The color has faded from Gabriel's cheeks, but not from his aura. The wildly swirling reds, blues, and blacks tell me that Giselle stirred up a complex brew of emotions in him.

"Was Giselle an Amélie?"

"Once," he says, pushing his fingers through his hair. "But that was before."

"Before?"

He smiles tightly. He's avoiding again.

"I am sorry. It's none of my business."

"Non, I am sorry, ma fleur. Giselle was rude, and she made you feel uncomfortable. I hope it hasn't put a damper on our evening."

I think about his non-answer to my question, and I realize Giselle's sudden appearance hasn't put a damper on the evening, but it has poked the beast of mistrust that had been sleeping in the darkest basement of my heart. The beast that tells me I shouldn't trust a smooth-talking, handsome French man.

"No, it hasn't."

"Bon." He raises my hand to his lips and kisses my palm. "It would upset me greatly if a specter from my past cast a shadow over my future. Now I will order us another glass of wine, and you will tell me about your life in Colorado."

Gabriel goes to the bar to order our wine, and I take several deep cleansing breaths. I try to quiet the beast roaring inside me, the beast roused by the ghosts of Gabriel's girlfriends past. I remind myself of the sensei's teachings on jealousy.

"Jealousy and suspicion are houses built on foundations of insecurity," she said. *"They are sad, bleak dwellings with air so toxic it kills bigger, more beautiful emotions."*

I take another deep breath and close my eyes. I exhale and imagine my breath blowing those rickety, miserable dwellings away, like stick houses in a tornado.

Chapter 20

I am standing outside La Belle Hortense, the two glasses of wine coursing through my veins and giving me a pleasant flush, despite the damp, chilly air, when Gabriel grabs the ties of my raincoat and pulls me to him.

"I don't want our evening to end yet," he murmurs, his breath hot against my ear. "Will you take a walk with me, ma fleur?"

I close my eyes and press my cheek against his, shivering a little as his warm, scruffy stubble grazes my skin.

"I would like that," I whisper.

"Merci," he says, kissing my cheek. "Let's walk to the river."

He wraps his arm around my waist, casually resting his hand on my hip, and we walk down rue Vieille du Temple toward the Seine. Most of the businesses along the road are closed at this time of night, their windows dark or hidden behind metal shutters. We move silently past Heaven, a boutique selling gauzy summer dresses, and Orphée, a music store that sells antique musical instruments from the baroque era. At the corner, we stand in the glow of a neon green *pharmacie* cross and wait until a rusty white van rattles by, its tailpipe belching noxious gray clouds. We cross the street, but Gabriel stops walking when we come to a gallery with a bright, shiny red façade and grainy black-and-white photos propped in the window. Except for the photographs in the window, the gallery is empty, the doors firmly shuttered with heavy red panels. I look up at the faded gold script painted above the door.

"Galerie Agathe Gaillard," I read aloud. "The spelling is close to your last name, Gabriel. Is Madame Agathe Gaillard a distant cousin?"

"No," Gabriel says. "Agathe Gaillard opened this gallery in 1975 after falling in love with Jean-Philippe Charbonnier's photographs." He removes his hand from my waist just long enough to point to a beautiful black-and-white photo of a little girl in a pinafore standing in a Parisian alley, hugging a kitten and laughing. "That is one of Charbonnier's images. Do you see the way the light reflects off of the cobblestones and the way the *vélo* leaning against the back wall is in the shadows, yet still illuminated? Brilliant."

"This is a happy photograph, isn't it?"

"Oui."

"It is one photograph, one little girl, and yet it seems to tell a story about Paris after World War II, the hope and return of joy."

He looks at me, his brows knit together, his lips curled up in a smile. "Brava, ma fleur. Beautifully said. Charbonnier was a master at capturing humanity during its impulsive and unrehearsed moments. His images were essential in spawning the humanist photography movement, a philosophical effort to document social change."

"Are all of his images so happy?"

"Non." Gabriel pulls me along, and we cross the quai de l'Hotel de Ville and walk over the pont Saint-Louis onto the Île Saint-Louis. "Many of Charbonnier's photographs depicted the harsh realities of life after World War II, the poverty, the lack of housing, and the struggles of the urban working class."

"You sound like you admire his work."

"Oui," Gabriel says. "I carry Charbonnier's images in my mind and use them as a yardstick to measure my own work. I aspire to his level of storytelling."

"You measure up."

"How do you know? You haven't even seen my work."

I keep my gaze fixed on the glowing windows of a brasserie at the end of the street and pretend I didn't hear his question. He squeezes my waist.

"Laney?"

He stops walking. I stop walking.

"I googled you," I mumble, looking at my feet.

He lifts my chin until our gazes meet. "I didn't hear you. What did you say?"

"I googled you."

His eyes sparkle in the lamplight, and his mouth parts in a beautiful, breathtaking, toothy grin.

"You googled me?"

"I was curious about your work, so I did a little Internet search. Please don't worry, though, I promise I'm not a creepy stalk—"

He leans down and presses his lips to mine in a kiss that makes my cheeks flush with blistering heat—like, volcanic heat. I am no longer standing on a bridge spanning the Seine; I am floating on a lava flow, being swept away by a river of molten red desire, consumed by a force too powerful to resist. It is so excruciatingly—

—and just like that Gabriel stops kissing me, leaves me spinning in a whirlpool of unfulfilled desires.

When I open my eyes, he is staring at me with a look that will forever be painted on my mind. He isn't smiling exactly, but he's not frowning, either. The predatory glimmer in his eyes makes clear his intention to possess me. It terrifies me . . . and thrills me.

I realize, with sudden clarity, with the clarity of a sharply focused inner eye, that I will give my virginity to Gabriel Galliard.

"Merci, ma fleur," he says, raising my hand to his lips. "I am flattered by your interest. You can stalk me anytime you want."

He puts his arm around my waist again, and we continue walking, following the road until we come to the pont Saint-Louis, the bridge leading to the Île de la Cité and Notre Dame Cathedral. We cross another bridge and take stairs leading to a path that runs alongside the river, the lights of the cathedral glowing golden on the smooth surface.

We stop walking when we come to a row of moored riverboats. A beautiful blue-painted wooden boat is filled with dinner cruisers sipping wine and eating lobster by candlelight. A man is standing on the deck, pushing and pulling the bellows of a concertina, playing a *bal-musette* tune, music that evokes romantic Parisian cafés and bistros.

Gabriel spins me toward him so my chest is pressed against his chest, my thighs pressed to his thighs.

"Dance with me?" he murmurs, his lips on my earlobe.

I nod my head because the feel of Gabriel's muscular body, of his warm breath on my neck, has snatched the breath from my lungs.

We sway to the music, making slow, intoxicating circles over the path. I rest my head on Gabriel's broad shoulder and let him lead me around and around, until I feel drunk and dizzy and consumed with desire.

The music finally stops, but we stand in an orb of silvery moonlight, pressed against each other as if we have been lovers for years.

The heat of Gabriel's body warms me to the bone, reminding me of what it felt like to step out of a brutal Colorado winter into a warm, cozy cabin.

"Are you cold, ma fleur," he asks, holding me at arm's length. "You're shivering."

"A little."

He reaches his hand into his pocket and pulls out a scarf, the kind of scarves stylish Parisian men wear, and wraps it around my neck. He's still holding the ends of the scarf and uses them to pull me close against him again, kissing me with a slow, sensuousness that matches our dancing.

He deepens his kiss, snaking his arm up my back, sliding his hand into my hair, thrusting his tongue between my lips, and I moan, low, deep in my throat. A moan of pure, unchecked desire.

I want . . .

I want . . .

I want things I have never had, things I have only imagined, things I have hoped for since that day in place des Vosges, when I looked into Gabriel's slate-blue eyes and felt a spark ignite deep inside me.

I suddenly feel a wetness on my cheeks, like tears, and realize it is raining. Gabriel takes my hand, and we run, laughing, to take shelter in a nearby tunnel.

We are standing in the archway, watching the rain fall in big, silvery drops, plopping into the river, creating wide ripples, when Gabriel grabs me around the waist, presses me against the wall, slides his leg between my thighs, and kisses me again. That tiny spark of desire that had been gently glowing bursts into flames inside of me, like an ember touched by a breeze.

I wrap my arms around him, snaking my hands inside his coat, beneath his shirt, up the broad expanse of his muscular back. I dig my fingernails into the smooth, taut skin of his shoulders, and he lifts his knee, spreading my thighs so I am forced to straddle his leg. The sweet, tender kiss we shared on the bridge is a distant, hazy memory, replaced by this scorching urgency.

I pull my hand out from under his shirt and slowly, hesitantly slide it inside his waistband. I've barely worked my way beneath his briefs when my fingers touch the head of his large, swollen cock, and he groans against my lips, muttering something in French.

"Let me take you home, ma fleur," he growls.

"Y . . . you want to take me back to the gallery?"

The world is spinning. The tunnel. The raindrops. The glow of the lamplight against the rain-slick cobblestones. Spinning. Spinning. Spinning at dizzying speed. If Gabriel didn't have his leg between my thighs, I would pull a Victorian and faint dead away.

"Non, my love," he moans against my lips. "Not to the gallery. I want to take you back to my apartment."

He doesn't wait for my response. He flicks the tip of his tongue over my lips, tracing, teasing, while slowly moving his knee against my clitoris. Slow, maddeningly slow, masterful circles that let me know Gabriel must have surrendered his V card long ago.

There are multiple layers of clothes between us. The cold night air is nipping at our skin, icy rain is needling our cheeks, but still Gabriel has me burning up like a woman suffering the worst kind of fever.

What would it be like if we were naked in his bed? How feverish would I feel then, if the threat of being discovered in a tunnel by strangers wasn't niggling at my conscious?

Am I ready to give up my virginity to a man I have known for only a week? A man clearly skilled in the arts of seduction? A man with a willowy Giselle hanging onto his shadow?

"Please, my love." He kisses my lips. "Say you will come home with me."

I drop my forehead to his shoulder and draw a shaky breath. Nothing in my uneventful, unfocused life has prepared me for a moment like this. What do you say when a man asks you to go home with him? Not a Johnny Josephs—not just some silly, fumbling man-boy—but a handsome, charming, wonderful man who makes you go all flushy-crushy and turns your knees to Nickelodeon slime with a single glance. What do you say to *him*?

Fanny would say something sophisticated and sexy in her native French that would drive Gabriel mad. Vivia would throw her inhibitions to the rainy wind and make love to Gabriel right here in this tunnel. I am not Fanny. I do not have her sophistication. I am not Vivia. I do not have her fearlessness.

Gabriel doesn't want Fanny or Vivia; he wants me. What's more, I want him. I want him because he makes me feel sophisticated and fearless and sexy. I want him because he brings out parts of me I have kept hidden for . . . well, forever.

Gabriel reaches up, pushes my hair aside, and whispers in my ear. "We don't have to make love, ma fleur, if that's what frightens you. We don't have to do anything you don't want to do. I just want to hold you in my arms until the night fades away to day."

"I . . . I'm sorry, Gabriel, but"—I lift my head and look at him, my eyes filling with humiliated tears—"this is happening too fast and—"

"Shh." He kisses my lips, cheeks, eyes. "C'est bon. We have all of the time in the world. There will be other nights."

"You promise?"

He rubs my cheek with his thumb and smiles.

"I promise, ma fleur."

We hold hands and walk out into the rain, climbing the steps to the street with our heads down, bodies close. I wonder if tonight will become my great regret. I wonder if Gabriel will quietly disappear from my life, frustrated by my rejection.

A guy I dated throughout my junior year in college got so angry when, after seven months of dating, I still wouldn't let him get beyond the heavy-groping stage, he called me Fridge. *"Damn, girl, you're colder than a refrigerator,"* he said. *"You don't just give a guy blue balls, you freeze his fucking nads right off."*

Gabriel hails a taxi, and it pulls to a stop at the curb, splashing puddle water onto our feet. Gabriel opens the door and lets me climb in first. We ride to the gallery together in silence. His arm is around my shoulders, but there's a distance between us. I don't think I am imagining it.

I am such an idiot. When I am a lonely, dusty, sixty-three-year-old virgin, I will look back on this evening with painful regret. I will close my eyes, rest my head against the back of my rocker, and remember the dark tunnel and Gabriel's hard body. I will mourn my lack of courage and long for a chance to go back in time, to feel Gabriel's knee rubbing against my clitoris, to hear his voice in my ear, begging me to go home with him.

You know what Sensei says about regret. . . .

Oh, shut up.

I am so lost in thought and choking on bitter regret, I don't realize we have arrived at the gallery until I hear Gabriel ask the driver to wait.

He climbs out, promises the driver he won't be long, and walks me to the wooden door leading to the courtyard.

He lifts my hand to his mouth and kisses it. "Will you miss me while I am gone, ma fleur?"

The bitter lump of regret is still lodged in my throat, so I merely nod my head.

"I will miss you, but I will remember the way you look right now, your cheeks pink from the cold, your eyes as wide and blue as the Mediterranean, your lips swollen from my kisses"—he draws a jagged breath—"I will think of you, and I will count the minutes until I see you again, until I can kiss you like this."

He leans down and presses his lips to mine, dragging them slowly, sweetly back and forth until we are both out of breath and clinging to each other again.

The taxi driver honks his horn. Two loud toots that shatter the intimacy like a break through a plate-glass window.

"Go now, go inside where it is warm, before I pick you up, carry you over to the park, and make love to you on the very spot where we first met."

Chapter 21

Laney's Life Playlist
"Lullaby" by Paradise Fears
"Long Distance" by Bruno Mars

TEXT FROM GABRIEL GALLIARD:
You are still asleep under a starry Parisian sky and I am already miles away, staring at the same stars and wishing our nights apart weren't so long. Be well, ma fleur. Don't forget there is someone half a world away thinking about you, fondly and often.

TEXT TO GABRIEL GALLIARD:
I would stay awake if it would make the nights go faster, if it would make you come home sooner. How could I possibly forget you, when I spend every moment thinking about you and what we will do when you are back in Paris?

TEXT FROM STÉPHANIE MOREAU:
How was your date, Laney-Bo-Baney?

TEXT FROM VIVIA PERPETUA DE CAUMONT
So, did you take my advice and *do* you? Better yet, did you do the über-hot French guy?

TEXT FROM GABRIEL GALLIARD:
Back in Paris or back in your arms?

TEXT TO VIVIA PERPETUA DE CAUMONT:
You're in my arms, even when you are half a world away.

TEXT FROM VIVIA PERPETUA DE CAUMONT:
Jesus, Mary, and getting jiggy w'it Joseph! I had no idea you felt that way about me. Thanks for keeping me in your arms. LOL

TEXT TO VIVIA PERPETUA DE CAUMONT:
I, like, can't even right now. Sorry. That was meant for Gabriel.

TEXT FROM VIVIA PERPETUA DE CAUMONT:
Don't be sorry. I am actually relieved it was meant for Gabriel. You had me contemplating leaving Luc.

TEXT TO GABRIEL GALLIARD:
You're in my arms, even when you are half a world away. Be safe, Gabriel.

The next few weeks pass like honey through a straw. Like, seriously, tortuously slow. I've never done the long-distance thing before. Or maybe I've just never done the in-love thing before. Is it supposed to be excruciatingly painful? Is it supposed to monopolize your every thought, make you feel an itchy restlessness, cause you to lose your appetite, sleep, hair?

Fanny called to check on me, and I asked her the same question. She laughed and said, "You're either in love, ma cherie, or critically ill. Have you run your symptoms through WebMD?"

I e-mailed Vivia to ask her if she had any advice on how to cope. Vivia did the long-distance thing with a Frenchman for a year. Now, she's married to that Frenchman. She wrote back in typical Vivia fashion—thoughtful, funny, and filter-free.

To: DreamsInPaint@yahoo.com
From: Vivia Perpetua de Caumont
Subj: Re: Long-distance Relationships

Laney,

Keeping it real? The long-distance thing sucks. What helped me was to have crazy hot monkey sex as often as I could—with Luc when he was available for a quick booty-call, with myself when he wasn't available.

Kidding. Sorta.

When monkey sex and masturbating didn't work, I would try to keep busy. Focus on your internship, artwork, friends, and building a new, independent life in Paris.

Some days, you will try everything I have mentioned and still feel miserable. You might even wonder if the long-distance thing is worth it. Remind yourself that you only feel miserable because you love someone, intensely. It's better to feel the pain of missing someone than the pain of not having someone to miss, isn't it?

Bon chance!

Vivia

I take Vivia's advice by spending extra hours in the atelier, using paint to express the complexly shaded emotions in my heart. When the light is too weak and watery to paint, I take long walks with Rigby.

We walk to every corner of Paris, swapping trivia about artists who lived and worked there. We dream about what it would be like if we stayed in Paris forever, started an art-themed tour company, and settled down with our French boys. We climb the hills of Montmartre and drink cheap red wine in outdoor cafés. We meet other Bobos—bourgeois bohemians—and discuss the esoteric.

We stay until the bistro lights flicker on and the cobalt, velvet curtain of dusk lowers. Then we walk back down the hill and make our way to Bâtard de Valadon for a bowl of onion soup and crusty baguettes. Robert has become our foster father, ladling us free bowls of fishy bouillabaisse or peppery ratatouille, and plying us with outrageous stories about life in the Marais.

When our bellies are full of cheap wine and free food, and our heads full of delicious conversation, we stagger home to our beds. This is my favorite time of the day, when the gallery is still and the din of the world beyond our walls falls silent, because I lie in bed and read my nightly e-mail from Gabriel.

This is going to sound like my sanity train jumped the track and is tumbling down, down, down the mountainside toward Crazyville, but I bought a spiral sketchbook and am calling it my Journal d'Amour. I have begun filling it with copies of Gabriel's e-mails and photographs he sends me and my own little wistful, wishful sketches. On the nights when I am really, really missing him, like tonight, I start at the first page and read all of the e-mails.

To: DreamsInPaint@yahoo.com
From: Gabriel Galliard 05/05/16
Subj: Missing You

I rode in a convoy with the UN and Red Cross as they delivered food and medical supplies to the people in the besieged, rebel-held Damascus suburb of Qudsaya. The people in this dusty hillside town have been cut off from the world for over a year. I can't imagine what these people have suffered, some of them separated from loved ones since the siege began. I have been away from you for less than a week, and I feel disoriented, lost, and a little sad.

Be well, ma fleur.

G.

To: DreamsInPaint@yahoo.com
From: Gabriel Galliard 05/08/16
Subj: My Rainbow

A brief note today, and that to tell you how happy I am to have you in my life. It rained all day. A heavy, deafening downpour that kept me from my task. When the skies finally cleared, a rainbow arched from one side of the shelled-out city to the other. The bold, beautiful colors made me think of you, ma fleur, and the way you suddenly appeared in my life, bringing unexpected joy. I have attached a photograph I took of the rainbow. How are you? Have you had time to work on Minority of Souls? I can't wait to see it . . . and you.

G.

To: DreamsInPaint@yahoo.com
From: Gabriel Galliard 05/12/16
Subj: E-mails

I returned to my hotel, hungry, sweaty, and exhausted. Before
I met you, I would have eaten, taken a shower, and fallen into
bed. But food could wait. All I wanted to do was check my
e-mail. I am glad you miss me. Keep missing me, ma fleur.
I certainly miss you.

To: DreamsInPaint@yahoo.com 05/14/16
From: Gabriel Galliard
Subj: Tell me

You've shared with me the large parts of your life, but I often
wonder about the million small parts. The inconsequential.
Pieces that seem too insignificant to share. I want to gather
them all, those tiny pieces. Open my arms and sweep them
into my lap, study them one by one. Until I know all of you.

When I was a boy, we played a game called ten questions. You
ask the first ten questions that come to mind, and the other
person must answer, spontaneously and without reservation.
Want to play?

G.

That was the last e-mail I got from Gabriel. It's been five days.
Five long, agonizing days filled with wonder and worry that he has
forgotten about me—or, worse, been captured, shot, or beheaded by
a wild-eyed, totally twisted rebel.

I was chill the first day.

I was pretty chill the second day.

I was less chill the third day.

By the fourth day, I was completely without chill.

Today, the fifth day, chill has become this totally mythical state
of being, as fantastically mythical to me as fairies and unicorns are
to others. Chill? That only exists in kids' books and Antarctica.

This morning, I spent two hours staring out the rain-streaked window at the empty park, replaying the few, dreamy moments I spent with Gabriel. The first day in the gallery, when he was just a suitsexual stranger with a devastating smile. The day we met. The day he brought me daisies. The night he kissed me in the rain.

No matter how hard I tried to focus on the daisies and kisses, my mind kept replaying the scene in La Belle Hortense, when willowy Giselle wrapped her willowy hand around Gabriel's arm and cooed, "Come now, we are more than mere friends, are we not?"

Are they more than friends? Is Gabriel a player? Did he have a hot and heavy with me in a tunnel on the left bank and then hook up with willowy Giselle in some chic right-bank apartment?

Fanny once told me that the French philosophy about monogamy is quite different from the American philosophy.

"In France," she said, "women do not weep and wail at the thought of their husbands or boyfriends taking another lover, because they understand fidelity is a cultural phenomenon. Monogamy is not natural, ma cherie; it is cultural. We are the only creatures in the animal kingdom to impose ridiculous notions of fidelity and monogamy upon our mates."

She went on to tell me about how bonobo apes regularly engage in sex with multiple partners, male elephant seals typically have a large concubine of female seals, and how even swans, long believed to mate for life, aren't always monogamous. Swans! Myth cruelly shattered.

So who has it right? The mate-for-life Americans or the free-loving French? Is Gabriel a bonobo ape, swinging from mate to mate, or a mostly monogamous swan, hooking up with one feathery female at a time?

I wish I could affect the casual manner of a French woman, a glass of champagne in one hand, a long, slender, theatrical cigarette holder in the other, a bored *What do I care?* expression on my face, but I am not an elephant seal. I don't want to be in a concubine. I don't want to share Gabriel with Giselle or Genevieve or Gislaine . . . I want to be the only blubbery, barking seal on his beach.

Chapter 22

Laney's Life Playlist
"I Will Possess Your Heart" by Death Cab for Cutie
"Tattooed Love Boys" by The Pretenders

To: DreamsInPaint@yahoo.com 05/19/16
From: Gabriel Galliard
Subj: I am sorry

There have been several suicide bomb attacks in the Shiite suburbs of Damascus. I have been busy photographing the wounded and the family members of the dead. It is a senselessly tragic story without a foreseeable end.

Earlier this week, I was in the north, photographing the last remaining obstetric hospital in Aleppo. Even though it is frequently the target of missile attacks, pregnant women arrive every day to deliver their newborns. It is a sad setting for a happy event.

You wrote in your recent e-mail that you are worried because you haven't heard from me. I am sorry, ma fleur. I should have warned you that there would be times when I would not able to communicate. I do not want you to worry about me—even though it feels good to know you care enough to worry. I have to go now, but I will send ten questions as soon as I can.

G.

To: DreamsInPaint@yahoo.com 05/20/16
From: Gabriel Galliard
Subj: Good Morning, Beautiful

I would like to say that these are spontaneous questions, but I have had several long days (and nights) to think about them (and you).

1. If your house was on fire and you could only save one thing, what would you save?
2. What is your happiest childhood memory?
3. If you could have a superpower, what would it be?
4. What is your greatest fear?
5. You have a long weekend, where do you go and what do you do?
6. If you could live in one fictional place, where would it be?
7. What's the bravest thing you have ever done?
8. What's the best present you've ever been given?
9. Tell me one dream you have for the future.
10. What are you passionate about?

To: GabrielGalliard@laposte.net 05/20/16
From: Delaney Brooks
Subj: Re: Good Morning, Beautiful

1. If your house was on fire and you could only save one thing, what would you save? My dog, Dalí.
2. What is your happiest childhood memory? Camping with Theo and my Pops. We would look at the stars through his telescope, eat s'mores around a campfire, and catch fireflies in a jar.
3. If you could have a superpower what would it be? The ability to fly, like a fairy.
4. What is your greatest fear? Fear is negative, and I try not to dwell in negative spaces. Sometimes, though, I worry that I will wake up one day and realize my mom was right, that I wasted time with prepubescent diversions, that I have no real talent in art or music, and am destined to spend my life working as a singing unicorn. I will be my parents' biggest embarrassment:

a talentless, homeless drifter who doesn't own a car or a toilet plunger.

5. You have a long weekend, where do you go and what do you do? I would go to the south of France and walk in the footsteps of Van Gogh and Cézanne. I would find Van Gogh's *Yellow House in Arles* and Cézanne's light-dappled landscapes of Aix-en-Provence.

6. If you could live in one fictional place, where would it be? The Shire, where the hobbits live in Tolkien's books, because it is peaceful and a hobbit house would be cozy, or Neverland, because I would stay young forever, swim with mermaids, and fly with fairies!

7. What's the bravest thing you have ever done? Move to Paris to be a starving artist.

8. What's the best present you've ever been given? A bouquet of daises tied with a polka-dot ribbon.

9. What makes you happy? A lot of things make me happy. Scoring a pair of Lucite sunglasses. Vintage clothes. Indie bands. Singing silly songs to kids. Driving in Theo's Bananarama. Coming home after a long day and putting on my bunny onesie. Reading your e-mails.

10. What are you passionate about? I am passionate about many things: art, music, unicorns, individuality, the environment, John Hughes movies.

To: DreamsInPaint@yahoo.com 05/21/16
From: Gabriel Galliard
Subj: Answers to your questions

I enjoyed reading your answers to my questions, especially question nine. I am glad my e-mails make you happy. Before I answer your questions, I need to respond to your biggest fear. You could never be a failure, ma fleur. You are honest, original, brave, and beautiful. You are already a success.

1. If you could travel back to any point in time, what would it be? The day I met you. I could relive that moment a thousand times.

2. If you could fix one of the world's problems, what would you fix? End violence.

3. If you had to describe your childhood in one word, which one would you use? Rebellious.

4. If you could make a wish upon a star, what would you wish for? I have a job I love, a home in the most beautiful city in the world, and a sexy woman sending me e-mails. What more could I wish for?

5. If you were marooned on an island, what are the five things you would take with you? A survival knife, books, my camera, wine, and someone who lifts my spirits.

6. Do you have any tattoos? Yes.

7. What's your idea of a perfect Saturday? Sleep in late, hit the gym, go for a ride on my motorcycle, drink wine, make love.

8. What are some traits you find appealing? Loyalty. Honesty. Confidence. Kindness. Originality. Spontaneity. Childish wonder.

9. Do you believe in monogamy? I believe it is possible, for some.

10. What makes you happy? You.

Chapter 23

Laney's Life Playlist
"Will You Still Love Me Tomorrow?" by The Shirelles
"Sweet Talk" by Samantha Jade

"What does that even mean: 'Monogamy is possible for some?' Is he saying it's a theoretical concept? Is he part of that *some*?"

It has been a week since I first read Gabriel's answer to my monogamy question, and I have twisted it around in my brain at least 43 quintillion times. I have analyzed every little word, every nuance, but it remains as confounding as a Rubik's Cube. So, I thought I would toss my confounding cube at my new friends and see if they could solve it. We are sitting on the terrace at Carette, an inexpensive brasserie tucked beneath the colonnade of place des Vosges, sipping tea and munching *chausson aux pommes,* flaky apple pastries, before we head to the Pompidou Center for a lecture and workshop on the birth of abstraction.

"You like this man, no?" Giorgio asks.

I nod my head.

"You are in Paris to improve your art, not to marry and have the *bambini*. Am I right?"

I nod my head.

"Okay," Giorgio says, slapping the table. "If he is a love rat, does this matter?"

"Uh, yeah," I say. "It matters."

"It is most important in France, as in Italy, that you don't take love affairs too seriously. In Italiano, we say, 'Figurati.' This means, 'It is nothing,'" Giorgio says, his voice rising and falling in time with his wildly gesticulating hands. "A love affair, she is simply a sweet nothing, bella. You enjoy her and move on."

Maybe Giorgio is right. Maybe I am taking this all too seriously. Maybe I should borrow a page from Vivia's book and look at Gabriel as one tall, dark, super-hot holiday fling.

Then again, Vivia's super-hot holiday fling turned out to be more than a chapter in her book . . . it turned into her happily ever after.

"What do you think, Julia?"

"Seriously?" Julia rolls her eyes, before taking a long drag from her cigarette and blowing the smoke in my face. "You're asking my opinion about a guy you've known for, what, a month? It hardly signifies." She narrows her gaze. "Have you even fucked him yet?"

My cheeks flush with heat.

Rigby looks at me, her eyes open so wide her fluttery lashes touch her pale, arched brows. She mouths, "What the?"

"Have you?" Julia prods.

I shake my head.

"Well, then," she snorts, "why all the drama? What do you care if he is monogamous? Like Giorgio said, you're here for your career. Three F's, baby. Flirt, fuck, and forget."

"Julia!" Rigby gasps.

"Rig-by!" Julia mimics, fluttering her clumpy black eyelashes. "Don't tell me you've never heard the eff word before? Don't people curse in Topeka?"

"Tacoma," Rigby corrects.

"What-ever." Julia takes another drag from her cigarette, tips her head back, and blows a smoke ring in the air. She extinguishes her cigarette by flicking it into her teacup, grabs her purse, and stands. "I'm outta here. See ya, losers."

We watch Julia walk away, her hips swiveling, the pointy heels of her stiletto booties stabbing the slate.

I only asked Julia's advice to be inclusive. It's not like I really expected her to step out of her tough, city-chick role and into the role of soft, caring big sister. Sagacity and empathy aren't really her bag.

I turn to Gunthar, the stoic German, and ask him what he thinks about Gabriel's vaguely worded answer.

"Does monogamy matter to you?"

"Yes."

"Then vat does it matter vat I say?" Gunthar pops a piece of apple pastry into his mouth and swallows it without chewing. "Listen to your heart, Laney. You have good heart."

"Thanks, Gunthar."

He nods his blond head.

"I have an idea," Rigby says. "Do you want to hear it?"

"Sure."

"He gets home tomorrow, right?"

"Yes."

"Why don't you meet him somewhere super casual, like that sandwich stand he took you to, and ask him if he believes in monogamy. Just be totally cool and matter of fact about it."

"Ask him? To his face?"

"Yeah, why not?" Rigby shrugs.

"I don't even know what I would say."

"You practice with us, no?" Giorgio grins.

"Like, role-play?"

"That's a great idea!" Rigby cries. "Giorgio can be Gabriel."

"I am your love rat, Bella." Giorgio pats his chest. "Ask me anything."

"I don't know—"

"Do it!" Gunthar commands.

"Yeah, do it," Rigby says.

I puff my cheeks up like a chipmunk and exhale slowly, trying to think of the words to ask a flirty Italian pretending to be a flirty French man if he is monogamous.

"Giorgio, are you—"

"Giorgio?" he asks, looking around confused. "Who is this Giorgio? I am Gabriel."

I sigh. "Fine. Gabriel."

"Oui, ma fleur," he says, leaning his elbows on the table and staring deep into my eyes. "What do you wish to ask me?"

"Are you—" Giorgio suddenly grabs my hands and brings it to his lips, kissing the fingertips one by one. I pull my hand away. "This is ridiculous."

"What is ridiculous, ma fleur? That I am making love to you with my eyes, my lips, my—"

"Be serious."

"I *am* serious." He reaches across the table and takes my hand. "Now, what did you want to ask me?"

I look at Rigby. She nods her head encouragingly.

"Gabriel," I say, looking back at Giorgio, "are you interested in . . . I mean, do you think a man and a woman should—"

"Make love?"

"No!"

"*No?*"

"Yes."

He winks. "Yes?"

I look into Giorgio's chocolate-brown eyes, and my mind goes as blank as a chalkboard. I've got nothing. Nothing. If looking into Giorgio's eyes wipes my slate clean, what is going to happen when I look into Gabriel's eyes? I'll go catatonic.

I close my eyes and take a deep, cleansing breath. *Sensei says authenticity requires vulnerability and transparency. Be authentic. Be vulnerable. Be transparent.* I open my eyes, take another deep breath, and tap into my deepest, most authentic stream of consciousness.

"Gabriel," I say, my voice trembling, "we have only known each other for a month, but I am crazy about you, like, grab the hug-me jacket, one hundred percent certifiable crazy. Here's the thing: I'm a virgin. I want to be with you, but not if you are a European love rat. I am one-man girl. So, how about it, will you be monogamous with me?"

Giorgio just stares at me, a horrified expression on his face.

"Absolument."

My cheeks flush with a familiar flushy-crushy heat, and I know, without even turning around, that Gabriel is standing behind me. It was his deep, French-accented voice I heard, not Giorgio's. *This is not happening. This is not happening.*

I look over at Rigby. Her expression confirms my fears. Her eyes are Rigby-wide, her mouth is hanging open, and she's staring at a spot over my head.

A trickle of sweat beads and breaks, sliding between my breasts. I swivel in my seat.

Gabriel is standing behind me holding a big bouquet of daisies, a dangerous, sexy, dimple-punctuated smile on his handsome face, a battered duffle bag and heavy, silver camera case at his feet.

"Gabriel." I stand up. "What are you doing here?"

He tosses the daisies on the table and pulls me into his arms, kissing me full on the mouth. He smells like the desert and heated flesh and exotic cologne. The world tilts, and I reach up, holding the lapels of his jacket so I don't fall like some silly, flushing, swooning virgin. The stubble that normally shadows his jawline and upper lip is thicker, coarser, and it grazes my cheeks as we kiss, a deliciously, delightfully painful feeling that I know will linger long after we stop kissing.

Gabriel pulls away just far enough to look into my eyes. His face is brown from the sun, and his dark hair is streaked with auburn. "I came here from the airport because I wanted ask you a question, but now it seems as if I must first answer your question."

"M . . . my question?"

"Yes, ma fleur." A smile curves his lips. "I would very much like to be monogamous with you."

I feel like Samantha in *Sixteen Candles,* when she walks out of the church after her sister's wedding to find super-sexy Jake leaning against his shiny red Porsche. I want to look around and mouth, *"Me?"* because I can't believe Scoville-scale-hot Gabriel wants me—dorky, dyslexic Laney. Gabriel is a shiny red Porsche and I am a Mini Cooper.

"What was your question?"

"I wanted to know if you would come home with me and let me hold you in my arms until the night fades to day."

My cheeks flush again.

"Yes," I whisper, "I will."

He kisses me again, long and deep, his tongue moving in and out of my mouth with slow, purposeful sensuality, as if we are already alone in his apartment, not standing in a crowded outdoor café surrounded by my friends and picture-snapping tourists.

It's the kind of kiss that lets me know we aren't just going get in his Porsche, drive to his house, sit cross-legged on his dining room table, and eat birthday cake.

Chapter 24

Laney's Life Playlist
"Right Now" by Akon
"Let's Spend the Night Together" by The Rolling Stones
"Let's Wait Awhile" by Janet Jackson

When I arrive on Gabriel's block, the sky is the color of a bruised plum, and the streetlights are casting golden halos on the rain-slick pavement. His apartment is located in one of the old limestone buildings bordering Parc Monceau, a green space famous for its English garden and romantic architectural follies.

We agreed to grab a bite to eat first, so Gabriel is waiting for me on the sidewalk in front of his building, the collar of his coat flipped up, a scarf around his neck.

I stop walking and stand beneath a tree, admiring his exciting masculine aura and dark beauty. His hair is wet from the rain, and my fingers itch to push it off his forehead, to feel the silkiness of it against my skin. His cheeks are clean-shaven, but his upper lip and jawline are shadowed with light stubble.

Stubble that will soon graze your lips, cheeks, breasts . . .

Gabriel notices me, and a look of relief crosses his face. He closes the distance between us in three powerful, long-legged strides, pulling me into his arms in a warm, wet hug.

"I'm sorry I'm late," I whisper against his ear.

I consider making a joke that being ten minutes late is really more like being on time in Laneyland, but the feel of his hard, manly body against mine is sobering and makes my joke sound girlish and unsophisticated.

"Ça ne fait rien," he whispers.

It doesn't matter.

"It does matter," I say, kissing his smooth cheek. "It's not respectful to keep you waiting."

"I am just glad you are here, ma fleur."

He brushes his lips over mine before wrapping his arm around my waist and leading me down the street. I am hyper-aware of the weight of his arm against the small of my back, the warmth of his hand on my hip, the wetness of his kiss still on my lips. It's doing things to me, stoking a heat inside of me that is building, building. I hear a low, throbbing, backbeat in my head like the refrain of a nasty R&B song, *sex-sex-sex.* It's the kind of song that would play as a backtrack for a down-and-dirty sex scene in a movie—not a sweet romantic-comedy pairing in a charming bed-and-breakfast, but an urgent hookup with a mysterious stranger in a subway car or some other shadowy, slightly illicit place. I suddenly imagine Gabriel pushing me up against the wall in a dark Metro tunnel, hiking my skirt up, and . . .

Gabriel squeezes my hip.

"Are you hungry?"

My cheeks flame with guilty heat, and I wonder if I am emitting some kind of horny virgin vibe.

"What do you mean?"

"Are you hungry? I haven't eaten since my layover in Zurich last night, and I'm starving."

Food. He's asking me if I am hungry for food, not his hot body. *Chill out, Laney. He can't hear your nasty backbeat or see your nasty fantasies.*

"Yes, I'm hungry."

A new wave of heat flushes my cheeks, and I pretend to study the crosswalk signal as we wait for the traffic to cross the street.

"Bon," he says, pulling me to his side. "I know a great Italian place about five minutes from here, just off boulevard de Courcelles. We will grab something and go back to my place."

Back to my place. My place. My place. His words play in my head, mixing with the R&B refrain, *sex-sex-sex.* When we finally arrive at the restaurant, I am more amped up than a Viking warrior getting ready to enter the battlefield. My veins are coursing with sexual adrenaline. I am excited, sweaty and . . . scared.

A waiter shows us to a table by the window, tells us the specials— white lasagna with spring vegetables, black truffle pasta, and linguine alle vongole—and asks if we would like to order anything from the wine menu. Fanny told me Parisian waiters liked to be asked recommendations, especially when it comes to wine, so I ask our waiter to recommend a full-bodied red. I don't know a lot about wine, but I assume a full-bodied wine is a more potent wine, and right now I need something potent to help me chillax. My legs are trembling, and my stomach is tied into a quintillion knots.

"We have a delicious, bold Touriga Nacional from Portugal with deep fresh blueberry and violet notes that pairs nicely with our savory mushroom pasta," he says. "Would you like a glass or a bottle?"

I consider asking for *une bouteille,* but Gabriel is already staring at me quizzically and I have never managed to consume more than a glass of wine. I am what Fanny calls a lightweight.

"A glass will be fine," I say, smiling. "Merci."

When the waiter leaves, Gabriel leans forward, looks into my eyes, grabs my hand, and whispers, "Are you okay, ma fleur? You are acting strangely."

"Am I?" My voice is unnaturally high and cracks, like a preteen boy. "Really?"

Gabriel nods.

I shrug. "I'm probably just . . . hungry."

The image of Gabriel lifting my skirt while pushing me against a tunnel wall flashes in my mind again, and I look out the window until the heat fades from my cheeks. My nerves are causing me to act like a totally awkward turtle. I'm, like, kind of embarrassed for myself. I wonder what Vivia would think if she could teleport herself into this sad little scene?

Ever since she found out about my virginity, Vivia has become my dating dealer, dispensing unsolicited, unfiltered advice. She calls her texts Straight Dating Dope from a Love Addict. Truthfully? Her advice is funny, honest, helpful, and as addictive as Malted Moose

Balls, this crazy-yummy candy I got hooked on when I lived in Sitka. She sent me a text this morning. *"Get him talking about himself. People love attention, and they love to talk about themselves, especially male people. If that doesn't work, pull out your phone and send him a naughty little sext that says something like, 'I know I am being super quiet, but that's only because I am doing super loud, naughty things to you in my head. Do you want to keep sitting here being quiet or go somewhere and get loud?'"*

I laugh. Vivia is too much, way, way too much. The whole unapologetically bold and sexy vibe works with her, but . . . I laugh again.

"Laney?"

"Gabriel?"

Great. If my awkward turtle thing didn't totally turn him off, my catatonic cackler thing will definitely give him the heebie-jeebies. He frowns, and I realize how crazy I must look staring out the window and laughing to myself.

"Are you sure you are all right?"

"I'm fine," I lie. "I was just thinking about something a friend said that made me laugh."

The waiter arrives with our wine, takes our dinner orders, and hurries back to the kitchen. I grab my glass of wine and hold it toward Gabriel.

"A ta santé, Gabriel!"

"Santé," Gabriel gazes into my eyes and gently clinks his glass to mine. "May your life always be as sweet as your wine."

Gabriel takes a sip of his wine. I drain my glass in one long swallow, lick the berry residue off my lips, and place my empty back on the table.

"Mmm," I say, licking my lips again, "that was tasty good."

Gabriel chuckles. "Would you like another glass?"

"Yes, please." I sit back and enjoy the relaxing warmth of the wine spreading through my body. "I would like that very much."

Gabriel nods his head at the waiter, and another glass of my full-bodied, limb-relaxing red appears on the table in front of me. I ask Gabriel to tell me about his trip, and the rest of the meal passes as smoothly as berry-flavored wine over the tongue. I feel chilled.

I am wrapped in a warm, hazy cocoon as I listen to Monsieur Tall, Dark, and Hot-Hot-Hot tell me about the shots he got in Damascus, his next assignment, and his plan to travel to the south of France later in the summer for a family gathering. Vivia is a genius. All I need to do is drink wine and keep Gabriel talking about himself.

I am about to order another glass of wine when Gabriel reaches into his pocket, pulls out a wad of euros, and tosses the bills on the table. He stands and slips his coat on.

"Shall we?" He walks around the table until he is standing behind me, bends down, kisses my neck, and whispers in my ear. "I have waited thirty days and eight hours to be alone with you, ma fleur. I am done waiting."

And just like that, my warm, berry-wine cocoon unravels. My nerves return in a roiling wave of nauseous. It takes all of my energy and focus to keep from tossing my mushroom pasta all over Gabriel's expensive leather boots.

We walk out of the restaurant hand in hand and stroll back to the brightly lit boulevard de Courcelles. I try to think of questions to get Gabriel talking again, but my tongue feels heavy in my mouth and tastes as bitter as the bile cresting and crashing against the walls of my tummy.

We are walking through the park, dark except for stepping-stones of light shining on the path from the street lamps, when Gabriel stops walking. He puts his hands on my waist and turns me to face him.

"There is something I need to say to you before we go into my apartment," he says, focusing his intense gaze on my face. "I heard you this morning when you said you were a virgin. I believe that is why you have been acting so strangely tonight, because you are frightened of what will happen when we are alone tonight. Am I right?"

"Yes," I whisper, my cheeks flushing.

"Relax, ma fleur." He kisses my lips softly, sweetly. "I have no expectations for tonight except to hold you in my arms, to talk to you until we fall asleep. I will not ask for anything that you do not wish to give. You have waited twenty-five years to give your virginity to someone—if I am lucky enough to be that man, I will receive it when you are ready, not when you are so nervous you have to drink wine."

"Really?"

"Really."

"You don't mind waiting?"

He lifts his hand from my hip and presses it against my face, stroking my cheek with his thumb.

"Do you remember what I texted you when you said you were going to be late the night we were to meet at La Belle Hortense?"

I shake my head.

"I said, '*Don't worry. I will always wait for you.*'" He lifts his other hand and cradles my face. "I meant it then, and I mean it now. I will wait for you because I know you are worth the wait, ma fleur."

"How? How can you know? We haven't known each other that long, Gabriel. I could be one of those crazy American girls who comes to Paris to take a selfie at the Eiffel Tower and harmlessly flirt with a cute French boy. Aren't you afraid I am just teasing you? That you, my French boy, are just my cute diversion?"

Gabriel drops his hands from my face, looks up at the dark sky, and laughs.

"Ma fleur innocente," he says, chuckling. "It is true that in Paris American girls have a reputation, but it is not for being harmless flirts."

"Really? Tell me."

He shakes his head.

"Come on. Give it to me straight, Gabriel."

He runs his hand through his hair and exhales.

"Parisian men think American girls are . . ."

"Oui?"

"Some Parisian men think American girls are des filles faciles."

I frown as I try to translate his French words into English. Easy girls.

"Sluts? Parisian men think American girls are sluts?"

Gabriel's cheeks flush red.

"You must understand. Parisian women are . . . sérieux." He looks down at his feet, making an arc on the path with the toe of his boot. "Pay attention, ma fleur, the next time you are in a restaurant, bar, or club. French women do not smile. They do not approach strangers. They do not flirt. They do not drink to excess. Many American girls laugh out loud, talk to strangers, and draw attention to themselves in the way they dress, dance, walk, and smile."

"Wow!" I whistle. "That's, like, super harsh. Just because a girl likes to flirt and smile doesn't mean she is une fille facile!"

"I know that, but many French men do not understand that the American girl has a different way of behaving. Her open behavior is as natural to her as a French woman's reserve." He runs his hand through his hair again. "I am making a mess of this, aren't I?"

I think about Vivia and her infectious joie de vivre, the way she greets every stranger as a friend, and then I think about Fanny, and the way she greets every stranger with wary skepticism, and I realize American girls and French girls are completely different creatures.

I shake my head. "I dig you."

"Bon," he says, smiling. "You see now, telling me you are a virgin and that you are not ready to let me make love to you is not the behavior of a fille facile. A tease would not be honest. She would play games because the game is what makes her happy. Comprendre?"

I nod.

He wraps his arm around my waist, and we continue walking down the path. The anxiety-churned nausea waves have subsided. I am again with chill. The pressure to be a sophisticated sexy kitten is gone. I can just be me, Laney.

"Gabriel," I say, resting my head on his shoulder, "I really dig you."

He chuckles. "You do?"

"Mmmhmm."

"How much?"

"Like, more than all of the John Hughes movies ever made. I just like being with you."

"I am glad," he says, kissing my forehead. "Because I like being with you too."

It's crazy. Gabriel is a virtual stranger, but he feels as familiar and comforting as Hoppy or Theo.

Theo.

I try to imagine what my best friend would say about me hooking up with a strange French man. I hope he would say, *"Dude! You and Gabriel are, like, craft beer and food truck tacos. You're the original one true pairing, Lane. Get your sex on, girl, and get up next to your*

man before it's too late and your moneymaker is as rusty as that old
Red Wing we found in the res at Valmont."

We arrive at Gabriel's building, and he unlocks one of the pair of carved wooden doors that are typical of these beautiful old Baron Haussmann buildings. He leads me down a narrow corridor and up a curving staircase to the top floor. He shoves a key into a lock and turns it until it clicks.

"Welcome to my home, ma fleur," he says, pushing the door open and stepping aside to allow me to pass.

His apartment is small, but crazy cool in an old Paris apartment gets a hip face-lift kind of way. One wall is floor-to-ceiling windows overlooking the park. Another wall has a built-in bookcase with a rolling ladder attached. The bookcase is painted a shark gray and has different-sized nooks. Some of the nooks feature stunning black-and-white photographs in metal frames, lit with sleek stainless-steel gallery lights. There's a high-backed, armless gray velvet sofa and a low industrial table with stacks of books and black-and-white prints.

I walk over to the bookcase and look at one of the photographs, a striking shot of place Vendôme with people moving through clouds of steam rising off the rain-slick granite pavers. The puffy white steam contrasts against the darkly silhouetted people and buildings.

"Is this place Vendôme?"

"Oui."

"Did you take it?"

"I did."

Gabriel is standing behind me. I can feel his warm, wine-sweet breath on my neck.

"Do you like it?"

"Very much," I say. "It's a beautiful, haunting shot, Gabriel. You are talented."

"Thank you." He kisses my neck. "Would you like to take your coat off?"

My coat. My dress. My panties.

This is crazy. Half of me wants to strip naked and beg Gabriel to make love to me, and the other half wants to button my coat to the neck and run from this apartment like a . . . like a . . . frightened virgin rabbit running from a confident fox and his erogenous-zone-stimulating den.

I unbutton my coat and hand it to Gabriel. He carries it over to the sofa and drapes it over the back.

"Make yourself comfortable," he says, walking through a darkened doorway. "I will be right back."

I sit on the edge of the sofa, running my hands over the soft fabric. Gabriel flicks on a light, revealing a small, sleek gray-and-white kitchen. I hear glasses clink together and the pop of a cork being pulled from a bottle. Gabriel returns, carrying two glasses of wine. He puts the glasses on the table and then walks over to the bookcase, grabs a slender remote, and pushes two buttons. The lights from the modern glass chandelier dim, and soft music plays from a slender speaker affixed to the wall.

He shrugs out of his jacket, tosses it over a chair, and sits down beside me, pulling me back against his chest.

"Come here, ma fleur," he says, wrapping his arms around me. "I want to hold you while you tell me something."

"Something?"

"Anything." He rests his chin on my head. "Tell me something, anything. I just want to hear your voice."

I don't know why, but I tell him the first things that come to mind. Serious and silly things. I tell him about my ADD and that, even though it is difficult for me to stay focused long enough to read a book from cover to cover, I started and finished the Alexandre Dumas book he gave me before he left for Damascus. I tell him about the first time I met Theo, about learning to drive stick by cruising Boulder in the Bananarama, and about the time Theo talked me into going to a concert in Denver. I had this ear infection, and I thought he said it was Mallay, which is this wicked techno rock band from Manchester, England.

"So I dressed for a rave. I dreaded up my hair and wore a neon spandex bodysuit and fluffies."

"Fluffies?"

"Furry leg warmers."

Gabriel chuckles. "Let me guess; it wasn't a Mallay concert?"

"Nope," I say, laughing. "Not even close. It was some group that played flutes and did interpretive ballet. It wasn't in an old warehouse, but the performing arts center. Everyone is walking in wearing semi-formal attire, and I'm kicking it in a glow-stick bra and glow-in-the-dark makeup."

Gabriel's chest rumbles as he laughs, a rich, warm sound that makes me feel like I am wrapped in fluffies.

"What did you do?"

"What could I do?" I look up at him and smile. "I waited until the music started and did my own little interpretive dance routine in the aisle."

"Show me."

"What? Now?"

"Why not?" He grabs the remote off the table and pushes the buttons until he finds a fluty, new-age tune. "Show me, please."

I laugh and start contorting my limbs to look like tree branches blowing in the breeze, whipping my hair back and forth, and making a rushing wind sound with my mouth. I keep twisting and contorting my body and face in time to the music until Gabriel lets out a booming laugh and pulls me back onto the sofa beside him.

"You thought I was just an artist, but you had no idea I possessed mad dancing skill, did you?"

"You continue to surprise me, Laney."

He pushes another button on the remote, and the flute music is replaced by a slow, sexy Ne-Yo jam. He stands and pulls me to my feet.

"What are you doing?"

"Show me some more of your mad dancing skills."

He lifts my hands to his shoulder and grabs my waist, moving my hips in time to the seductive beat. We move together in the dark. I rest my cheek against his collarbone and close my eyes, listening to the throbbing, thumping beat of his heart and his throaty voice singing the lyrics of the song, imploring me to *say-it, say-it*, say what I want him to do to me. Spiritual gurus talk about moments of divine clarity, when you receive insight into the universe. Here's some insight: if I live a hundred years and have a quadrillion lovers, I will never have a more erotic moment than I am having right now, dancing in and out of the shadows created by the city's twinkling lights with Gabriel's voice pleading in my ear to *say-it, say-it*.

One song fades into the next and the next, but we keep slow-grinding in the dark, making love with our clothes on. I am lost in a fevered delirium of berry wine and Gabriel's sweet kisses, dizzy and drunk on this crazy, improbable love. He kisses me, in a drugging rhythm that matches the music and the movement of his hips against mine. He thrusts against me, his tongue, his big, hard . . . until my legs are as loose and rubbery as stretched out rubber bands, until I feel like I am falling, falling, falling . . .

It takes me a few seconds to realize that Gabriel has lifted me into his arms and is carrying me into his bedroom. He carries me to his bed and lays me down on the feathery duvet, then walks over to his dresser, pulls out a plain white T-shirt, and hands it to me.

"The bathroom is right through there," he says, nodding in the direction of a small hallway. "Use whatever you want."

I carry the T-shirt into the bathroom and close the door. I am about to climb into bed with a hot, seriously experienced French man, but I am not nervous. Like, not even a little. I believed Gabriel when he promised we would only hold each other and sleep. I believe he won't ask me for something I am not ready to give.

I strip out of my dress and bra, hang them over the towel rack, and pull Gabriel's tee over my head. It's soft, smells like his cologne, and hangs to my mid-thighs. Next, I squirt some of Gabriel's toothpaste on my finger and brush my teeth.

When I go back into Gabriel's bedroom, he has already pulled the blinds and is waiting for me in bed, one bare, muscular arm behind his head, a reassuring smile on his handsome face.

He pulls back the covers, and I climb in beside him. My bare legs slide against his, and I shiver at the warm, roughness of his male skin.

"Are you cold?"

"A little," I whisper.

He pulls me closer so my head rests on his bare shoulder, my breasts press against his hairy, rippled chest, separated by a flimsy cotton tee.

"Relax, ma fleur," he says, his voice a low, rumbling growl in my ear. "You are as stiff as a board."

He rubs my back, his strong hand making slow, soothing circles between my shoulder blades until I relax, melt against him, melt into him.

"Bonne nuit, Laney," he says, kissing me on the lips. "Fais de beaux rêves."

"Sweet dreams, Gabriel," I say, closing my eyes and draping my arm over his chest.

The last thing I hear before I fall asleep is Gabriel's heartbeat in my ear. It sounds a lot like Ne-Yo singing, *say-it, say-it, say-it.*

Chapter 25

Laney's Life Playlist
"Too Afraid to Love You" by The Black Keys
"Scared to Death" by HIM

"Bonjour, ma belle."

Gabriel kisses and nuzzles my neck, his beard grazing my bare collarbone. I shiver and moan, then blink away the morning grit and arch my back, stretching my legs and rolling my shoulders.

"Every girl deserves that," I say, smiling.

"What?"

"Every girl should wake to a 'Good morning, beautiful' greeting. The world would be a happier place—like, way, way happier."

His chuckle echoes softly in my ear.

"I would be willing to do my part, but I don't think it would be possible for me to greet every girl." He sucks my earlobe into his warm, wet mouth, and I shiver again. "Besides, there's not enough room in my bed."

"Funny," I laugh, ruffling his hair. "You're very funny, Gabriel Galliard."

He kisses a path from my collarbone to my lips and then does a push-up over me so he is staring at my face.

He whistles and shakes his head.

"What?"

"You are really beautiful."

I cover my face with my hands. "You've got to be kidding! I didn't remove my makeup or wash my face last night. I haven't brushed my hair or my teeth. I must have crazy scary morning face."

The mattress shifts, and Gabriel straddles me. The only things separating his manly bits from my girly parts are my Victoria Secret panties and his Calvin Klein briefs. *Hello, Vicki, meet Calvin!* My cheeks flush with skin-singing flushy-crushy heat. He pulls my hands from my face. I keep my eyes closed because I, like, can't even right now.

"Look at me, ma fleur."

I shake my head. "So not gonna happen."

"Really?"

I nod my head.

"Challenge accepted."

He trails his fingertips over the curve of my breast, making slow, shivery circles around and around.

"Laney," he coaxes in a deep, husky voice, "look at me."

I open my eyes, because, like, for real? Who can resist a handsome man imploring you to obey him in a voice that is panty-dropping sexy and accented with French? Not this girl.

He doesn't speak. He doesn't smile. He just stares into my eyes, a deep, soul-probing look that feels like he is slowly peeling off my tee and VS panties. Exposed. I am so totally exposed.

"You are so beautiful," he says, pressing his hand to his chest. "You make my heart ache. Ache because I know soon you will kiss me good-bye, and hours will pass before I can look at you again."

"Thank you," I whisper, blinking back tears. "That is the sweetest thing anyone has ever said to me."

"De rien." He rolls off me and climbs out of bed. "I'll be right back."

I try to avert my gaze, but Gabriel's chiseled body is a serious eyeball magnet. His broad shoulders and back taper to a narrow waist. The white band of his Calvin boxer briefs contrasts with his tanned skin. My gaze move up his back, following the deep valleys on either side of his spine, the sharp planes of his shoulder blades. He is an ancient statue of a Corinthian warrior, a carved god who has leapt off his pedestal to walk among the mortals.

"Would you allow me take your picture, ma fleur?" he asks, striding back into the room with a camera in his hands.

"What?" I shriek, pulling the blankets up to my chin. "Why would you want to take a picture of me now, looking like this?"

"Because this," he says, holding the camera up his face, "is beautiful."

He pushes the shutter release, and the shutter makes a soft clicking sound as my image is recorded again and again. I narrow my gaze like a sloe-eyed vixen, cross my eyes and stick out my tongue, and finally blow him a kiss. He laughs and clicks a last shot before setting the camera on the nightstand and climbing back into bed with me.

"Merci, ma fleur," he says, pulling me against his chest. "Now, I can look at your face when you aren't here."

We make out, kissing each other, sliding our hands up and down each other's bodies, exploring warm curves. Gabriel grabs my breast, wrapping his big hand around my soft flesh, squeezing and kneading it until I don't care if I have epic, Sasquatch bed head and mascara smudged under my eyes.

I am floating high-high-high in the Nethersphere of desire, lost in a hazy, cloudy dimension way, way beyond reality when Gabriel stops kissing me.

"Merde," he swears, rolling out of bed, grabbing his jeans, and shoving his legs into them. "I'll be right back."

What? What just happened? Where is he going?

The doorbell buzzes—*buzz, buzz, buzz*—and I realize someone is at Gabriel's door, someone super-eager to speak to him.

I look at the clock on Gabriel's nightstand and jump out of bed. Oh my god! It isn't really twenty after seven already, is it? I have to work a shift at the gallery at nine, and I am going to be late.

I hurry into the bathroom, strip out of Gabriel's tee, and take a lightning-fast shower, scrubbing my body with his gritty, manly scented soap, and drying off with a hand towel (because I am *so* not going to rummage through his drawers).

Three minutes later, I have dressed, finger-combed my hair, finger-brushed my teeth, and slapped some color into my cheeks.

I hear the breathy female voice as soon as I step out of the bathroom and freeze in my tracks. Well, this is awkward. Should I wait in the bedroom and risk being late for my shift at the gallery or join

Gabriel and his early-morning, breathy visitor and risk appearing jealous?

What would Vivia do? I wish my iPhone wasn't in my purse in the living room because I could text her and ask her.

A badass woman would walk into the living room with confidence, chest out, nose up, lips pursed like, "Mmm-hmm, I own this room . . . and this man." A badass, confident woman wouldn't cower in the bedroom worrying about what some stranger will think about her.

I walk out of Gabriel's bedroom with my best interpretation of a badass, confident woman and trip right over Gabriel's boots where he kicked them off last night, before our slow-jam dance sesh. *I hear you, universe. I am not a badass bitch. Got it.*

I look over at the door, hoping Gabriel didn't see me trip. He has his back to me and missed my gawky near-pratfall. Giselle saw me, though. Willowy, *we are more than friends* Giselle. She smiles a closed-mouth reptilian smile at me and thrusts a *boulangerie* bag into Gabriel's hands, cooing in French, "I know how much you adore the bichon au citron from Maison Honoré, so I thought I would bring you one, mon cherie."

Pointy, sharp arrows of distrust find a tender target in my heart, and I have to silently repeat the sensei's admonition about jealousy. *Jealousy and suspicion are houses built on foundations of insecurity. They are sad, bleak dwellings with air so toxic it kills bigger, more beautiful emotions. Jealousy and suspicion are . . .*

Not working. *So* not working.

Giselle widens her eyes, pretending as if she only just noticed me. "La! I am sorry, Gabriel. I didn't know you had a visitor. I have only brought pastries for two."

Gabriel turns around.

"Laney!" Is it my imagination, or was his tone a little harsh, his expression a little angry? "You remember Giselle?"

"Yes," I say, slipping my feet into my shoes and grabbing my coat and purse. "It's nice to see you again, Giselle."

A total lie, but even willowy, reptilian French female creatures bearing pastries for two deserve social niceties. It's good karma to be friendly, especially when your inner snotty girl is screaming at you to stick your tongue out and say something super-snotty.

"I'm sorry, but have we met?" Giselle asks, all innocent tone and eyes.

"This is Laney," Gabriel says. "I introduced you to her last month at La Belle Hortense. She is my . . ."

He stops talking and looks at me. There's a question written all over his face, but I can't decipher it. Great! Is he asking me to explain who I am to him—the girl who works in his family's gallery, a flirty little American girl trying to sink her talons into a French boy? Is he asking me why I haven't left yet? Is he asking me to play it cool and not let on that we spent the night together?

Ffffttttth. Thud.

Another arrow impales my heart, and I gasp with pain. It is excruciatingly obvious that Giselle was right; they are more than friends, so much more, *mon cher.*

"I have to go," I say, maneuvering around Gabriel. "Good-bye, Gabriel."

"Laney, wait . . ."

I brush past Giselle and run down the stairs, taking them two at a time. It's a total virgin move. An experienced woman, a badass, confident woman wouldn't run away. She wouldn't surrender her claim on her man to some willowy, lisping, pastry-toting woman with a serious case of anorexia. She would have stood her ground and engaged in a fierce, silent battle of wills until the other woman retreated.

But I am not a Giselle or a Vivia or a Fanny, so I keep running—down the stairs, out of the building, down the street, onto a bus—until I am slumped on a hard plastic seat, head against the cold window, tears streaming down my face.

By the time I make it to the gallery, I am a sniveling, mascara-streaked mess. My fears about Gabriel—that he is a major player—have returned with a vengeance and are devouring my confidence.

Rigby takes one look at me and pulls me into my room, closing the door behind us.

"What happened?"

I fall onto my bed, press my balled-up hands against my closed eyes, and sniffle out the whole humiliating tale.

"You shouldn't have left before giving Gabriel a chance to explain. He might have had a perfectly logical explanation."

"His horrified expression said it all, believe me."

"I don't know, Lane. Are you sure you don't want to talk to him, to hear what he has to say?

"No," I sniff.

"Oh-kay."

"Okay, what?"

"Okay what, what?"

"You might have only said okay, but your meta text said you don't think it is okay."

"It's just"—she sits on the edge of my bed and pries my fists from my eyes, forcing me to look at her—"a player wouldn't have said he was happy to wait until you were ready. He wouldn't have respected your virginity. He would have pushed and pressured and massaged and manipulated. Then, when he was finished nailing you, he would have shown you to the door and said, 'Next!'"

"What are you saying?"

"I am saying, my sweet, naïve friend," she says, brushing a tear-damp tendril from my cheek, "that you acted like an over-emotional virgin. You let your fears grab you by your skater skirt and yank you away from a situation that felt scary and overwhelming."

She's right, of course. Maybe I used Giselle's appearance as a convenient excuse to end something that felt too grown-up and steady. I don't do steady. I do flighty, unfocused, and unfettered. I am beginning to think holding onto my virginity was a way to push guys away and keep myself from going steady, from being steady. *Whoa!* That's heavy. Like, way, way too heavy so early in the morning.

"You're right." I take a deep breath and exhale a shuddering breath. "What am I going to do now?"

She stands up, walks over to my sink, turns the water on, and sticks a washcloth under the stream. "You are going to wash your face and go to work, that's what you are going to do right now. This afternoon, you will meditate on the situation, and the right words will come to you. Then, you will go to Monsieur Tall, Dark, and Hot, and you will tell him what's in your heart."

She hands me the washcloth and walks to the door.

"Rigby?"

She looks over her shoulder. "Yes?"

"Thanks."

"No worries," she says, grinning. "That's what a PBFF is for, right?"

"Right."

"Oh yeah," she says. "I almost forgot. You got a package."

"Me?"

"Yes, you." She chuckles. "Unless you think there might be another Laney 'Dude' Brooks in Paris?"

"Theo!" I jump up. "It must be from Theo. He's the only one who calls me Laney Dude. Where is it?"

"It's downstairs in the warehouse because it was too big to carry up the stairs."

I frown. "Serious?"

"As serious as a Frenchman promising to wait to take your virginity."

"Ouch."

"Too soon?"

I laugh. "Maybe just a little."

Chapter 26

Laney's Life Playlist
"The Way I Am" by Ingrid Michaelson
"Where Is My Mind?" by the Pixies (Daniela Andrade cover)
"Count on Me" by Bruno Mars

TEXT TO THEO WILDE:
You are beyond. I got your package today, and the timing couldn't have been better. I love, love, like, crazy love the bike. The black-and-white striped seat, the red basket, the red spokes, the blingy bell. It is très chic. Thank you, Theo.

TEXT FROM THEO WILDE:
You're welcome. What's wrong?

TEXT TO THEO WILDE:
What do you mean?

TEXT FROM THEO WILDE:
My Wonder Twins telepathic link is alerting me about a potentially dire situation. That, and you said my gift came at a good time, like you were bummed and needed a gift or something. Let's hear it, Jayna. Are you homesick? Hating Paris? Wishing you were driving with me in the Bananarama to get FroYo?

I haven't been homesick until now. Theo's text makes my eyes fill with tears and a big old phlegmy lump form in my throat. I miss my best friend and the easy comradery we have always shared. If only all of my relationships could be as easy and straightforward as my friendship with Theo.

TEXT TO THEO WILDE:
I met a boy.

TEXT TO THEO WILDE:
Ew. I get it. Boys are gross.

TEXT TO THEO WILDE:
Ha. Ha.

TEXT TO THEO WILDE:
So, you met a boy. BFD. What's the prob?

TEXT TO THEO WILDE:
I like him.

TEXT TO THEO WILDE:
How much?

TEXT TO THEO WILDE:
Like, a lot. Like, I am thinking of *gulp* sleeping with him.

TEXT TO THEO WILDE:
Duuuuuude. This is huge.

TEXT TO THEO WILDE:
IKR? Dorky Dookie Brooks has a man.

TEXT TO THEO WILDE:
Shut up. You're not dorky. You've never been dorky Dookie Brooks. You've always been amazing, intuitive, compassionate Delaney Lavender Brooks. You have to believe that, Lane. YOU. You have to own it.

TEXT TO THEO WILDE:
Okay, so what if I sleep with him and he breaks my heart? What if we date for years and he asks me to marry him and then one day he wakes up and says, "When did you turn into such a hipster geek?" What if my parents don't like him?

Text to Theo Wilde:
What if you don't trust him? What if you don't sleep with
him? What if you end something awesome before it has even
had a chance to begin?

Theo is right. A net of fear has fallen over me and is keeping me
from swimming freely in the sea of love, from finding my own special Nemo. Maybe sometimes you just have to venture forth and risk
getting hopelessly lost.

Text to Theo Wilde:
I am going to pretend like you didn't even ask that last
question because I refuse to believe my Wonder Twin still
can't break her 'rents' mind control. You have the ability,
Jayna, so break the influence.

Chapter 27

"This painting is titled *Illumination,* and it is by a brilliant, revolutionary artist named Nancy B. Randt. For this piece, she used pages from ancient texts to form the background, then added layers of acrylic paint, more text, and gold leaf. It's stunning, isn't it?"

The Japanese businessman nods his head. Mister Takazaki handed me his glossy black business card when he entered the gallery. The embossed letters spelled out HIROSHI TAKAZAKI, COLLECTOR OF ART. That was it. No e-mail address or telephone digits. He told me he visits Paris several times per year to acquire pieces for his collection. His aura hints at brilliance, imagination, discipline, and social awkwardness, so I am guessing he is probably some brainiac who earned his bazillions in the tech industry. Tokyo's version of Bill Gates, maybe.

"This painting intrigues me. I would like to know more, Mademoiselle Brooks."

I am about to tell him about the artist when the door opens and Gabriel strides into the gallery. My heart pulls a quick loop-de-loop.

"Mademoiselle Brooks?" Mister Takazaki frowns. "Are you unwell? The color has left your cheeks."

I stand there like a wide-mouthed carp, my lips opening and closing, my eyes round and unblinking. Gabriel stands to the left of the door, his muscular arms crossed over his chest and a blank expression on his handsome face. I close my mouth and fix my wide-eyed gaze on Mister Takazaki.

"Although the artist refuses to explain the meaning behind any of her pieces, I believe the she was influenced by Dadaism," I say, forcing myself to blink.

"Dadaism?"

"Yes." I turn my back on Gabriel and focus on the painting. "Notice the rough, textural application of the acrylics combined with the simple text and the carefully placed rich gold leaf? It suggests a kind of artistic anarchy, doesn't it?"

Mister Takazaki tilts his head, his obsidian eyes narrowing as he focuses solely on the artwork. He studies the image for several minutes before finally smiling and nodding his head.

"Yes, Mademoiselle Brooks," he says. "I see it. How astute, very astute indeed."

"The central figure is Saint Francis de Sales, the patron saint of writers. See how the text and gold leaf seem to swirl around him, as if he is in the center of a gathering storm?" I wait for Mister Takazaki to nod his head before continuing with my hypothesis. "I believe Ms. Randt is making a statement about the duality of words, their divine and destructive nature."

"I will take it."

And like that, I make my first sale at the gallery. Mister Takazaki fills out the paperwork necessary for the sale and shipment of an expensive piece of artwork, thanks me kindly for my assistance, and departs with a nod of his head to Julia, who has been standing behind the desk scowling ever since Mister Takazaki entered the gallery and approached me.

Gabriel closes the distance between us in two strides. He offers Julia a perfunctory greeting and focuses his gaze on me.

"Laney," he says, "we need to talk."

"I know." I move out from behind the desk. "Wanna go to the park? We can find an empty bench and pop a squat."

"You can't go," Julia snaps.

"I won't be gone long, I promise."

"I know you won't, because you're not going. Your shift isn't over for another fifteen minutes."

Gabriel ignores Julia, puts his hand on the small of my back, and leads me out the door. I look over my shoulder at Julia, who pretends to flick something off her sleeve and mouths, "See ya, Flake."

Flake. Julia said I am as flaky as a croissant because I was late for my shift this morning. She said I am not focused enough on my art, which is bogus. But what-ev. I forgive her because I believe, deep down, beneath the crackly crust, Julia is an ooey-gooey toasted marshmallow.

Gabriel leads me to an empty bench beneath the clipped branches of a lime tree. Several people are sprawled out on the grass squares, their shoes off, shirtsleeves rolled up, hoping to catch some midday rays before they return to their shops and offices nearby.

"What happened this morning? Why did you run away?"

"I was going to be late for my shift at the gallery. Besides, you were busy with your"—I pause and take a breath so I don't sound like a sulky toddler—"Giselle."

"She is not *my* Giselle," he asserts. "She was my Giselle, once, but that ended last year."

"So, she's your ex-girlfriend?"

"Yes."

"Does *she* know she is your ex?"

"But of course." He frowns at me. "Do you think I would ask you out on a date, send you flowers and texts, and invite you to stay the night if I were still involved with Giselle?"

I replay the morning's events in my head and hear the urgent, persistent ring of the buzzer and Giselle referring to Gabriel as *her dear*.

"I don't know," I say, shrugging. "She certainly acted like she had some kind of proprietary claim on you."

"Judge me by my actions, not Giselle's." He stands up and squats down in front of me so we are facing each other. "You said you read auras. Have you read mine? Do my emanations tell you that I am a liar and a cheat?"

When I first read Gabriel's aura, I likened it to Van Gogh's *Starry Night* because it was swirling with mysterious colors. Now I realize it was also because he has a lot of devoted, loyal blue and joyful, loving yellow.

"You have a beautiful aura, Gabriel. It is not the aura of a liar or a cheat." I smile sadly. "Even so, I don't think this is going to work. We aren't going to work."

"We *are* working."

"Now, but you can't fight fate."

He frowns. "What does that mean?"

"It means the fates are against us."

"Why?"

I shrug. "Because you're . . . you're . . ."

"What?" He leans forward, looking deep into my eyes. "I'm what, Laney?"

"You're French!"

"What does that mean?" he asks, softly.

Tears flood my eyes. "It means you're handsome, charming, sophisticated, worldly, sexy and . . . and . . ."

"And what?"

"You're, like, *everything*. Everything I am not. You belong with someone who is as sophisticated and beautiful as you are, someone like Giselle."

"That's a terrible thing to say, ma fleur."

"Why? She is beautiful and chic."

"It's true. Giselle is physically beautiful, but she's also faithless, heartless, manipulative, and dishonest."

"Wow." I sniff. "Harsh."

"Not harsh, mademoiselle, accurate." He sits back on the bench and runs his hand through his hair. "Harsh is cheating on your boyfriend with his brother."

"Wait. What?" I turn to look at Gabriel. "Giselle cheated on you with your brother? Alexandre?"

He nods his head.

"When? Why?"

Gabriel shrugs. "Giselle is a vain flirt who . . ."

"Who?" I prompt.

"In French, we say dormir sur ses deux oreilles."

"I don't know what that means."

"The literal translation is *sleeping on one's two ears*, but in this case it means Giselle is someone who does things with little fear of getting caught."

Wow. Wow. I mean, *wow!* I can't even, right now. Monsieur Alexandre's aura has a lot of competitive brown, like Brueghel's *The Land of Cockaigne,* but I assumed he channeled that into his career as curator for one of the world's most prestigious galleries, not against his brother. Poor Gabriel!

I hold his hand. "I am sorry, Gabriel. That must have hurt."

"It did."

"Did you love Giselle?"

"Mon dieu, non." He laces his fingers through mine and squeezes gently. "I loved my brother, not Giselle."

"You haven't forgiven him, have you?"

"Not yet, no." He exhales, and the hair partially hanging over his right eye lifts. "I am trying, but it doesn't help that he never apologized. It would be easier, I think, if he showed some remorse for betraying his only brother."

"You don't forgive someone to release them from a net of guilt or remorse." I stroke the back of his hand with my thumb. "You forgive them because it releases you from a net of bitterness and pain."

"You are wise, ma fleur."

"Me?" I chuckle. "Nah! I am just repeating something Sensei Roshi once said to me."

"Who is Sensei Roshi?" he asks.

"He is a cosmically enlightened Zen master who teaches at the Welcome Ohm Wellness Center in Boulder. My mom signed me up for his Observe the Breath class when I was in fourth grade because she thought it might help with my reading disability." I give a whatev shrug and roll my eyes. "It didn't magically transform me into a fluent reader, but it gave me some insight. Sensei is, like, *it.* I don't think I would have survived life without his lessons."

"Then I am glad he was in your life."

"Gabriel?"

"Oui?"

"Will you forgive?"

"Alexandre?"

I shake my head. "Me. I was wrong not to trust you. I am sorry. Will you forgive me?"

"Desolée, ma fleur." He sighs and shakes his head. "It is not possible for me to forgive you."

I gasp because it literally feels like Julia just jabbed one of her pointy heeled booties into my heart. I was so busy worrying that Gabriel would commit some unforgivable act and break my heart, it never occurred to me that I would be the one seeking forgiveness.

"I get it," I say, pulling my hand free from Gabriel's grasp and standing. "I was, like, a total suspicious jerk. Why would you forgive me?"

I need to go. I need to leave right now, because I am devastated. The inside of my heart probably looks like a post-nuclear apocalyptic scene, all scorched walls and withered ventricles, a hollow shell of the organ it used to be. If I don't leave right now, I am afraid I might do something humiliating, like drop to the ground, curl up in the fetal position, and wail that I am a zombie, one of the living dead moving through this world without a heart, without a love.

"Adieu, Gabriel."

I turn away and am about to follow the path back out of the park when Gabriel grabs my arm.

"Unless . . ."

I turn around.

"Unless?"

He pulls me onto his lap and wraps his arms around my waist. "I will forgive you if you also apologize for what you said earlier."

I scrunch my nose, squint my eyes, and try to recall anything I said during our conversation that might have been hurtful, but my dyslexic mind is still racing to process everything that has happened since Gabriel led us to this bench. "What did I say?"

"You said you were not beautiful or smart or sophisticated or sexy." He tilts my chin up so I look at him. "That upsets me more than your jealousy and mistrust, because I think you are belle comme un cœur."

Pretty like a heart.

"I have only scratched your surface, ma fleur, but already I see that your beauty extends down deep to your heart. You are a beautiful soul, and I love you."

"You love me?"

He kisses me sweetly, slowly, tenderly. It is the kind of kiss that washes away the ashes in my post-apocalyptic heart. A kiss that feels as warm and welcoming as the first rays of sun after a sudden, nearly devastating nuclear winter.

I feel it. The tender sprouts of my love for Gabriel have taken root and are growing stronger every minute I spend with him.

Chapter 28

Laney's Life Playlist
"I'm Yours" by Jason Mraz
"Crazy in Love" by Daniela Andrade (cover)

To: Delaney Brooks
From: Dr. Elisabet L. Brooks
Subj: Your Future

I am sorry I wasn't home when you called. Your dad said you are enjoying your time in Paris and that you have made a lot of new friends. He also mentioned you have a boyfriend. I am very happy for you, Laney, but have you thought about what you will do after this latest diversion?

You only have a few months left on your internship. Now might be a good time to start submitting applications and searching for a studio apartment. It might be time to stop dreaming and start planning. Remember what Alan Lakein said, "Failing to plan is planning to fail."

Love,
Mom

To: Dr. Elisabet L. Brooks
From: Delaney Brooks
Subj: Re: Your Future

Remember what Gloria Steinem said, "Without leaps of imagination, or dreaming, we lose the excitement of possibilities. Dreaming, after all, is a form of planning."

"Laney," Rigby says, "you should go up there and sing. Let these Frenchies hear your mad vocals."

It's a Friday night, and we are on the terrace of an old-style bistro in the Oberkampf district listening to one of the impromptu jam sessions that have made the area a hot and happening scene with hot and hip Parisians. The lively Oberkampf attracts Bobos and artists and glorious gays and is now my favorite place in all Paris. The sultry summer air is pulsating with bass and the vibes emitted by creative people.

"Mad vocals?" Gabriel looks at me, eyes wide. "You are a singer?"

I shrug.

"Don't be so modest," Rigby admonishes. "Laney was in a super popular band back in Boulder."

"We have been together for months, and this is the first I am hearing of this?" Gabriel asks. "You sing?"

"Un peu."

"A little?" Rigby laughs. "Are you kidding me? You sing a lot."

"She is true," Giorgio says. "Laney, she sings to the woman who bakes her favorite croissants, the man who changes the lightbulbs in the lamps around the place, the homeless woman—"

"Is this true?" Gabriel interrupts. "Why didn't you tell me you were a singer?"

"It's no big deal."

"Yes, it is," Rigby argues. "Two of Laney's songs are at the top of iTunes Cool Children's Songs chart."

"Shut up!" I say, slapping Rigby playfully on the arm. "They are not."

"Yes, they are!" She frowns. "Laney, haven't you even checked to see how your songs are doing?"

I shake my head.

I look around the table, first at Giorgio, then at Gunthar, Rachelle, Rigby, Rigby's fiancé (who is sweet, btw), and finally Gabriel. I am waiting for one of them to burst out laughing or yell, "Psych! We are punkin' you, Lane!" But they don't.

"Come on," Rigby says, grabbing my hand and jumping up. "You are going to sing."

She leads me through the crowd and to the corner of the makeshift stage, and waits until the musicians finish performing a cool French electropop song.

"Excuse me," she says to the guy on the keyboards. "My friend is the lead singer of a popular band in America and wants to know if she could sing with you."

I am about to correct her for continuing to describe my band as popular, because, really, we were popular-*ish*—in Colorado—when the keyboardist breaks into a huge smile and says, "Bien sûr!"

"Good luck," Rigby says, squeezing my hand.

She leaves me to join our group, who have managed to carve a place for themselves in the crowd at the front of the stage. The keyboardist pulls a microphone from a hard plastic case at his feet.

"Je suis Michel," the keyboardist says, handing me the mic. "Quel est ton nom?"

"Nice to meet you, Michel. I'm Laney."

We bump fists.

"What do you want to sing, Laney?"

I look at the crowd of street performers and trendy Parisians and try to think of an edgy song that would entertain them, but all I can think of is poppy-happy tunes that reflect what I am feeling in my heart. I am not sure this crowd will dig the notes I am about to lay on them—but if I have learned anything in the last year, it's that I have to own who I am. Gabriel smiles at me, and a melody plays in my head.

"Do you know 'Love You like a Love Song'?"

"Selena Gomez and the Scene?" Michel asks, squishing his nose up as if he just got a whiff of a bad round of camembert. "That one?"

I nod my head.

"Sure."

"Okay, I want to slow it down—like, way, way down, until the second verse. Just you, me, and a guitar."

Michel plugs the mic cord into an amp, slides the mic into a stand, and lowers the stand so I can sit on the stage. I walk over to a girl holding an acoustic guitar and ask her if I could borrow it, and she hands it to me. I sit on the edge of the stage, adjust the mic, and strum the cords, getting my fingers used to the unfamiliar instrument. When I am ready, I smile at Michel.

"Ready?"

Michel nods and begins playing an extended intro on the keyboard, slowing the song down and stripping it of its usual synthesized, techno-beat sound. I take a breath, close my eyes, strum the guitar, and begin singing "Love You like a Love Song." I strum and sing the first verse as if it is a sorrowful ballad about heartbreak, not a catchy, upbeat pop song about love and lust. I sing like I have all of the time in the world, stretching out the syllables.

When I come to the chorus—which is really just the title repeated in two sets of three—I open my eyes and look at Gabriel. I look into his eyes, only his eyes, so he can see what I am thinking, what I am feeling. So he knows I am not singing for the other musicians, the drag queens in ball gowns swaying at the back of the crowd, the street performers in face paint making motions to match the lyrics. I am singing this song for him and only him.

When I sing the last word in the chorus, I set the guitar out of the way, grab the mic, and stand up. Michel picks up the tempo, switching from a mournful piano to a highly synthesized keyboard, and the crowd goes wild. I match my energy to Michel's, increasing my tempo and moving my hips to the beat, flipping my hair, and dancing like a pop starlet. Michel turns the auto-tune on, and my voice comes out of the speaker sounding remote and robotic.

Gabriel hardly waits for me to finish singing before lifting me off the stage and hugging me to him.

"You are beautiful, Laney," he whispers in my ear. "You are so beautiful you make me want to carry you back to my apartment, pull my mattress out onto the roof, and make love to you until the neighbors weep with jealousy."

He doesn't wait for me to respond, but presses his lips to mine in a primal, possessive kiss that makes me flush from my petunia-painted toenails to my powdered cheeks. When he finally stops kissing me, a new singer has taken the stage and is singing a reggae song.

We hold hands and sway to the music for two songs when he leans down and growls in my ear, "Do you want to go home?"

"Yes."

We weave our way through the crowd to the street. Gabriel hails a cab, and we climb in the back. Eighteen minutes later, we are climbing the stairs to his apartment. He opens the door, and I follow him into the darkened living room.

"There is something I want to show you," he says, he whispers in my ear. "Wait here."

He crosses the apartment to the bookshelf and flips a switch. The gallery of lights flicker on, spotlighting Gabriel's photographs. The striking shot of place Vendôme has been replaced with a photograph of me, one of the photographs he snapped weeks ago, when I first spent the night with him.

"Wait! What?" I say, moving across the room to look closer at the print. "That can't be me!"

I look from the photo to Gabriel and back to the photo. The woman in the photograph isn't a flaky, dyslexic, unfocused virgin. She is an ingénue. She is a French actress from the days of Brigitte Bardot, or a Catherine Deneuve, with tousled hair and cat eyes. Gabriel captured me with one leg sticking out from beneath the sheet and his T-shirt hanging off one shoulder. I am holding the sheet up to my mouth so the focus is on my eyes, which are narrowed and sparkling with a seductive invitation.

"It looks like I am naked!"

"Oui," Gabriel chuckles. "It does."

"That's so . . . *naughty*!"

His laughter echoes in the quiet apartment.

"Aren't you afraid of what other people might think when they visit you and see your naked . . ."

"Lover?"

My cheeks flush. "We aren't lovers."

"We will be."

He lifts me into his arms and kisses me deep, groaning when I put my hand on his neck, pull his head closer, and open my mouth wider. I tell him with my body what I have wanted to say since the second he flipped the light on to reveal my sexy portrait: *Make love to me, Gabriel. I want to feel as beautiful and desirable as you made me look in that picture.*

I know we are in his bedroom because I can smell his cologne lingering in the air and the feathers in his down comforter. He stops kissing me.

"Are you sure you're ready, ma fleur?" he asks, pushing my hair away from my eyes. "Will you allow me to make love to you?"

I nod.

"You are sure?"

I look at his handsome face, the stubble shadowing his strong jaw, the thick, black lashes framing his slate eyes, and my heart literally aches with joy. Images appear in my brain, one after the other, like someone is holding an old-school View-Master in front of my eyes and pressing the lever: *Gabriel holding an umbrella over my easel as I put the finishing touches on a canvas during an unexpected rainstorm. Laughing and sitting sideways on the back rack while Gabriel pedals my bike through the Marais. Sunday morning at the flea market, laughing as Gabriel slips a pair of crystal-covered sunglasses on his handsome face and blows me a kiss.*

"I have never been surer of anything in my life."

He pushes me back onto the bed, props himself up on his elbows over me, and asks me again, "Are you sure, ma fleur? If not, say so now. I don't think I will have to strength to stop if we go much further."

A bubble of apprehension forms inside my stomach as I imagine what it will be like to have Gabriel pushing inside me, but I look into his earnest, concerned eyes, and it pops.

"Make me a woman, Gabriel," I whisper, sliding my hand under his shirt, over the peaks and valleys of his muscular abs. "Please?"

He growls, reaches over his shoulder, and yanks his shirt off. I reach up and unfasten his fly, easing his pants over his narrow hips and shapely bum. Gabriel stands and kicks his pants off. He pulls his briefs off, and I catch a glimpse of his erect penis. We have fooled around. I've touched him down there, but seeing the thing I have touched and stroked exposed, inches from me, is shocking.

Gabriel falls back on top of me, pinning me to the mattress with his broad chest and heavy thighs. His big erection presses between my thighs, and a stream of apprehension bubbles form inside my belly, floating, popping, forming, floating, popping. My limbs begin to tremble. Gabriel puts his forearms on either side of my head and props himself up so he can look into my eyes.

"Please do not be frightened," he says, kissing me gently on the lips. "I love you, Laney. I won't hurt you, ever."

I lower the straps of my sundress and wiggle out of it. Gabriel slides his hand under my back, unhooks my bra with a deft flick of the fingers, and drops his head to my breast. I moan as his tongue circles my right breast, slow, ever-narrowing concentric circles that turn my nipples into brownish-pink pebbles. Then he moves to my left breast and laps at the nipple like a kitten lapping milk, lap . . . lap . . . lap.

I turn my head and watch him suck my nipple into his mouth.

"Oh . . . my . . . *god,*" I moan, pressing my hand to my hot cheek.

Keeping his lips around my breast, he looks at me and pushes the tip of his penis between my thighs. The slender strip of lace preventing Gabriel from entering me rubs against my clitoris, and I shiver, shudder, drop my head, and arch my back, silently encouraging him to keep going. He pulls away and pushes again, beginning a slow, teasing rhythm that has me moaning low in my throat, an animalistic moan that surprises me.

"Please . . . don't . . . stop," I beg, feverishly turning my head side to side. "Please . . . *don't* . . ."

I close my eyes and am lost in the delirium of desire, a vague, foggy place that feels familiar and entirely new all at once. I am in a dreamy, misty world, far, far from Paris.

I don't even realize Gabriel has stopped sucking my breast until I feel my moist panties sliding down my legs and his stubbly cheeks grazing my thighs, his tongue lap, lap, lapping my clitoris, slipping between my slick folds.

Something bright flashes in my dream world, a beautiful, bright firework, exploding over and over with each thrust of his tongue.

"Gabriel," I cry out, lacing my fingers in his hair and pushing his head deeper. "Oh my god, Gabriel."

He teases me with his mouth for a few more seconds before pulling his head free and climbing atop me, his body slick with a fine sheen of perspiration, his heart pounding against my breast.

"You feel so good," he whispers, his hot, wet mouth against my ear. "I don't know how much longer I can go without burying myself inside you."

He reaches for my hand and guides it to his erection. I wrap my hand around him and squeeze gently, feeling the veins throbbing against my fingers.

He groans low in his throat and slides his hand between my thighs, cupping my sex. He holds my womanhood in his hand, and I hold big, throbbing manhood in my hand. When he coaxes my folds apart by slipping a finger inside and rubbing his palm against my clitoris in a circular motion, I cry out with pleasure and thrust my pelvis against him, rolling my hips and moving my hand up and down his shaft.

"Mon dieu," he groans. "I can't wait any longer."

"Now, Gabriel. Take me now."

He removes his hand from between my thighs, reaches into his nightstand, and pulls out a condom, handing it to me. I rip the package and hand him the condom back to him.

"I'm sorry, but I've never put one of these—"

"Shh."

I close my eyes while he puts the condom on and slip back into that warm, foggy world. He props himself on his forearms, and whispers, "Look at me."

As soon as our gazes meet, he pushes inside of me. One quick thrust that causes me to bite my lip and dig my nails into his shoulders.

"Are you okay, ma fleur?"

I nod my head, and he exhales.

He drops his forehead to mine, and we stare into each other's eyes while he slowly moves in and out of my body, in and out, in and out, until the pain of the first thrust fades to a dull, distant ache.

In and out.

In. And. Out.

Gabriel's breathing becomes ragged, and beads of perspiration form on his face, but he keeps his rhythm slow and gentle until I feel something building, building inside of me, a pressure, an urgency, and then—my body tightens around him, and I climax, like white-hot, colorful fireworks exploding against a black sky.

I cry out and Gabriel collapses on top of me, unable to hold back any longer.

"Mon dieu, you are driving me crazy," he says against my mouth, plunging inside me again and again. "Laney. Laney. Laney . . ."

The sound of my name coming from his lips does something to me, and I start to cry, silent tears that slip from my eyes and dampen my hair. I sniffle and try to wipe my eyes. Gabriel stiffens and stops thrusting.

"What's wrong? Am I hurting you?"

I shake my head.

"What is it then? Do you regret giving me your virginity?"

"No," I sniffle. "It's stupid . . ."

"Tell me, please."

"When you say my name, it makes my heart hurt with happiness," I cry, fresh tears filling my eyes. "I love you. I love you more than I thought I ever could love someone, and I just want to stay here, in your arms, listening to you say my name over and over."

He smiles and moves inside me again. I wrap my arms around him and pull him down so his full weight is on me, his cheek against my cheek, his lips on my ear.

"Je t'aime aussi, Laney."

I feel him grow inside me, bigger, thicker. One last thrust and he orgasms, his body jerking against mine.

He rolls onto his back, pulls me onto his chest, and I rest my head on his shoulder. He kisses the space between my eyes, murmuring, "Laney."

Gabriel absently runs his fingers through my hair, and I use my finger to draw figure eights on his naked shoulder. We stay like that for a long time. Finally, Gabriel reaches down and pulls the feather cover over us.

"Bonne nuit, ma fleur," he yawns, kissing my forehead. "Je t'aime."

I fall asleep watching the trees outside Gabriel's window swaying in the breeze, their branches making coral-patterned shadows on the wall and listening to the steady thump of Gabriel's heartbeat in my ear. *La-ney. La-ney. La-ney.*

Chapter 29

Laney's Life Playlist
"Dog Days Are Over" by Florence and the Machine
"Good Morning" by Mandisa
"Money" by The Flying Lizards

TEXT FROM VIVIA PERPETUA DE CAUMONT:
Jesus, Mary, and Shia LaBeouf screaming, "Just do it!" Have
you done the bow-chicka-wow-wow with your Frenchman yet?
What are you waiting for? Just. DO. It!

"I can't even right now." Rigby squeals. "Gabaney finally
smooshed! You have to tell us every little detail."

"Spill it," Rachelle says. "I have a novel to write."

"Sorry, Rachelle," I grin, slipping my sunglasses off my head and
onto my nose. "Some things just aren't fit for print."

"*Ooo!*" Rachelle coos. "Now I have to know. Give me a reference
here. If it were a scene in a novel, would the novel be a sweet romance
or erotica?"

"Yeah," Rigby teases. "Was it *Fifty Shades of Gabriel?*"

"*Eww!*" I wrinkle my nose as if I have just smelled a rotten wheel
of Camembert. "That is so gross."

Rigby laughs.

We are sunning ourselves at Paris Plage, a pop-up beach on the
banks of the Seine. Each summer, the city imports sand and palm
trees to create a fantastic faux beach for city-bound vacationers.
There is even an ice cream stand and a volleyball net. We are lying
on our backs with our arms behind our heads and our legs dangling

over the ledge. I am wearing a tee that says, "My brain is 80% lyrics" with a pair of high-waist shorts and my fave cat's-eye sunglasses.

I haven't spent more than a few minutes with my friends, not since I left them at the café in Oberkampf to go home with Gabriel and let him take my—*you know*. Since then, I have spent every free minute with Gabriel, painting in the park, riding bikes along the river, reading books at La Belle Hortense, making—*you know*—in his apartment. Rigby threatened a hunger strike unless I promised to spend time with her today.

"Maybe she's lying," Rachelle says. "Maybe it didn't *really* happen."

"You mean, like they went back to his place and made s'mores and watched Disney flicks?" Rigby asks.

"Sure," Rachelle says. "The original Netflix and chill"

They laugh.

I know they don't mean anything with their razzing, so I just let them have their laugh. Besides, I don't really want to share the intimate details of the most important moment in my adult life with— anyone. I feel like I am at summer camp and have captured a lightning bug in a jar. I just want to keep it to myself and enjoy the glow. You know what I mean?

"I almost forgot," Rachelle says, jumping up and pulling a champagne bottle and paper cups from the basket attached to her rented bike. "I brought some bubbly to celebrate your night of . . ."

"*Bedknobs and Broomsticks?*" Rigby giggles.

"*Free Willy?*" Rachelle counters.

"*Holes?*"

"*James and the Giant Peach?*"

"*Whale Rider?*"

This perverted game of making innocent children's movie titles sound like bad pornos continues even though Rigby is gasping for breath and Rachelle is holding her sides. *Mr. Toad's Wild Ride. Up! Big. Once Upon a Mattress.* They have totally ruined Disney for me. I will never be able to listen the *Little Mermaid* soundtrack again. Like, ever. Sebastian the Crab singing, "Darling, it's better down where it's wetter. Take it from me." No. *Just, no.* I am about to press my hands over my ears and hum to drown them out when Rachelle slaps my arm.

"*The B . . . B . . . Biscuit Eater!*" she says, howling.

"Okay, now you are just making titles up," I say, rubbing my arm. "Disney did not make a movie titled *The Biscuit Eater*."

"Yes, they did!"

"What's it about?"

"Beats me," Rachelle says, popping the cork out of the bottle of champagne, pours some of the bubbly liquid into a paper cup, and hands it to me. "It's a wicked old movie. I saw it a long, long time ago. I just remember it has something to do with a boy and a dog."

I take the paper cup and frown skeptically.

"You don't believe me?" Rachelle asks, pouring champagne into another cup and handing it to Rigby. "Google it! The little redheaded kid from that TV show *Family Affair* starred in it. Johnny . . . Weissmuller."

"Johnny Weissmuller wasn't in *Family Affair*!" I say, smiling. "He was that Olympic swimmer who starred in the old-school Tarzan movies. You mean Johnny Whitaker."

"That's so random," Rigby says, chuckling. "How did you even know that name?"

I shrug. "My preschool teacher's name was Mrs. Beasley, and I totally loved her. When my mom told me Mrs. Beasley was also the name of a little girl's doll on an old TV show, I made her call the cable company and add TV Land to our lineup."

"Mister French was *it*," Rachelle says. "Wasn't he?"

I nod my head. "Shyeah, he was like, way, way cooler than Alice from *Brady Bunch* or Mrs. Garrett on *The Facts of Life*."

"Totally."

We sip our champagne and watch flat-bottomed boats glide down the river, leaving ripples that shimmer like quicksilver in the summer sun. The yogi who teaches my Sunrise Salutations class back in Boulder starts each lesson off by asking us to check in with our bodies and spirits. She says we should make it a habit to read the barometer of our well-being. Today, listening to the bells of Notre Dame tolling in the distance, feeling the warmth of the summer sun and my new friendships, my barometer is fixed to Joyful. I don't want the needle of my well-being barometer to spin in a different direction.

Rigby nudges me with her shoulder, and a small golden wave of champagne curls over the lip of the cup and splashes onto my thigh, evaporating on my hot skin.

"Whatcha thinking, Lane?"

I smile and shrug.

"If you won't tell us about your nuit d'amour, at least tell us what you are thinking," Rigby says. "You look all lit up inside."

"I feel all lit up inside!" I point my toes and lift my legs, fluttering them up and down with excitement. "My spirit is filled with a million effervescent, buoyant golden bubbles. I am drunk on life and love, and I don't ever want to sober up."

Rigby puts her arm around my shoulders and squeezes. "I am so glad, Lane. You're the sweetest person I have ever met. You deserve to be all bubbly and fluttery and in love."

I drop my head to her shoulder and sigh.

"It looks like we all have something to celebrate." Rachelle pours more champagne into each of our glasses. "To us!"

"To us!" I laugh, tapping the bottom of my paper cup first to Rachelle's cup, then Rigby's. "Wait! What are we celebrating?"

"You're in love with Monsieur Tall, Dark, and Hot, Matthias asked Rigby to marry him, and I have been offered an amazing part-time teaching position at a college that will still allow me time to write." She grins. "Life is Chinese takeout and we've just been given extra fortune cookies, my friends!"

"Wait!" I shake my head back and forth and make the noise a cartoon character makes when they shake their head. "Rigby, you're engaged?"

Rigby grins and holds up her hand. An engagement ring with a ginormous diamond is sparkling on her ring finger.

"Oh my god!" I say, grabbing her hand. "He must have stolen one of the Silmarils because that is the biggest, most brilliant stone I have ever seen."

"Way to work in a Tolkien reference."

We bump fists.

"I am crazy happy for you and Matthias," I say, hugging her. "You two were destined to be together, like Aragorn and Arwen. Beren and Lùthien."

"Frodo and Samwise," she says.

We sigh.

"Congrats on the job, Dr. Phil," I say, turning to Rachelle. "You're going to be an amazing professor. When do you leave?"

"Next week," she says, her lips turning down in a frown. "I need to be back before the new term begins."

I stare across the river. Rigby is getting married. Rachelle is leaving Paris to take an important, grown-up job. In two months, I am going to have to pack my daisy suitcase and roll it back to Boulder. *Adieu, independence. Adieu, Paris dreams. Adieu, Gabriel.* Some of the golden bubbles floating inside me lose their buoyancy and sink, sink, sink to the bottom of my soul.

"What is it?" Rigby asks.

"What is what?"

"Come on, Lane," she says, narrowing her gaze. "You're not the only one who can read people. You went from looking lit-up to burnt-out in, like, three seconds. What's eating you, Gilbert Grape?"

"I came to Paris believing the universe would reveal the path I am supposed to take next, but I have been here four months, and I still don't know what I am supposed to be doing with my life." I take a deep breath, hold it in for three seconds, and let it out. "Am I really destined to spend my life living in my parents' house, taking gigs as Luna the Unicorn just so I can hustle together enough scratch for gas money?"

"What are you talking about?" Rachelle says. "The universe has shown you the path you are supposed to take."

"It has?"

She nods her head.

I look at Rigby. She nods her head, too.

"I give. What's my path?"

"You're already on it." Rachelle says. "You've only been in France for four months, and you have made friends, fallen in love, improved your art, and made a few big sales at the gallery. I think the universe redirected you here for a reason."

"I can't stay in Paris."

"Why not?" Rachelle lies back down, looking at me over the rims of her Ray-Bans. "Give me one good reason why you can't stay in Paris after your internship ends?"

"I am broke."

"Bah!" Rachelle waves her hand. "Didn't you tell me Renoir was so poor when he started painting that he nearly starved?"

"Yes, but—"

"—and didn't you tell me Van Gogh had to trade his paintings for supplies?"

"Yes."

"Don't forget Pissaro!" Rigby shouts. "His wealthy father disowned him after Pissaro eloped with a housemaid. He spent the rest of his life in poverty."

"So what are you both saying? That I should stay in Paris and trade my paintings for day-old baguettes? What if I end up like Pissaro, impoverished and shivering in the cold, mean streets, ruing the day I ever left the warmth and security of my parent's home?"

"Don't be ridiculous!"

"Where would I live?"

"You could stay with me," Rigby says, throwing her arm around my shoulder. "Think of me as your Bazille."

The wealthy, amiable Frederic Bazille often provided food, shelter, and the use of his studio to his more impoverished artist pals. Rigby offering to be my Bazille is the kindest thing anyone has ever said to me.

"Thanks, Rigby, but . . ."

"But what?"

"My mom and dad would go intercontinental ballistic if I told them I was going to stay in Paris and sponge off my friend."

"Cut the cord, Lane," Rigby says.

"Snip. Snip." Rachelle makes a V with her fingers and mimics a cutting motion. "Snip. Snip. Snip."

"Okay, okay," I laugh, pushing Rachelle's scissor fingers away. "Let's say I take you up on your generous offer, Rigby. I would still need money for food and art supplies. What would I do to earn my bread?"

"Hmm." Rigby taps her lips with her finger. "Let me think about this. Think. Think. How could Laney make enough money to support herself in Paris? Come to think of it, how am I going to earn money? I refuse to be Matthias's dependent spouse."

"I know!" Rachelle sits up so fast she knocks her paper cup over, the champagne soaking into the sand. "Why don't you two start a tour company?"

"Who two?" Rigby asks.

"You and Laney."

Rigby looks at me and I shrug.

"A tour company?"

Rachelle nods.

"What kind of a tour company?" I ask.

"You know how you two are always swapping art factoids? *'Did you know Renoir stubbed his toe on this corner? Yes, but did you know Degas bought his bread from that boulangerie?'*"

I nod my head.

"Well, what if you guided tourists around Paris and showed them all of the places where artists worked and lived and . . ."

"Bought their bread?"

"Exactly!"

Rigby pushes her sunglasses onto her head and stares at me from behind her long Twiggy lashes. "What do you think, Lane?"

"I don't know," I say, pushing my sunglasses onto my head. "What do you think?"

"I think it's a brilliant idea!"

"Me too!"

"Serious?"

I nod my head.

"So you are going to stay in Paris. You are going to cut the cord?"

I make a scissoring motion with my fingers.

"Snip. Snip!"

We laugh.

Rachelle stands, brushes the sand from the backs of her legs, and shoves the empty champagne bottle back into her basket. "My work here is done, and now I must return to the bookstore. I have the evening shift."

We thank Rachelle for her brilliant idea and hug her good-bye, promising to meet up for dinner her last night in Paris.

* * *

An hour later, I am walking beside Rigby as we push our bikes through place des Vosges on our way back to the gallery when I think of my own brilliant idea.

"Rigby!" I stop walking and look down at my beautiful, one-of-a-kind Wilde Ride bike with its black-and-white striped paint job and Parisian black-and-white seat. Rigby stops walking and looks over her shoulder at me. "We are going to have to cover a lot of ground on our art tours, aren't we? From Montmartre to the Tuileries to the Louvre."

Rigby nods her head.

"Instead of a walking art tour, why don't we make it a biking art tour?"

"That *is* a brilliant idea."

"We could order the bikes custom from Theo and ask him to paint the bodies like an impressionist painting, like Morisot's *Summer Day* or Monet's *Water Lilies*."

"Do you think Theo would do that for us?"

"Of course! I'll e-mail him as soon as we are back at the gallery and ask him if he will make us twenty-four bikes. That should be enough, shouldn't it?"

"Definitely." She laughs. "But where are we going to store all of those bikes?"

"We will find a place," I say, feeling my confidence surge.

"We are going to have so much fun, and I just know it's going to be a huge success!"

We start pushing our bikes again and are almost through the park when reality creeps up and smacks me across the face. I stop walking. Rigby stops too. She looks at my face and frowns.

"What's the matter?"

"Twenty-four custom bikes with baskets and bells are going to cost a lot. Way more than I have in my bank account."

"How much do you have?"

I frown as I try to remember the last time I checked the balance on my checking account.

"Don't you know?"

I shake my head.

"Laney! You've withdrawn money from your account, haven't you?"

"Yes."

"Didn't you look at the receipt?"

"No," I say, shaking my head. "I crumple them up and throw them away without looking. Who needs the pressure? I know I am riding downhill toward the valley of poverty, so I am closing my eyes, lifting my feet, and just going, baby!"

"That's insane."

"I set a weekly budget before coming here, and I have been sticking to it, so I should have money left over."

Then again, I did splurge on pastels from La Maison du Pastel and a new bra and matching panties from a chichi lingerie shop in the Opera District. Then there was that birthday gift for Gunthar and an Exodus comic signed by the illustrator for Gabriel. I might be closer to the valley than I thought.

"Here," Rigby says, handing me her iPhone. "Check your balance."

"That's okay," I say, swallowing the thick, guilty lump in my throat. "I'll check the next time I take money out."

"Do it!" She waves the phone at me. "How are we going to be business partners if you are rotting away in debtors' prison?"

"Fine, but opening my eyes at the last second isn't going to keep me from crashing in the valley of poverty."

I take her phone, tap the Safari app, and type "Wells Fargo" into the search bar. I enter my login information, close one eye, and hold my breath while the page loads.

"Holy crap!" I say, opening my eye. "This can't be right!"

"How bad is it?"

"It's not bad," I say, staring at Rigby with wide eyes. "It says I have fourteen thousand nine hundred and sixty-two dollars in my account."

"That's great."

"No, it's not."

"It's not?"

"No!" I look at my friend. "Something is wrong, Rigby. Really wrong. I should have a lot less than that in my account."

"How much less?"

I tilt my head and my glasses slip down my nose.

"Like, fourteen thousand five hundred and twelve dollars less." I say, shoving my glasses back up. "Give or take a dollar."

She holds out her hand.

"Let me see."

I hand her the phone, and she slides her finger up the screen. Slide. Slide. Slide. Her eyes widen, and she looks at me, her long lashes curling against her pink skin.

"It's not a mistake."

"It's not?"

She shakes her head.

"Look," she says, holding the phone so we can both see the screen, "it says that iTunes deposited fourteen thousand and twenty-two dollars into your account on the first of this month."

"What?"

I grab the phone from her hand and look at the screen. Sure enough. The bold black line halfway down the screen confirms it. On August 1, iTunes Payments deposited over fourteen thousand dollars into my account.

"Fourteen thousand dollars divided by seventy cents . . ." I use my finger to do the math in the air. "That's twenty thousand down-loads! Are you telling me twenty thousand people downloaded me singing *Waddaliacha* and *The Unicorn Song?*"

Rigby laughs. "I told you that your songs were topping the iTunes Children's Chart."

"I know, but . . ." I shake my head. "This is crazy."

"Laney, everything about you is crazy. You're the most crazy, wonderful person I have ever met."

Chapter 30

To: Delaney Brooks
From: Theo Wilde, Wilde Rides
Subj: Re: My path

Dude! I can't believe you are going to stay in Paris and open an art bike tour business. That's such a super-badass, ballsy move. I am proud of you, Laney-Bo-Baney.

What did the 'rents say? Is Mama E losing her brain? She will probably try to talk you off of this path. She will tell you the terrain is too steep and rocky. Don't listen to her.

Remember what I told you when we were going to do the Boulder Monster? I warned you that it was an epic, 50-mile butt-kicking ride with death-defying climbs. I told you that you needed to attack the hills with the ferocity of a demon, but once you reached the top, there would be awesome landscapes. Follow this path. Get in the Zone. You're gonna shred this one.

Theo

P.S. Of course I will make the bikes for your new business. I can't believe you thought you had to ask, Hoser. If you haven't thought of a name for your company yet, how about Get Up and Van Gogh?

To: Delaney Brooks
From: Elisabet Brooks
Subj: Re: My path

I can't pretend your decision to remain in Paris and open a bike tour business has filled me with confidence and happiness. Everything we spoke about before you left Colorado remains a pressing concern—your ability to provide for yourself while building a respectable career.

However, the initiative and determination you have shown this last year have been refreshing. I am proud of you for completing the internship. Your father showed me the pictures you sent of the paintings you did during your internship. They really are very lovely, Laney. I know I haven't said this to you very often, but I am proud of you. You are a talented, passionate artist. I still don't believe you can make a career out of art, but I applaud your desire to try.

I have purchased a ticket to Paris and will be visiting you over my winter break. I hope we can spend some time together and maybe even start our adult friendship over.

Love,
Mom

Chapter 31

Laney's Life Playlist
"Style" by Taylor Swift
"Unconditionally" by Katy Perry

"He said he has something he wants to ask you?" Fanny holds her phone closer so her face fills the screen. "That's what he said?"

"Yes."

"How did he say it?"

"What do you mean *how* did he say it?"

"Was he casual or serious?" Fanny demands. "Did he say it like you were a bro he was asking to a football game, or did he say it in that deep, serious voice men use when they're trying to get you to slip out of your Louboutins and into your La Perla?"

"I don't know," I say, chuckling. "It was somewhere between bro and ho."

Fanny sighs. "Tell me exactly what he said."

"'Ma fleur, would you meet me at Bâtard de Valadon tonight at seven? There is something important I need to ask you,'" I say, repeating the words Gabriel spoke to me less than five minutes before. "What do you think it could be?"

"Are you serious? He said he has an important question to ask you and he is taking you to dinner at a chichi restaurant. What else *could* it be?" Fanny's voice, usually calm and carefully modulated, sounds like air escaping from a balloon. "He's going to ask you to marry him!"

"No."

"Oui!" Fanny shifts her phone from one hand to the other.

"You really think so?"

"Abso-bloody-lutely, as my British pal Poppy would say!" Fanny laughs. "I am so happy for you! Promise you will Facetime me after he's popped the big question? I want to be able to congratulate you both."

"I promise."

"Okay, let's get to the serious issue at hand: what are you going to wear?"

I shrug. "Dunno."

"Mon dieu!" Fanny mutters and shakes her head. "You're killing me, Laney. Kill-ing me."

"What did you wear when Hottie McScottie asked you to marry him?"

"He didn't ask me. I asked him, remember?" She grins. "And for the record, I wore impeccably tailored Armani pants, a constructed jacket with leather panels, and Christian Louboutin boots. Of course, I didn't know I was going to have to ride a horse over the Scottish countryside, or that I would be covered in mud and sheep shit when I asked him."

Fanny is drop-dead gorgeous and always, always fashionably dressed—even on Facetime! When I met her in Anchorage, she was about to climb out a hotel window to chase a couple of pill-popping jerries who had busted into her room and run off with her designer luggage. Some women would have cried and used their victim status as an excuse to dress down. Not Fanny. She marched to the nearest Nordstrom and pulled together a runway-worthy wardrobe from the ready-to-wear pieces hanging on the racks.

"You're the one who graduated from Parsons School of Design," I say, smiling. "What do you think I should wear?"

"Something timeless and feminine, so when you're sixty years old with blue hair and a gaggle of grandchildren at your feet, you can pull out your engagement selfies and not be humiliated," Fanny says, her tone serious. "Think Ava Gardner or Audrey Hepburn. Arched brows, flirty lashes, bold lips, and a classically tailored suit or dress. Heels are a must, but not too high. As Vivia would say, 'No Amy Winehouse fuck-me pumps.'"

"Got it," I say, making mental notes of Fanny's pointers. "Channel

Audrey, not Amy. There's a boutique near the gallery. If I go now, I should catch them before they close."

"Bon chance, mon amie," Fanny says.

"Merci, Fanny!"

"Oh, and Laney?" Fanny says, moving closer to the screen. "Remember what Christian said, 'The tones of gray, pale turquoise, and pink will always prevail.'"

I wrinkle my nose. Pink is not my color.

"Wait!" Fanny says. "Before you go, what did your parents say about your decision to stay in Paris?"

"My mom wrote me a nice e-mail."

"Really?"

"Well, nice-ish. She said she thinks I am a talented artist, but she doesn't think art is a real career."

"Ouch," Fanny says. "How does that make you feel?"

I scrunch my nose and stare up at the ceiling. Truthfully, I didn't take the time to process how my mom's e-mail made me feel. Not thinking about how things make me feel, really make me feel deep down, is a habit I formed many years ago. Eating lamb. Religion. Being an artist even if it means defying my parents. I have never focused long enough to figure out who I am, what I believe, and what I really want for my life. The non-processing habit formed neural pathways in my brain, pathways I have been reshaping since coming to Paris.

"I am fine."

"Really?"

"Yes," I say, smiling at Fanny. "I have spent twenty-five years trying to reshape my image into something that was a little more pleasing to my mom. I have failed and made myself miserable in the process. It's time I embrace my misshapen shape and stop worrying about how it makes my mom feel."

"It's your life, mon amie."

"And I'm gonna live it!" I disconnect the call, but continue staring at my phone as if the answers to the questions bothering me will suddenly appear on the screen, like a guiding text message from the universe. *Is Gabriel going to ask me to marry him tonight? And if he does, am I ready to clip the wings of my fledgling independence before I have truly tested their strength? Am I strong enough to follow the path I want to follow, even if it means disappointing and defying my parents?* Even if it means I end up starving and mad, like poor old Vincent van Gogh?

I close my eyes, take a deep breath, clear my mind of all chatter, and listen for that quiet inner voice that whispers wisdom. *Thump. Thump.* My pulse pounds in my ear. *Bark. Bark. Bang. Beep.* Outside a dog barks, a door slams, a car horn sounds. My inner voice is mute. Wisdom is eluding me.

I grab my wallet, slip my feet into my ballet flats, and head down the stairs. Maybe I will find the perfect wisdom to go with my classic Audrey Hepburn–inspired dress at La Pâmoison, a consignment shop that promises swoon-worthy vintage clothes (*Pâmoison* is swoon in French).

La Pâmoison closes at five o'clock. Prompt. Since it is already a quarter past four, I decide to run the five blocks to the shop. If my inner voice was trying to whisper a warning about running on uneven cobblestones in slick-bottomed ballet flats, I didn't hear it. My shoe slips over a wet cobble, and I pitch forward like a comedian performing an absurd pratfall. Only it's not very funny. It's humiliating and painful. I land hard on my knees and palms, the gritty stones braising my skin like sandpaper.

Blood trickles out of the cut on my knee and down my leg, turning my buttery-yellow leather flats an ugly rusty orange. If I had any sense, I would hobble back to my room, curl up in my bed, and lick my wounded pride like an animal in her den, but something is urging me on, a primal adrenaline. I can't quit. I have to find a classic, feminine dress that will make Gabriel's heart go *ba-boomp, ba-boomp, ba-boomp* and leap out of his chest like Jim Carrey's did when he played Stanley Ipkiss in *The Mask*.

My desperation to make it to La Pâmoison, to find the perfect dress, tells me more than a whispering inner voice ever could. Instinct is leading me to love. Who am I to argue?

Chapter 32

Laney's Life Playlist
"Marry You" by Bruno Mars
"Complicated" by Avril Lavigne

The Year of Learning Dangerously. If Rachelle makes good on her promise to write a fictional account of my life in Paris, she should seriously consider titling it *The Year of Learning Dangerously*. To say this has been a time of growth is an understatement.

For instance, I have learned you shouldn't operate a motor vehicle while wearing a unicorn costume, Sunny D and painkillers don't mix, Frenchwomen don't run through the streets of Paris and you shouldn't either, yoga pants aren't acceptable attire anywhere in Paris (even a yoga studio), a Parisian waiter will definitely give you a Spitter if you tell him his chakras are totally out of whack, and no matter how late you are, never, ever forget to put on underarm deodorant.

I learned the last one, oh, about three seconds ago, when I lifted my arm to open the door to Bâtard de Valadon and saw a ginormous pit stain on my newly acquired dress reflected in the glass.

True to their motto, La Pâmoison had the perfect swoon-worthy dress, a pink satin fit and flare gown with a light teal ruffled petticoat and matching elbow gloves. It's what Audrey Hepburn would wear if she was asked to star in an indie music video with Zoey Deschanel and Joseph Gordon Levitt. The swingy skirt makes me happy—so happy I had to resist the urge to twirl all the way here.

I step inside Bâtard de Valadon and discreetly flap my arms so the cool air will dry my damp satin pits.

"There you are, cherie!" Robert suddenly appears at the end of the hallway. He greets me with kisses to my cheeks. "Monsieur Galliard is waiting. Follow me."

"Wait," I say, grabbing his forearm with my gloved hand. "I need a minute to . . . to . . ."

Robert smiles. "You are nervous? But why should you be nervous, cherie? You look magnifique. Monsieur Galliard is fortunate to have you as his date tonight."

I smooth my hair and then my skirts.

"Merci, Monsieur Robert," I say, lifting my chin. "Lead the way."

Robert walks through the velvet curtains into the dining room, which is already humming with the low, subdued conversation of elegantly clad Parisians. Soft jazz music plays in the background, and candles flicker at each table.

Gabriel stands when he sees us. He's wearing tailored slacks and a vest, his shirtsleeves casually rolled up to reveal his muscular forearms, his suit jacket tossed across the back of his chair. With his impeccably tailored suit, tall, solid physique, slicked-back hair, and closely trimmed beard, he could be a Dolce and Gabbana model posing on a yacht or beside a roadster. I look into his stormy blue eyes, and the bones in my legs turn into rubber. I am wobbly, weak-kneed. He steps out from behind the table and pulls me into his arms.

"You look beautiful," he whispers, kissing my neck.

"So do you."

He chuckles and pulls my chair out. I sit and remove my gloves while Gabriel orders us a bottle of wine. You know how your stomach feels when you are riding a roller coaster and your car reaches the top of a climb, that split second of thrilling weightlessness before it plunges down, down? That's how my stomach feels right now.

"I missed you today," Gabriel says, reaching for my hand.

"You did?"

"Bien sûr," he says, smiling sweetly. "I always miss you when you are not with me. Did you miss me?"

"A lot."

"Bon." He lifts my hand and kisses my fingers. "What did you work on today? Did you finish *Sunday Morning*?"

Sunday Morning is a painting I started a few weeks ago after I woke up in Gabriel's arms and saw a golden, mote-filled shaft of morning light streaming through his bedroom window. I wanted to capture the warmth and wonder of that moment on canvas.

"Yes," I say, swallowing the lump of emotion clogging my throat. "I finished it this morning."

"That is wonderful, ma fleur," he says, smiling. "Congratulations. What will you do with it? Sell it?"

I plan to give *Sunday Morning* to Gabriel so he can always remember our special time together, but I don't want him to know that now, so I just shrug.

The sommelier returns with our wine. He removes the cork and pours a splash into Gabriel's wineglass. Gabriel does the whole sniff, swirl, sip thing that always makes me feel like I am child playing grown-up with a big, sophisticated Frenchman.

We are ordering our first and second courses when my iPhone rings. I pull it out of my purse and look at the screen. It's Fanny. I send it to voice mail and slip it back into my purse.

I ask Gabriel about his next assignment, and he tells me that in September he is headed to Cannes to cover the Yachting Festival. Our conversation flows as freely as the wine, so that by the time he reaches across the table and takes my hand, I am totally chill and my roller-coaster tummy has returned to earth.

"I have something important to ask you, ma fleur."

I lean closer to him. "Yes."

I am ready to say *yes-yes-yes,* and I haven't even heard his question yet.

"The gallery will be closed for the next two weeks, which means you will be free of obligations. Yes?"

Ohmygod. Is he going to ask me to elope?

My iPhone rings again. I pull it out of my purse, push the button to decline the call, slide it to mute, and set it on the table.

He grabs my hand again, looks into my eyes, and . . .

. . . my phone rings again.

"Would you like to answer your phone?"

I shake my head. Bruno Mars is singing "Marry You" in my head, and I am having visions of beautiful nights spent doing stupid things, like sipping dancing juice and running off to a little chapel. I'll wear a '50s-inspired bridesmaid gown in cotton candy pink or seafoam green, and Gabriel will rent a convertible. I'll throw my scarf out the window, and we'll sing, "*Yeah, yeah, yeah, yeah*" at the top of our lungs.

"Very well." He takes a deep breath and exhales. "My family is gathering at our house in Provence to celebrate Aunt Fantine's ninetieth birthday next week. Would you go to the south of France with me, ma fleur?"

The needle scratches across the Bruno Mars album playing in my head, and the romantic visions fade. Most girls would be thrilled if their super-hot boyfriend asked them on a vacay to Provence. So why do I feel like someone has just repeatedly jabbed a record needle in my heart?

My phone starts to vibrate. I look down and see Fanny's name on the screen and look back up, blinking, but not really seeing, not clearly. Gabriel nods his head at the phone.

"I can wait to hear your answer. Take your call."

When I reach for the phone, my thumb accidentally hits the round green answer button and Fanny's face pops up on the screen.

"Félicitations, Monsieur et Madame Galliard!" Fanny says. "Did you set the date yet? Will it be a winter wedding?"

I quickly disconnect the call and throw my phone in my handbag, snapping it shut and dropping it onto my lap. Gabriel is staring at me with wide eyes and raised brows. He is waiting for me to say something that will explain my friend's outburst, but what can I say? I must have been drunk on the dancing juice when I let Fanny convince me Gabriel was going to ask me to marry him. I am not the kind of girl a guy like Gabriel marries. I am the kind of girl who rides through the streets of Paris on a bike with streamers and a childish red bell. I am the kind of girl who wears Heidi braids and recycled gowns with ridiculous ruffled petticoats.

"Laney?"

He reaches for my hand again, but I grab my gloves and pull them on, finger by finger. It buys me the time I need to visualize a ship on a stormy sea sailing into the shelter of a harbor. I am calm. I am strong. I am anchored in truth and light.

"I would love to go to the south of France with you, Gabriel," I say, smiling. "Thank you for asking."

Gabriel pays the bill, and we leave Bâtard de Valadon, walking beside each other without touching or talking. Gabriel opens the gate to the park, and I walk through it, my expensive new heels sinking into the gravel path. We are walking back to the gallery instead of catching a cab back to his apartment. I am trying not to read more into that.

"Laney," Gabriel says, grabbing my hand and pulling me off the path and beneath the shadowy canopy of a tree, "can we talk?"

I lean against the tree and stare at my pink-painted toenails peeking out from the open toes of my heels. Tears fill my eyes, and I blink them away before looking at Gabriel.

"Sure," I say. "What do you want to talk about?"

Gabriel pulls me into his arms, spins us around, and leans against the tree. I have no choice but to lean against his broad chest and look up into his handsome face.

"Let's talk about our trip. Are you excited?"

I think about Gabriel's family and feel a moment of panic. As far as I know, they don't know Gabriel is dating me.

"Yes."

He kisses me.

"Your lips say yes, but your eyes say no." He tilts my chin up so I am forced to meet his gaze. "What is bothering you, my love?"

I ran through the streets of Paris, fell and skinned my knees, spent a ridiculous amount of money on a gown and sexy heels, because I thought you were going to ask me to marry you, but you just want to take me on a romantic vacation to the south of France and introduce me as your girlfriend to your family. Wah! Poor me. Break out the Kleenex.

"I am fine," I say, kissing him back. "When do we leave?"

I rest my head on his chest and listen to his voice rumbling in my ear, but I don't hear his words. It's hard to hear what he is saying when my doubts are screaming in my head. *You aren't sophisticated. You lack focus. Your eyes are too big, and your hair is too thick. The Galliards will take one look at you and turn their perfectly sculpted, aristocratic French noses in the air, sniff, and say, "Ne sois pas stupide, Gabriel. You take an American girl to Vegas for the weekend, you don't bring her home."*

Chapter 33

Laney's Life Playlist
"Come Away with Me" by Norah Jones
"Just Give Me a Reason" by Pink with Nate Ruess

TEXT FROM STÉPHANIE MOREAU:
I am sorry again about that Facetime. I'm also sorry you are disappointed that Gabriel didn't pop the question, but I am sure he will ask you when you're in Provence. I can't wait to hear all about it. Don't forget Vivia and I are coming to Paris to celebrate the end of your internship (and your engagement). See you soon.

Three days later, we are in the Comfort à la Carte compartment of a TGV train speeding to the south of France. Gabriel is napping, and I am staring out the window, watching blurry yellow fields of sunflowers whiz by while listening to Norah Jones.

Every time I hear Norah sing about waking up in her lover's arms while rain falls on their tin roof, I think about waking up in Gabriel's arms as the light of dawn streams through his bedroom window. I think about those tiny motes of dust dancing through the golden rays and how I felt just as weightless and free in Gabriel's love.

I had no idea falling in love with Gabriel would complicate things so much. My heart and mind are all twisted up like the macramé bracelets I used to make at summer art camp.

I look at Gabriel sleeping in the seat beside me. His long, thick black lashes against his tanned cheeks. The swoop of his hair hanging to one side. The full lips that kiss me awake in the middle of the night, when the moon's silver light is the only thing covering our naked bodies. I etch this scene on a blank canvas in my mind just in case . . .

. . . in case, what? Say it. Say what you have been thinking ever since you walked out of Bâtard de Valadon without an engagement ring on your finger.

I am gathering many images, fixing them in an album in my mind, just in case this thing with Gabriel turns out to be another of those clichéd American girl–French boy short-lived romances. Not that I want it to be a short-lived romance, but I still find it difficult to believe a man as sophisticated as Gabriel would want to settle with me.

Gabriel wakes up when his phone rings. He yawns, stretches his arms over his head, winks at me, and pulls his phone out of his pocket.

He looks at the screen and clenches his jaw.

"What is it?" I say, putting my hand on his leg. "It's not bad news, is it?"

"You could say that," he says, slipping his phone back into his jeans pocket. "That was Alexandre. He has invited Giselle to join us this weekend."

"I am sorry, Gabriel."

"Me too."

He pulls his sunglasses out of the collar of his shirt, slips them on his face, and stares out the window for the rest of the journey.

I listen to Norah singing "What Am I to You?" and wonder if Gabriel feels butterflies when he looks into my eyes, or if he's filling my heart with lies. I wonder if the thought of seeing Giselle again is what has him acting withdrawn and moody.

A private car is waiting for us when we arrive at the Marseilles train station. We climb into the back of the car and hold hands. Gabriel points out interesting sites as we drive from the train station to his family's home near Moustiers-Sainte-Marie, a beautiful hilltop village overlooking the green waters of the Gorges du Verdon.

Small, stone country houses are called *bastides* in the south of France. The Galliard home is whatever you call several *bastides* connected by colonnades and surrounded by Cyprus trees and ancient vineyards.

The car pulls around the house and stops near what looks like stables. The driver jumps out and opens our door. Gabriel grabs my hand and helps me out of the car.

"That's okay, Jean-Paul," he says, taking our bags from the driver. "I can manage these."

I follow Gabriel across the gravel drive and into the house. He drops the bags on the tile floor and pulls me into his arms.

"Bienvenue La Bastide de Sainte-Marie, Laney," he says, kissing me. "I am so happy you are here with me. This is my favorite place in the world."

We kiss again until the back of my neck gets that tingly feeling it gets when I think someone is watching me.

"What's wrong?"

"Your family doesn't know we are dating," I whisper, pulling away. "I don't want them to walk in and catch us making out."

He laughs.

"No worries, ma fleur," he says, a wicked smile curving his lips. "My family doesn't arrive until tomorrow afternoon. We have the place to ourselves until then."

He lifts me into his arms and carries me up the stairs, nudging a door at the top of the landing open with his foot and dropping me onto a big canopied bed.

"You know what that means?"

I shake my head.

"It means," he says, sliding his hands up my skirt and pulling my panties down my legs. "We have twenty-four hours to try each of the beds in the bastide and decide which one we like best."

The next morning, I wake to the sound of a rooster crowing outside our bedroom window and Gabriel's sleep-rough voice in my ear.

"Wake up, my love," he growls in my ear, his beard scratching my collarbone. "We have a busy day ahead of us."

I turn toward him, pressing my bare breasts against his side, wrapping my leg over his muscular thighs, sliding my hand up his chest, into his hair, moaning softly when I smell the scent of our lovemaking lingering on his warm skin.

He kisses my forehead and rolls out of my embrace, standing and walking to the window, throwing open the heavy curtains. "It's a beautiful day, ma fleur. If you don't get out of bed, I will close the curtains, and we will spend it under the covers."

I roll onto my stomach, lift my bum like a Victoria's Secret model, and look back at him over my shoulder.

"We wouldn't want that, would we?" I gasp, batting my eyelashes.

He groans, yanks the curtains closed, and climbs back into bed.

Two hours later, I am sitting on the back of Gabriel's shiny red BMW motorcycle, my legs wrapped around his waist, as he maneuvers the powerful machine over the hills and around the snaking roads that cut through Provence.

After we made love, showered, and dressed, he grabbed my hand and led me to the stables behind the house. He opened a set of wooden doors, handed me a helmet, and told me to get ready for the ride of my life.

I thought about telling him he'd already given me the ride of my life . . . but that seemed like something Vivia would say, not me, so I strapped the helmet on my head and climbed onto the back of his bike.

I rest my head on Gabriel's shoulder and squeeze my eyes shut, thinking about all of the firsts I have experienced with this gorgeous man: First time making love. First time visiting Provence. First time riding on the back of a motorcycle. First time feeling like my heart is being pumped, pumped, pumped full of so much love it is surely going to pop like a balloon and come flying out of my chest.

We ride for another hour until we come to a round, blue-and-white sign welcoming us to Arles. Gabriel maneuvers the bike into the city center, parking it in a narrow spot on the street. He lets me get off the bike and then kicks the kickstand down, kills the ignition, and climbs off.

He removes his helmet, takes mine, and hooks them to the back of the bike using a long, twisty cable with a lock.

"Ready?" he asks, taking my hand.

"Sure, but where are we going?"

"You'll see."

He holds my hand, and we walk down the street to a green square bordered with tall plane trees.

"Voilà!" he says, gesturing to the square.

"Okay," I say, looking left and right. "Where are we?"

"You see that building on the other side of the square, the one with the black awning?"

I nod.

"That is where Van Gogh's *Yellow House* once stood." He grins. "It was bombed during the liberation of Arles and demolished shortly afterward, but he spent time in this park. You told me once you wished to walk in Van Gogh's footsteps. So, start walking, ma fleur."

I look around the green square and notice little things from Van Gogh's painting, a bridge in the distance, a building. The scene becomes cloudy as tears fill my eyes.

"I read online that the site where he painted *Starry Night over the Rhône* is a few minutes away," Gabriel says. "Do you want to try to find it?"

I look up at Gabriel, and a tear spills down my cheek.

"What's wrong, ma fleur?" he asks, brushing my tears away with his thumb. "Aren't you happy?"

I stand on my tippy-toes and kiss his stubbly cheek.

"I am crazy happy," I say, sniffling. "This is, like, the sweetest thing anyone has ever done for me."

"I've only just begun to make you happy, Laney."

"Promise?"

He smiles. "Promise."

We walk to the site that inspired Van Gogh to paint *Starry Night over the Rhône* and are totes bummed to learn that the space is now occupied by a Monoprix, the French grocery store chain.

On the way back to Gabriel's motorcycle, we stop in a shop and purchase a bottle of wine, some cheese, and a crusty baguette, still warm from the oven.

Gabriel stows our purchases in the hold affixed to the back of his bike, we put our helmets on, and we are off, speeding out of town and into the countryside.

Gabriel turns off the main road onto a narrow dirt track bordered with wheat fields, the slender golden stalks bending in the breeze like graceful ballet dancers. A ramshackle stone farmhouse with an orange-clay tile roof stands at the end of the track.

Gabriel stops the bike and kills the ignition. We get off the bike.

This time, I don't need him to tell me where we are. I pull my helmet off my head and grin.

"*Farmhouse in Provence,* right?"

Gabriel smiles and nods, his black hair falling over his forehead.

"I thought we could have a picnic here in the field," he says, pushing his hair off his forehead.

He pulls our picnic and a rolled blanket out of the hold, and we make our way through the wheat field until we find the perfect spot, the tall grasses shielding us from passersby.

We drink wine and eat warm, buttery bread beneath a blazing yellow Provençal sun and cobalt Van Gogh sky. We make love and then lie in each other's arms, listening to the wind whispering through the fields of wheat, watching the day fade into a starry night. While Gabriel is packing up the remains of our picnic, I stare up at the heavens and make a wish on a shooting star.

Please God, let the love we have for each other remain as vibrant and enduring as Van Gogh's paintings.

Chapter 34

Laney's Life Playlist
"Pop Punk Pizza Party" by Sunrise Skater Kids
"Death of a Bachelor" by Panic! at the Disco

We make it back to La Bastide de Sainte-Marie in time to shower and change our clothes before meeting Gabriel's family for dinner. Gabriel told me dinner is always casual at the *bastide,* held in the backyard under the stars. I don't know how the French do backyard meals, but I am picturing a smoking BBQ grill, Solo cups filled with lemonade, and chill reggae music. A flip-flops and tees scene.

What I find when we step out of the *bastide* and into the garden is definitely not a flip-flops and Solo cups scene. A long wooden trestle table set with fine china, crystal wineglasses, and elaborate floral centerpieces is situated beneath a pergola strung with fairy lights. Sweet-scented lilacs hang from the pergola like clusters of grapes. A string quartet is playing Saint-Saëns's "The Swan" beneath the bowing branches of a wisteria tree, also hung with dozens of twinkling fairy lights. I stop walking and stare at the cellist plucking her strings.

"Gabriel," I whisper, looking up at him, "I thought you said this was a casual dinner?"

"Oui."

I look at the elegantly clad people sipping aperitifs and munching hors d'oeuvres beside a glimmering turquoise swimming pool and thank the universe I decided to wear my black ruffled chiffon sundress instead of my Namast'ay in Bed tee and shorts.

"This is not a *cazh* backyard dinner. Where is the lemonade in plastic cups? Where is the Bose speaker blasting reggae?" I make the Vaayu Mudra hand pose for calmness, placing the tip of my index fingers at the base of my thumbs, and take a deep breath. "There's a string quartet and"—I squint, peering into the darkness—"are those Grecian statues around your pool?"

"Bof, ce n'est rien," he says waving his hand.

"Nothing?"

Gabriel frowns at me. "This isn't like you, Laney. Where is the free-spirited girl I met in the park? That girl was too confident and audacieux to let some champagne and a string quartet make her feel inferior. Where is that girl?"

Where is that girl? That girl lost her audaciousness when she gave her heart to a boy from a family so rich and cultured they put statues as old as Socrates in their garden as if they were merely plastic garden gnomes.

"You're right," I say, taking a deep breath. "I am without chill. I need to take a deep breath, reclaim my chill, and just do me."

He presses a kiss to my forehead.

"Oui, ma fleur," he says, chuckling. "Just do you." He leans over and whispers in my ear. "And tonight, when we are back in our room, I will do you."

"Gabriel!"

Gabriel stiffens, and the flirty twinkle in his eyes dims. He doesn't turn in the direction of the voice. He stares straight ahead, a muscle working on his angular, whiskered jaw.

I don't need to turn around to know Giselle is standing behind us. The air left my lungs the second I heard her voice and caught the whiff of her bold perfume circling around us like a jasmine-scented cloud.

She steps around us, a six-foot Gallic beauty in a silk Hermès minidress and gladiator sandals, hair scraped back into a fashionable knot, her makeup accentuating her almond eyes and pouty lips.

"You look beautiful," I say sincerely, smiling. "Giselle, isn't it?"

She flicks her gaze from Gabriel to me and chuckles with her mouth closed, the humor never reaching her dark, unreadable eyes. Gabriel removes his hand from the small of my back and the spot feels suddenly cold, bare.

"Je suis Giselle," she says, smiling tightly. "Mais, qui êtes-vous encore?"

I am Giselle, but who are you again?

"Why are you here, Giselle?" Gabriel asks, pointedly using English.

"Come, darling," Giselle coos in French, placing her manicured hand on his forearm. "You know how much I love spending time at La Bastide. Do you remember when we came here to celebrate—"

"There you are, my dear," Alexandre strides up, looking every bit the heir to the Galliard fortune in his black tailored slacks, a shirt, and a white dinner jacket. He kisses Giselle's cheek. "You mentioned you were bringing a special date, Gabriel, but you didn't say it was our very own Mademoiselle Brooks."

"Bonsoir, Laney." Alexandre moves in, resting his hand on my waist and kissing both of my cheeks. "Comment vas-tu?"

"I'm all good," I say, moving my hip so Alexandre's hand falls away. "How are you?"

A man in a white chef's coat steps onto the patio and rings a tiny bell.

"Ah, dinner," Alexandre says, putting his hand on the small of Giselle's back. "Shall we?"

Alexandre and Giselle move over to the table, and we follow, though Gabriel doesn't take my hand or put his arm around my waist. He clenches his jaw and presses his lips together to create an angry slash across his handsome face.

We find the place cards with our names written on them. Gabriel is seated across from me, between Giselle and someone named Philou. I am seated between Aunt Fantine and someone named Coco. Of course, I recognize Gabriel's grandfather, parents, siblings, and dear, old Aunt Fantine, but the other dozen people gathered around the table are strangers to me.

The fish course is served, seared tuna with Provençal vegetables and lemon aioli. Aunt Fantine introduces me to Coco, her oldest and dearest friend. In a hushed voice, Aunt Fantine gives me the lowdown on Coco, who was apparently a gifted singer.

"Coco started her singing career when she was only nine years old. Can you imagine? She sang in Louis Leplée's nightclubs. You know, Édith Piaf's mentor? Anyway, Coco had a marvelous voice, but who could compare with La Môme Piaf?"

Aunt Fantine sips her wine until she has a burgundy moustache, the liquid seeping into her many lip wrinkles, as though someone dipped crumpled-up waxed paper into grape juice.

I leave Aunt Fantine to her wine and turn to chat with Coco. By the time the main course is served, Coco has shared a few stories about her rivalry with Édith and confessed to her late-life love affair with a much younger Johnny Hallyday.

"Have you heard of Johnny?" she asks, a twinkle in her cloudy brown eyes.

I shake my head.

"La!" She shakes her head. "America had her Elvis. France has her Johnny."

Coco keeps me riveted with stories about France's music scene all through the main and salad courses. She excuses herself when the cheese course is served and helps herself to a wedge of bleu d'Auvergne and several apple slices.

It's the first time I have had a chance to look at Gabriel, and I am surprised to find him toying with his wineglass, tipping it back and forth, his sullen gaze fixed on the burgundy wave of wine rolling one way and then the other. I nudge him under the table, but he doesn't even look up. I kick my sandal off and slide my foot inside his pants leg.

He finally looks at me.

I mouth, "What's up?"

He shakes his head and returns his attention to his wine. I look over the table at Giselle. I don't want to believe that she is the cause of Gabriel's bad mood, because that would mean she still has some hold over his emotions, but I can't deny that he changed the second she stepped into the garden and cooed his name.

Actually, I noticed an almost imperceptible shift in his 'tude yesterday on the train, when Alexandre texted him to say that Giselle would be joining us at the *bastide*.

Gabriel said he broke up with Giselle when he found out she was sleeping with his brother, but he never said he was over her.

Alexandre stands and taps the edge of his wineglass with his butter knife. The conversations around the table fade away as all eyes focus on the tall, handsome heir to the Galliard throne.

"A Galliard gathering would not be complete without a toast," he says, lifting his wineglass. "Won't you please raise your glasses?"

Everyone complies—everyone except Gabriel. He stops tipping his wineglass back and forth and crosses his arms over his broad chest. I nudge him under the table. He sighs and, with a great show of reluctance, raises his wineglass.

"When I was a boy, my mother told me I should give thanks for small blessings, large blessings, and everything in between. Tonight, let us give thanks for the small blessings: this lovely evening, the meal we just enjoyed, the wine in our glasses," he says, smiling at his mother. "And let us give thanks for the large blessings, too: our good health, our great fortunes, and our expanding family."

Gabriel's face drains of color. He sits up and leans his forearms on the edge of the table, fixing his brother with a dark gaze.

"It seems we will soon welcome a new member to our family." Alexandre pauses and looks over at his brother. Gabriel shakes his head as if to stop Alexandre from revealing his news. Alexandre chuckles and lifts his glass higher in the air. "I am truly blessed today as the love of my life, Giselle Sournois DéLoyalle, has agreed to become my wife."

Gabriel sits back so hard I can hear the air leave his lungs from across the table, even over the cheers and applause. While his relatives congratulate Alexandre and Giselle, Gabriel quietly stands and walks into the house.

I stand to go after him, but Aunt Fantine rests her thin, wrinkled hand on my arm and shakes her head.

"Let him go, ma cherie," she whispers. "Right now, there is nothing you can do to ease Gabriel's suffering. He must heal this latest wound himself."

A minute later, the sound of a motorcycle engine roaring to life and tires devouring gravel echoes through the garden.

Chapter 35

Laney's Life Playlist
"Stupid Me" by Magic!
"Maps" by Maroon 5
"Rude" by Magic!
"Distance" by Christina Perri with Jason Mraz

I sit up waiting for Gabriel to return and listening to every track on *Don't Kill the Magic,* sniffling along to "Stupid Me" and crying when the lead singer, Nasri Atweh, wonders if his love is unrequited.

I feel you, brother Nasri.

I want to sing similar lyrics to Gabriel. *Do you love me the way I love you? Do-do-do-do you need me the way I need you? Do you? Do-do-do-do you want me the way I want you?*

Gabriel rode off three hours ago. I don't know if he is sitting on the shoulder of some Provençal road, staring into the darkness and wondering why his love life took such an unexpected, treacherous turn, or if he is on his way back to the *bastide* and me. Each minute that passes feels like another mile between us.

I turn off the light and curl up on top of the blankets, one ear listening to Magic! and the other ear listening for the growl of Gabriel's motorcycle.

When I wake the next morning, Nasri is singing "Mama Didn't Raise No Fool" softly in my ear and Gabriel's spot in our bed is cold and empty. I pull my iPhone out of my pocket and check for messages, but there are no missed calls or texts from Gabriel. The fear coiled in the pit of my belly springs up, filling every space of my body, twisting around my heart and lungs. Losing Gabriel to another woman doesn't terrify me nearly as much as losing him to a horrific motorcycle accident. What if he missed a hairpin turn and is lying at the bottom of some hill, too bloody and broken to call for help?

Leaping out of bed, I pull my earbuds from my ears and hurry over to the window. I throw open the curtains, push the French doors apart, and step onto the small Juliet balcony, leaning against the wrought-iron railing as I look toward the stables. The massive wooden doors are closed, so I can't tell if Gabriel's bike is parked safely inside. I am about to head back inside to get dressed and go look for myself when I hear voices below. I peek over the railing and see Celine and another woman sitting on the patio, sipping espresso and puffing on cigarettes.

"Poor Gabriel," Celine says. "Alexandre's news came as such as shock."

"Did you see his face?" the other woman asks. "I don't think I have ever seen him so upset."

"But of course he is upset," Celine says, taking a long drag from her cigarette and blowing the smoke over her slender shoulder. "He loved Giselle, and she broke his heart."

"What about his new girlfriend?"

"What about her?"

"Do you think he loves her?"

"Who can say with Gabriel?" Celine says, flicking her cigarette on the ground and grinding it against the flagstone with her heel. "He's always been . . . different from us. More reserved and private. Though . . ."

"Oui?" The other woman replaces her espresso cup on its matching saucer and leans across the table. "Tell me."

Celine lowers her voice. I have to sit on the balcony and press my ear to the space between the sections of wrought-iron to hear her.

"Gabriel came in late last night and went to one of the empty guest bedrooms."

The coil of fear wrapped around my heart releases. I say a little prayer of thanks that Gabriel isn't lying in a vegetative state in some hospital.

"Can you blame him?"

"Not at all," Celine says. "I mean, how painfully awkward. I wouldn't want to make love to someone new if I was still nurturing a broken heart for another."

It's crazy how fast uncoiled fear can twist and writhe and turn into something sharper, something far more lethal. Celine's words sink into my heart, releasing a fast-acting sorrow that has me pressing a hand to my mouth to keep from crying out.

"Her presence here this weekend is rather inconvenient . . ."

I crawl back into the bedroom and quietly shut the door. I think about calling Fanny for advice, but decide to listen to my inner voice instead, the one that is saying leave, leave, leave.

It doesn't take me long to throw my clothes and toiletries into my backpack. I creep down the stairs like a thief about to make away with the Galliard treasures and out the front door.

I am halfway to Moustiers-Sainte-Marie when I suddenly realize the trees lining the road have fat, green olives growing on their branches.

And just like that, the ghost of my happy past reminds me of the silly, sappy love song I wrote after I met Gabriel.

Oh, let's run away to the south of France,
Where the music of love makes us want to dance.
We'll eat olives by the light of a silver moon,
And sing silly songs and kiss 'til we swoon.
Oh, let's run away to the south of France.

Chapter 36

Laney's Life Playlist
"Basket Case" by Green Day

"This is bonkers, like "Blank Space" Taylor Swift crazy. Like, mascara streaked down your face while you caress a poison apple crazy," Vivia says. "You know that, right?"

Fanny arrived yesterday with her straight-talking best friend in tow. We sat up all night drinking champagne cocktails Vivia made using a recipe she got from a bartender at the Hotel Martinez in Cannes and talking about what happened at La Bastide. Now we are eating scrambled eggs and sipping super-black coffee at a café near Fanny's father's apartment.

"It's not that crazy," Fanny says, squeezing my hand.

"Uh, yeah it is! Laney, you are this close"—Vivia raises her hand, leaving a tiny space between her thumb and index finger—"to bashing the hood of a Jaguar with a golf club."

"Vivian!" Fanny cries.

"Don't Vivian me," Vivia says. "Someone needs to feed this girl the straight dope before she lets the wack voices in her head talk her into doing something crazier than she has already done." She reaches across the table and grabs my hand, fixing me with the full force of her 1,000-watt intense Vivia gaze. "Trust me, Laney, you don't want to go full Tay-Tay. You *never* go full Tay-Tay."

Fanny sighs. "I don't even know what you are saying anymore, Vivian."

The filter that exists between stream of consciousness and the mouth is broken in Vivia, which means her thoughts flow without censor or reservation. Some people might find such candor off-putting, but not me. I like Vivia. She is genuinely caring and totally hilarious. Her aura is as pretty and soft as a Renoir landscape.

"Look, all I am saying, Laney, is that you overheard a couple of cell warriors talking out the sides of their necks. They could have been monkey mouthing it, but you don't know, because you ran away like a little bitch."

Fanny rolls her eyes.

"English, Vivian."

"Sorry," Vivia says, grinning. "I am interviewing Taylor Schilling next week—the star of *Orange Is the New Black*—so I binged watched the first two seasons before coming to Paris. Basically, I said Laney overheard two women going on and on about shit they don't know."

"What would you have done?" I ask.

"Well, I sure enuf wouldn't have run away," Vivia rubs her nose and sniffs like a gangster. "Those bitches gave you a hoe check."

I shake my head.

"They ganged up on you to see if you would stand up for yourself."

"I don't think they even knew I was there."

"They knew," Vivia says. "Even if they didn't know you were there, you took the coward's way out by running back to Paris instead of confronting Gabriel with what you heard. You should have asked him if he was still in love with Jizz hole."

"Giselle."

"Whatever."

"You're right."

"Damn straight, I'm right." Vivia says. "You gotta stand tall and claim your space, girl."

"So what are you going to do now?" Fanny asks. "I mean, now that you have finished your internship at the gallery?"

"I was going to stay here and start a bike tour business with Rigby, but I don't know. Maybe I should just go back to Boulder. I mean, who was I kidding? I am not sophisticated enough for Paris."

"Are you *freaking* kidding me?" Vivia says, waving her butter knife at me. "What about all of this aura mumbo jumbo?"

"What about it?"

"You're going to let some man change your aura?"

I frown. "What do you mean?"

Vivia drops her butter knife on her plate. She squints and hold her arms up, moving them through the air as if feeling for something. "When I met you in Alaska your aura was *lit*."

"Lit?" Fanny asks.

"It's slang for effing amazing," Vivia says.

Fanny rolls her eyes. "You live in a tiny village in the south of France. How are you able to keep replenishing your supply of ridiculous American slang?"

"I am on fleek"—Vivia blows on her fingernails and polishes them on her shirt—"fluent in all that is cool and current."

"Yeah, *fleek* I have heard, and I am pretty sure it was on the list of words that should be dropped from our vernacular, along with *squad, bae,* and *preach*."

"Uh-uh." Vivia wags her finger. "*Preach* is sacrosanct. Don't *even* go there."

Fanny rolls her eyes again. "Can we go back to Laney, please? She is on the verge of making a decision that could impact her future happiness and success. She needs a couple of empowered women to jolt her with a shocking dose of reality until she has the power to make the right decisions."

"Preach," Vivia mumbles.

"Vivian!" Fanny cries. "Would you be serious?"

"I am being serious." Vivia leans forward, resting her elbows on her knees. "Laney, do you know for sure that Gabriel is still in love with Jizz hole?"

"Giselle," Fanny corrects.

"What*ever*." Vivia waves her hand at Fanny, but keeps her gaze fixed on me. "Well, do you?"

I open my mouth to speak, but she doesn't wait for my answer.

"Bzzzz," she says, making a buzzer sound. "Wrong answer. You don't know if he is still in love with her because you didn't give him a chance to explain what he was feeling. Instead, you ran away, which is what you said you did the first time you thought he was into Giselle. Right?"

I nod.

"How do you think that made *him* feel?" she asks. "You dated for—what—six months? Are you telling me that after all of that time, he still hadn't earned the benefit of your doubt? You canceled him as if you were swiping left for some uggo on Tinder."

"When you put it that way, it sounds harsh."

"That's because it was a little harsh." She sits back. "Sorry, but I believe in keepin' it real. Aint no time for pulling a Kylie."

Fanny frowns. "Kylie?"

"Jenner." Vivia sighs. "Fake lips, fake cheeks, fake boobs. A big, silicone-injected fake."

"You're oversimplifying the situation, Vivian."

"No," I say, jumping to Vivia's defense. "She's right. I have been acting like a child, riding around Paris on my silly bike, wearing ridiculous T-shirts, talking about unicorns and pixie dust, expecting my fairy godmother to swoop in, wave her wand, and fix my broken heart. It's time I grew up and acted like an adult and fixed my own broken heart."

I look at my reflection in the café window, and tears fill my eyes. I have been such a foolish child, fighting maturity like a toddler fighting a nap.

"Fanny," I say, taking my glasses off and wiping the tears from my eyes. "Starting a business is a grown-up thing to do. And if I am going to start a new business, I need a new, grown-up wardrobe. Will you help me change my style?"

"Wahhhhhh!" Vivia sings, her mouth a perfect O, her gaze cast toward Heaven. "Did you hear that? That's the celestial choir singing. That's the sound Fanny hears in her head anytime someone asks her to go shopping."

Fanny laughs. "I think you are beautiful just the way you are, but if you want a makeover, I would be happy to oblige."

"Look," Vivia laughs, standing and grabbing her sunglasses off the table, "I have an errand to run."

"You can't go!" Fanny cries. "We are in the middle of a makeover."

"Fashion is your bag, baby." Vivia slips her sunglasses on her face. "I'll meet you guys at the restaurant for the gallery graduation. Just make sure our Dizzy Princess is über-glam for the ball tonight, okay?"

Chapter 37

Laney's Life Playlist
"Marry Me" by Train

Vivia is pacing the sidewalk in front of Bâtard de Valadon in black cigarette pants and matching black jacket. Her '80s Mötley Crüe tee and impossibly high sparkly heels transform the conservative outfit into something totally edgy. It's totally Vivia.

She stops pacing and mumbling to herself when she sees us approaching.

"There you are!" she says, striding over to us. "You were supposed to be here fifteen minutes ago. You're late."

"Chill, White Rabbit," Fanny says, grinning. "We will make it to the Mad Hatter's Tea Party."

"Fanny!" Vivia's mouth falls open. "Did you just make a pop culture reference? A Disney pop culture reference?"

Fanny nods.

Vivia closes her eyes, presses her hand to her forehead, and sways back and forth on her heels. "What's happening? Am I hallucinating? Do I have a brain tumor?"

"Ha! Ha!" Fanny says, laughing. "I watched Calder's best friend's daughters last weekend, and all they wanted to do was watch Disney movies. No big deal."

Vivia keeps her hand pressed against her forehead, but opens her eyes. "Ohmygod! I do have a tumor. I thought you just said you babysat . . . *children.*"

"Shut up, you dork!" Fanny laughs, pulling Vivia's hand from her forehead. "Besides, if I am going to be an auntie to Vivia Perpetua de Caumont's children, I need to know the lyrics to every Disney musical."

"No worries there, mate. As you can plainly see"—Vivia opens her jacket to reveal her flat abdomen—"I am without bump and intend to stay that way. So you can just go back to being pop-culturally challenged Fanny."

Fanny told me Vivia had a little pregnancy scare earlier this year. She thought she was pregnant and due to deliver around the time of Fanny's wedding to Calder, but it turned out she made some error when she tried to synch her iPhone calendar to her new iPad so the dates of her menstrual cycle got all jacked up.

"Well, maybe *I* will be working a bump soon."

"Wait! What the what?" Vivia shakes her head. "Ohmyfreakinggod! Fanny, are you pregnant?"

Fanny shakes her head. "Not yet."

"Not yet?" Vivia cries. "Are you sure I don't have a brain tumor? Maybe there was a rip in the space-time continuum. Something is wrong."

"Technically," I say, removing my glasses and sliding them into my little clutch, "there is no way the fabric of time could be ripped because there is no theory about time being like fabric."

Vivia blinks. "What are you saying? Doc Brown's theory was bunk?"

"Well, technically speaking, yes. The phrase 'ripping a hole in the space-time continuum' is a theory perpetuated in science fiction."

"Great Scot! What is happening here?" Vivia cries, covering her mouth with her hand. "My child-hating best friend is quoting Disney flicks and talking about having babies. You're debunking Doc Brown's theory about the space-time continuum. I need a drink."

Fanny laughs and links her arms through ours. "Let's go then. I am pretty sure Bâtard de Valadon can accommodate your alcoholic needs."

"Wait!" Vivia says, turning to look at me. "Before we go in, I have something to say to you, Laney-Bo-Baney Brooks."

"Yes?"

"You look fabulous."

"Gee, thanks."

"You're welcome."

Fanny grins, clearly pleased that the results of my miraculous makeover were worth her efforts. We spent the morning shopping for a new wardrobe, sleek slacks, pencil skirts, leather leggings, cashmere turtlenecks, polka-dotted silk blouses, Breton striped tops, a pair of pink satin pants, swingy little skirts, and a bright, colorful scarf that looks like something a grown-up artist would wear. She even let me get a slouchy cashmere beret and minidress with an ultra-mod Picasso-esque print. A neutral palette with occasional pops of color. Somehow, she managed to give my immature wardrobe a mature update while still maintaining what she called the *Laney je ne sais quois*.

After our shopping spree, we headed to Fanny's favorite salon. They wanted to cut several inches off my hair and give me the perfectly tousled, sexy bed-head look popular with très chic Frenchwomen, but I opted for a shorter, chicer version of my own style, with fringy, side-swept bangs and chin-hugging layers. Fanny gave me smoky eyes and thick, pin-up-girl lashes, and brushed Nars Orgasm blush over my cheekbones, and I hardly recognized myself.

We walk into the restaurant, and Robert takes one look at me and whistles, waggling his shaggy eyebrows suggestively.

"Ooo, la-la, la vache!"

I blush. "Does that mean I look okay?"

"Cherie," he says, kissing both of my cheeks, "it means you look like a sophisticated, sexy French screen goddess."

"Merci, Robert."

"De rien!"

He leads us to a long table in the atrium where the other interns have already gathered. They take one look at my chic black sheath dress, buttery-soft peacock blue leather jacket, and Amy Winehouse fuck-me pumps and burst into applause. Giorgio lets out a loud catcall. Rigby jumps up and wraps her arms around me.

"You look amazing, Lane," she says. "Like if you smooshed Sophia Loren and Audrey Hepburn."

"Thanks, Rigby," I say, hugging her back.

Fanny orders us bottles of champagne, and we toast to the future. Vivia entertains us with stories about her assignments with *Gogirl!* magazine. Rigby asks Vivia about all of the famous celebrities she has interviewed for the magazine. Vivia tells a funny story about how she slipped onto a set where they were photographing a Dolce and Gabbana underwear campaign with super-sexy male model David Gandy, and how she pretended to be the oil girl, slathering baby oil onto David's chiseled pecs until she was discovered.

"So what happens next?" Vivia asks. "Where will you all go, and what will you do?"

Giorgio tells us he is going home to Bedizzano and will work part-time in his family's business, spending the rest of his time opening a gallery.

"I am going to New York with Julia," Gunthar says.

I look at Julia and see her as if for the first time. Her aura is different from what it was when we met. She is *glowing*.

"A strong voman needs a stronger man," he says, the corners of his lips twitching as he resists smiling.

Julia laughs and kisses Gunther, "And I suppose that is you, my big Viking lovah?"

Gunthar nods his head.

"When did this happen?"

Gunthar shrugs.

"It just kinda happened," Julia says, beaming.

"What about you, Rigby?" Julia asks.

Rigby throws her arm around my shoulders. "We are staying in Paris, aren't we, Lane?"

I nod.

"What will you do?" Giorgio asks.

"We are going to start an art bike tour business, leading people to places artists lived and worked. I have some money from my car insurance settlement, and my iTunes royalties keep rolling in, so"—I shrug—"why not?"

"Everything is working out for you," Vivia says, grinning. "Isn't it?"

I think of Gabriel, and my heart aches.

"Come on," Vivia says, grabbing my hand. "We have somewhere to be."

"Where?"

"You have a date with destiny, Dizzy Princess."

We follow Vivia out of the restaurant. She leads us down the street and into the square at place des Vosges, but pauses before pushing the gate open.

"I want to talk about Gabriel and what happened in the south of France," she says, positioning herself in front of me. "What if there's a perfectly logical explanation for the way Gabriel behaved? What if he wasn't upset because Alexandre asked Giselle to marry him, but because he had planned on asking *you* to marry him that weekend and his weasel-ass brother stole his glory?"

I blink at her because I don't have an answer to her questions.

"What if he didn't come back to your room that night because he was über-pissed at weasel-boy and didn't want you to see him all raged-out and shit? What if he just wanted to take some time to pull his shit together so he didn't ruin your trip?" She narrows her gaze. "Do you think those are plausible what-ifs?"

"Sure."

She steps aside, and I am able to see into the park. The square is usually empty at this time of night, but crowds have gathered around the fountain, which is surrounded by easels with artwork on them.

"What's going on?"

"Come on," Vivia grabs my hand. "Your fairy godmother has been wearing her wand arm out working magic for you."

We walk through the gates and follow the gravel path leading to the fountain at the center of the park. Fanny and Vivia stop walking and smile at me.

The crowd parts, and my heart skips a beat, my cheeks flush with serious flushy-crushy heat.

Gabriel is standing by one of the easels. His black hair is hanging over one eye, but I can see that he is staring at me.

"Your Prince Charming is waiting," Vivia says, putting her hand on my shoulder and pushing me toward the crowd. "Go get 'im, Dizzy Princess. Your happily ever after is waiting."

My Amy Winehouse pumps sink into the gravel, and my knees wobble, but I keep walking until I come to the first easel. There's a large framed photograph on the easel. I look around the circle and see that there are framed photographs on each of the easels. Gabriel's photographs. There is a black-and-white shot of the bench we sat on during our first date, not too far from where I am standing. I walk to the next easel and look at a photograph of the sandwich stand where we went for lunch on our first date and many dates since then. I move around the circle, staring at photographs of the places we visited throughout our relationship—special places, our places— until I come to the last shot. I don't recognize this place. It's the inside of a church, with gleaming pews and intricate stained-glass windows.

I turn around to find Gabriel standing behind me, a bouquet of daisies in one hand and a black velvet ring box in the other.

He hands me the bouquet of daisies and then gets down on one knee. He flicks open the velvet box.

"Delaney Lavender Brooks, ma fleur," he says, holding the box out to me. "Will you make me the happiest man in the world and say that you want to marry me?"

The crowd goes wild.

"Gabriel," I whisper, "get up."

He shakes his head, and a lock of his black hair falls over his cheek. "I am not going to get up until you answer me. Will you marry me, Laney?"

"You can't be serious?"

"Why not?"

I look around, beyond the crowd, to the beautiful seventeenth-century buildings surrounding the square and then back at Gabriel.

"You don't want to marry me, Gabriel," I say, my cheeks flushing with a new wave of heat. "You're punctual, focused, and successful. You're the sophisticated son of a distinguished family, and I am . . . Laney Brooks, late all of the time, forgetful, scattered Laney."

He stands up and puts his hand on my waist, looking into my eyes.

"I love scattered Laney. Don't you love me?"

"Of course I love you. I am, like, way, way over the moon and back again in love with you."

He smiles, and my heart does a somersault.

"I don't care if you are late all of the time, as long as you are coming home to me, and I don't care if you're forgetful, as long as you don't forget to kiss me hello every time you see me."

"You're serious? You really want to marry me?"

"Totes," he says, grinning. "What about you, ma fleur? Do you want to marry me?"

"Are you kidding?" I say, throwing my arms around him. "Did Samantha want Jake to pick her up from the church in his shiny red Porsche? Did Andie want Blain to kiss her outside the dance? Of course I want to marry you. You're my OTP!"

He kisses me, and the crowd cheers.

Cue cheesy, synthesized end music, and roll credits, please. The gawky, goofy, middle-class girl is about to ride off into the sunset with the boy of her dreams.

Laney's Biking (or Walking) Tour
of Artistic Paris

Jardin des Tuileries

If you could pull a Doctor Who and travel back in time to nineteenth-century Paris, you would probably encounter Édouard Manet in the Tuileries gardens. In Manet's time, the Tuileries was *the* hang spot for Bobos, the *foule élégante,* and anyone hoping to *see* and *be seen.* The fashionable set would sip coffee in the cafés, lounge on yellow-painted deck chairs, and admire posters tacked to one of the many kiosks positioned throughout the gardens. Manet immortalized his fave hang spot in *Music in the Tuileries Gardens.* An interesting side note about the Tuileries: It is reported that a ghost haunts the gardens. Called the Red Man, he is believed to have been Catherine de Medici's executioner and confidant. Worried that he knew too many of her dastardly secrets, old crafty Catherine had him executed in the gardens. Marie Antoinette and Napoleon claimed to have seen the Red Man. Spiritualism, particularly the belief that the spirits of the dead haunt the world unseen, was huge in the nineteenth century.

46 rue Laffitte
Café de la Nouvelle-Athènes

In the nineteenth century, 46 rue Laffitte was the home to Café de la Novelle Athènes, a wicked popular meeting place for impressionist painters. Degas, Matisse, Valadon, Manet, and Van Gogh frequented this café, where they would sit at one of the long tables and get a little hammered on wormwood—aka absinthe, an addictive, hallucinogenic green alcohol poured over sugar cubes. Edgar Degas chose Café de la Novelle-Athènes as the setting for one of his most famous paintings, *The Absinthe Drinker*, depicting a neatly dressed, slightly dejected woman zoning out, a half-consumed glass of absinthe on the table in front of her. The café was transformed into a strip club in the 1940s and was a popular hangout for Nazi soldiers. It was demolished in 2004. Today an apartment building stands in its place.

171 boulevard du Montparnasse
La Closerie des Lilas

In the early nineteenth century, La Closerie des Lilas was merely a humble open-air café situated in a garden of lilacs. By the end of the century, it would become a meeting place for artists like Modigliani, van Dongen, Man Ray, and Picasso. Cézanne and Émile Zola often met under the café's wide green awning to discuss their works in progress. Today the tables in La Closerie bear plaques engraved with the names of its most illustrious patrons.

46 rue du Bac
Maison Deyrolle

It was here, in this tiny taxidermy shop, crowded with stuffed animals, preserved skins, insects, and botanical specimens, that Salvadore Dalí and other surrealists gathered to discuss their philosophical views on politics, society, and art. Deyrolle was also one of the filming locations used by Woody Allen when he shot his movie *Midnight in Paris*.

14 rue Clauzel
Père Tanguy

In the nineteenth century, Julien-François Tanguy owned and operated a small paint-supply shop at 14 rue Clauzel. Often, starving artists would exchange their paintings for supplies. Soon Tanguy had a warehouse full of paintings, some by artists who would go on to become crazy famous. Vincent van Gogh was one of those starving artists. He painted the rotund, bearded "color grinder's" portrait in exchange for supplies. Today you can see Van Gogh's *Portrait of Père Tanguy* at the Musée Rodin, located at 77 rue de Varenne.

6 rue de Furstenberg
Home and atelier of Eugène Delacroix

This pretty, three-story brick building with glossy green doors was once the home and studio of Eugène Delacroix, the most important and colorful painter of the French romantic movement. Delacroix moved from rue Notre-Dame-de-Lorette to rue de Furstenberg in 1857 because it was closer to Saint-Sulpice; earlier that year, Delacroix had been commissioned to paint the interior walls of the church. Delacroix lived and worked at this location until his death in 1863. The building was saved from destruction in 1929, when a group of artists banded together to form a society for the preservation of Delacroix's "sacred abode" and the promotion of his inspired works. Today it is a museum dedicated to Delacroix.

77 rue de Miromesnil
Caillebotte's Crib

The wealthy impressionist painter Gustave Caillebotte lived at 77 rue de Miromesnil, and his studio was located on the top floor. Caillebotte's family purchased this home from Baron Haussmann, the ambitious prefect who gave Paris a massive face-lift, pulling her out of the Middle Ages and into the Belle Époque by renovating her parks, roads, buildings, and public works. Caillebotte painted one of his most famous pieces here. *The Floor Scrapers* depicts three shirtless men, hunched over as they scrape the dark varnish from Caillebotte's new studio floor. Caillebotte commissioned the floor scrapers to remove the dark varnish because artists appreciate light, and studio floors are rarely dark. Caillebotte also painted *Young Man at the Window,* a beautiful, bright portrait of his brother staring out a window from a corner room overlooking the intersection of rue de Miromesnil and boulevard Malesherbes.

20 rue du Rambuteau
La Maison du Pastel

La Maison du Pastel is the oldest pastel manufacturer in the world. Founded in the eighteenth century by Henri Roche, who sold his "pigment sticks" to artists like Maurice Quentin de La Tour and Jean-Baptiste Siméon Chardin. In the nineteenth century, Degas purchased his pastels at La Maison du Pastel, including the ultramarines he used in his *Blue Dancers* and the *vert vif* he used in *The Green Singer.*

49 rue Notre-Dame-de-Lorette
Pissaro home and studio

The Danish-French impressionist and post-impressionist painter Camille Pissaro lived and worked at 49 rue Notre-Dame-de-Lorette before moving with his family outside of Paris to Pontoise and Louveciennes. Cool little factoid: rue Notre-Dame-de-Lorette was named after the women who lived around that street. A *lorette* was a loose woman.

8 rue Notre-Dame-de-Lorette
Home and atelier of Eugène Delacroix

Eugène Delacroix lived and worked at 8 rue Notre-Dame-de-Lorette from 1844 until 1857. Sadly, Eugène's home was destroyed to make room for a Carrefour, a chain supermarket.

56 rue Notre-Dame-de-Lorette
Birthplace of Paul Gauguin

On June 7, 1848, Eugène Henri Paul Gauguin was born at 56 rue Notre-Dame-de-Lorette to Clovis Gauguin, a journalist, and Alina Maria Chazal, the daughter of a socialist leader and radical feminist. Today 56 rue Notre-Dame-de-Lorette is home to a Middle Eastern restaurant.

8 rue Carcel
Gauguin's space

In 1881, Gauguin lived at 8 rue Carcel with his wife and four children. It was here that he painted one of his most famous paintings, a dark, moody piece depicting a cozy room in his home, complete with a still life of flowers and his wife playing an upright piano.

11 boulevard de Clichy
Pablo Picasso's posh pad

In 1909, after Picasso graduated from struggling artist to painter with some serious cash to splash, he moved from a dreary apartment in the hills of Montmartre to this light-filled studio-apartment combo with a view of Sacré Cœur.

82 boulevard de Clichy
Moulin Rouge

The Moulin Rouge, perhaps the world's most famous cabaret, opened its doors in 1889. With a swish of their ruffled skirts and a kick of their shapely legs, pretty young dancing girls would delight (and inspire) Henri de Toulouse-Lautrec, Paul Gauguin, Charles Conder, and Edgar Degas. Back then, the cabaret was dark and slightly seedy. Toulouse-Lautrec developed a friendship with one of the dancers, a slender, mentally ill girl named Jane Avril, and featured her in many of his works.

16 rue du Repos
Père Lachaise Cemetery

This cemetery is positively crowded with the headstones of famous corpses—Molière, Chopin, Wilde, Maupassant, Morrison. One grave, its headstone faded and crowded between encroaching neighbors, belongs to Jane Avril, the Moulin Rouge cancan dancer immortalized by Toulouse-Lautrec. After entrancing the artist with her high kicks and skirt tosses, she married a faithless German artist and died in poverty.

17 rue Jean-Baptiste Pigalle
Jean-Baptiste Pigalle home

From 1756 to 1782, the sculptor Jean-Baptiste Pigalle lived and worked in a modest limestone building on this road, later named after him. Today the building houses a super-swank upholsterer and interior decorator.

18 boulevard Pigalle (aka boulevard de Clichy)
Whistler's whore

American artist James Abbott McNeill Whistler painted a portrait of Joanna Hiffernan, an Irish painter and artists' model, here in the winter of 1861–1862. Whistler and Hiffernan spent days cloistered away in his warm, cozy studio, which suited them just fine since they were already in the midst of a scandalous love affair (Whistler's puritanical family didn't approve of the relationship because Hiffernan posed nude for various artists, which, in their eyes, meant she had to be a whore). One of Whistler's portraits of Hiffernan, *The White Girl,* is now housed at the National Gallery of Art in Washington, D.C.

3 rue Royale
Maxim's

This fashionable restaurant was the gathering place for luminaries of the Belle Époque, particularly artists and writers. Jean Cocteau frequented the opulent art nouveau restaurant, where he would dine on *boeuf braisée bourgeoise* and admire the beautiful female patrons.

22 rue des Saules
Lapin Agile
Long before Picasso immortalized this cabaret with his painting *At the Lapin Agile,* it had a reputation for attracting the sketchiest members of society—pimps, criminals, indigents, anarchists, and struggling artists. The volatile Italian painter and sculpture Amedeo Clemente Modigliani lived nearby in Le Bateau-Lavoir, a commune for penniless artists. Lapin Agile is where he would consume absinthe, smoke hashish, and dally with prostitutes.

13 place Emile-Goudeau
Le Bateau-Lavoir
7 place Jean-Baptiste Clément
Modigliani's heads
The hotheaded Italian painter and sculptor Amedeo Modigliani lived and worked at both of these locations. Some nights, under the cover of darkness, he would slip silently through the streets until he came to the Barbès-Rochechouart Metro station, which was under construction. He stole railroad ties, dragging them back to his dingy studio, where he would use them to sculpt human heads. Modigliani suffered from tuberculosis and used drugs and alcohol, especially the wicked wormwood, to ease his pain. At his home on place Jean-Baptiste Clément, he would get totally liquored up and then get into loud, knock-down, drag-out brawls with his girlfriends, Beatrice Hastings and Jeanne Hébuterne.

44 rue Pointe Cadet
Hôpital de la Charité
In this dreary, gray-brick building, on January 24, 1920, Modigliani took his last breath, his body totes wasted from tubercular meningitis and the excessive consumption of alcohol. A few days later, his young pregnant lover, devastated with grief, would take a leap from a five-story building.

6 rue Lucien Gaulard
Cimetière Saint-Vincent
This is the final resting place of Maurice Utrillo, a French-born artist famous for his Parisian cityscapes and excessive drinking. In life, Utrillo hung at the seedy Lapin Agile with Modigliani and

writer Guillaume Apollinaire. In death, he hangs at this cemetery, conveniently located across the street from the Lapin Agile, along with French author and playwright Marcel Aymé and director Marcel Carné. Tourists can't visit Montmartre without seeing at least one of Utrillo's paintings, which are prodigiously reproduced in postcard form.

20 rue Visconti
Atelier of Frédéric Bazille

In 1867, the wealthy artist Frédéric Bazille invited his impoverished friends Auguste Renoir and Claude Monet to bunk at his atelier. It was in this studio that Bazille and Renoir painted each other's portraits; today the two portraits hang in the Musée d'Orsay.

7 rue de Guichard
Berthe and her birds

In 1873, Berthe Morisot moved to an apartment in a bourgeois, four-story apartment building at 7 rue de Guichard. Although Morisot was an extremely talented painter and one of the founding members of the school of impressionism, she lived and worked in the bedroom of her light, humble apartment. A visitor at the time described her studio as having white slipcovers and curtains, hooks holding straw shepherdess hats, and a cage filled with chirping parakeets.

37 rue Vaneau
Galerie Minsky

Argentinian surrealist painter Leonor Fini is often described as the bohemian "it girl" of Paris. Most people haven't heard of her, but in the early half of the twentieth century she dominated the Parisian art scene, ran with Picasso and Dalí, and conquered more men than Napoleon. The prolific artist, party girl, and lover would often hold wild raves at her house here at 37 rue Vaneau.

Love Leah Marie Brown?

Be sure to keep an eye out
For her NEW SERIES
Coming soon wherever
Print and e-books are sold

And don't miss any of
THE IT GIRLS series!

Finding It

Faking It

Working It

Available now from
Lyrical Books

ABOUT THE AUTHOR

LEAH MARIE BROWN has worked as a journalist and photographer. An avid traveler, she has had adventures and mishaps from Paris to Tokyo. She doesn't buy cheesy T-shirts or useless bric-a-brac, but prefers friendships and memories as souvenirs from her travels. She lives a bike ride away from the white sand beaches of Florida's Emerald Coast with her husband, children, and pampered poodles. She is hard at work on the next novel in the It Girls series, but loves to hear from readers. Please visit her website at www.leahmariebrown.com. You can also visit her blogs: leahmariebrownhistoricals.blogspot.com and leahmariebrown.blogspot.com, and follow her on Twitter @18thCFrance and @leahmariebrown.

An It Girls Novel

Faking it

Love and lies don't mix...

LEAH MARIE BROWN

Haven't you ever told a little lie in the name of love?

Vivia Grant couldn't be happier. She has her dream job and is about to marry her dream man. Does it really matter that she's led him to believe she's a virgin? After all, being in love makes every experience feel like the first time anyway! But an unexpected encounter with an ex-lover is about to expose her embarrassing lie . . .

When Vivia's fiancé discovers the truth, he ends their engagement—via text—and uses his connections to get her fired. Unemployed and heartbroken, Vivia begins planning her new future—as a homeless spinster. But her best friend has a better idea. They'll skip the Ben & Jerry's binge and go on Vivia's honeymoon instead. Two weeks cycling through Provence and Tuscany, with Luc de Caumont, a sexy French bike guide. Too bad Vivia's not a big fan of biking. And she's abysmal at languages. Will she fib her way through the adventure, or finally learn to love herself—and Luc—flaws and all?

* An It Girls Novel

shine

Finding it

Sometimes what you're looking for is right in front of you...

LEAH MARIE BROWN

Falling in love is the ultimate faux pas.

Anything can happen in a year! Unemployed, homeless, and left at the altar, Vivia Perpetua Grant could see her future as a flannel-pajama-wearing spinster—or worse, a bag lady, shuffling around Golden Gate Park. But for a girl obsessed with rock music, Chinese takeout, and the color pink, misfortune is another word for opportunity. Vivia has found her niche as an international travel writer and the long-distance lover of Jean-Luc de Caumont, an über-hot French literature professor and competitive cyclist.

Still, even with so much going right, Vivia can't help but wonder if something is missing. The long-distance thing is taking its toll on a girl who didn't have that many tokens to begin with. And fate seems to be tempting her at every turn, first with a hunky Scottish helicopter pilot, and then with a British celebrity bad boy . . . Will Vivia continue to keep it real, or will she discover that some old habits die hard?

Falling in love is always in fashion . . .

With her trust fund and coveted job at Christian Dior, Fanny Moreau believes she has it all. But when her best friend finds a fulfilling new career abroad—and a dreamy relationship with a great guy—Fanny's fabulous life suddenly feels empty. Inspired to find her true purpose, she trades her cushy lifestyle in San Francisco for an adventure in the Alaskan wilderness.

Everyone thinks Fanny has gone off the deep end. What's a girl with a PhD in Prada doing teaching in an Inuit village? Even Fanny is wondering, especially when she comes face to face with Calder MacFarlane. The Scottish search-and-rescue pilot is everything Fanny is not—selfless, heroic, and used to living on the edge. He's also the man who once loved her best friend. Yet something in Calder's sexy gaze has her believing that she's a woman capable of great things—a woman who might just find her own happily-ever-after, in a place where she least expects it . . .

www.ingramcontent.com/pod-product-compliance
Lightning Source LLC
Chambersburg PA
CBHW020745250626
47155CB00003B/934